HOUSE OF ANGUISH

David W. Gammon

House of Anguish David W. Gammon
Published by CanAida Publishing
Distributed by Create Space & Amazon
Copyright 2018 David W. Gammon
All rights reserved.

ISBN: 1775231429
ISBN 13: 9781775231424

For Aida, in gratitude, thank you for taking a step towards me

ACKNOWLEDGMENTS;

So many people to thank, so little space. I want to take opportunity to express my undying gratitude to all my friends and family that supported this endeavor. It means more than I can say that you had all believed in me. While of course many things have changed since the conception of this novel. You'll note the endearing author's note upon conclusion. While Aida and I had come to the conclusion we're best suited to remain worlds apart, don't be saddened for us, we'll always hold one another in the highest regard. A huge shout out to be dear friend Brooke Lewis, who had scribed the heartfelt forward you're about to read. Most of all thank you, the reader for deciding to knock upon House of Anguish.

FORWORD

In 2017, life and career can be crazier than ever! As an actress, producer, and life coach in Hollywood, I am more overwhelmed than ever before. I feel like I am dialed in 24/7 and the constant flow of social media messages, emails and requests for media interviews never ends. As we all know, and have felt at times, the internet can be a blessing and a curse. With over 100K followers and fans, it is sometimes difficult to distinguish between the two. Then, on rare occasion, a follower will pop up on Twitter who, in time, will prove to be a blessing and a friend, as I have found in author and writer Dave Gammon.

Dave and I began following one another on Twitter about two years ago. At first, Dave was more of a quiet observer, liking many of my posts. He was an incredible supporter of my career and always created the most eloquent and prolific responses to my tweets. Soon after, I came to learn that Dave and I were highly connected by the ever loyal and amazing horror genre and community. Dave had messaged me to request an interview for his column on HorrorNews.net (HNN) and that is when I learned his true talents and kind and loving soul! Dave is one of those true gems of a human being who wants to better himself and his creative endeavors. He dreams big and works super hard to keep moving forward as a writer in an industry that can be thankless and disappointing, at times. But, Dave is the type of person in the creative industry who inspires me the most... the type who never quits and is FEARLESS on his journey... especially when times are tough. I, too, share his journey of taking many beatings in this business, so I respect and relate to the tenacious ones who never give up! Dave shared some personal information with me and came to me for some coaching and advice. Humbly, I hope and feel that something I said mentored, supported, and encouraged him to be here with you today and share his talents through House of Anguish. Every one of us needs a positive push and acknowledgement sometimes. We want to BELIEVE again! We want reassurance to know that anything is possible, and dreams can come true! When Dave published one of the most heartfelt, detailed, honoring interviews I had ever done in the horror media, I was compelled to honor him in return. When he approached me to create a foreword for his masterpiece House of Anguish, my heart immediately accepted this honor and I only hope I do him proud.

House of Anguish is a read that keeps you intrigued and wanting to follow the main character, Damien, as he discovers horrific truths of his life and childhood that have never been revealed. As a committed horror actress and fangirl, I am often drawn toward the stories and films that contain an element of the "supernatural". House of Anguish hits the mark when dealing with the old-fashioned supernatural elements we all know and love...good vs. evil! As the author, Dave created a sophisticated plot with the perfect amount of "twists and turns" to keep me impatiently waiting to turn each page. Dave's storytelling and writing talents allow him to share his genius with the reader through descriptive visuals and raw dialogue. The story touches on both light and dark components of life, including love, trust, memories, sacrifice, lies, deception, abuse, and PTSD, yet, never loses its sense of a horror story.

House of Anguish is a "thinking" and "soul-searching" reader's pleasure. Damien's journey has the ability to ignite emotion in each of us, as we all have the possibility of "looking back at our lives in search of truth". Along with Damien, we have all experienced life's pain and disappointment on our natural journey. A few of my favorite excerpts from the book display the emotions Dave intended to evoke:

"He crept towards the bathroom. Each step more cerebral than the last. He cared not to wake his love. For more selfish reasons than courtesy, Damien couldn't stand to admit to yet another nightmare. Clinging to the past had never been his style. After countless years of therapy, psychiatrists, medication, and more therapy, the young man couldn't bear admitting that he needed further help. Jade's intentions were always the best, but he'd rather blow his brains out, than be coddled over something she clearly didn't understand."

"Damien honey, go back to bed. Mommy and Daddy, we're just..." she stammered from over father's shoulder. Maternal as her instincts were, her pleas lacked any sense of conviction."

I was inspired to end my foreword with the latter excerpt above, as Dave does not know it yet, but I WILL be playing the role of Damien's mother, Joy, in the film version of House of Anguish one day (typed with a big devilish grin)! Until then, it has been my honor to endorse this book and the very special person who authored it...Dave Gammon. May your House of Anguish be one abundant home! - All my horror love, Brooke Lewis

*Brooke Lewis is an award-winning actress, producer and author who has appeared in many different genres, but is most known for the mystery, thriller "iMurders" (2008), mobster movie "Sinatra Club" (2010) and her comedic mobster Vampire "alter-ego" character and passion project "Ms. Vampy". After growing up and beginning her creative dreams in Philly, she moved to New York City and got her first little/big "break" playing Donna Marsala in the Off-Broadway hit comedy "Tony n' Tina's Wedding". She made her living acting in New York for four years, before packing it up and

heading to Hollywood. Never forgetting her ties to the LOVE statue and Geno's Steaks, she launched Philly Chick Pictures in 2002 to create more opportunities for herself as an actress. In 2007, she played Dr. Grace Sario in the horror, mystery "Kinky Killers", which aired on Showtime, and had the title 'Scream Queen' bestowed upon her in the entertainment industry. In 2010, she was honored with the 'B Movie Golden Cob Award for Scream Queen Of The Year' for her work in "Slime City Massacre". In 2016, she was honored with the Mary Pickford Award to "Highlight Women in The Film Arts" who both produce and act at Zed Fest. In 2017, she was honored by the prestigious Actors Awards with the 'Best Actress In A Drama Award' for her work in "Sprinkles". In 2017, she was also acknowledged with the honorable Stella Adler Acting Award at Action On Film International Film Festival, Grace Kelly Gold Actor Award at West Coast International Film Festival and Awards, as well as Los Angeles Film Awards 'Inspiring Woman in a Film' Award. She has been fortunate to work opposite a long list of talented veteran actors, which includes, Mark Ruffalo, Andy Richter, Charles Durning, Michael Pare, Michael Madsen, Tony Todd, Billy Dee Williams, William Forsythe, Gabrielle Anwar, Danny Nucci, Jason Gedrick, Michael Nouri, Joey Lawrence, Dominique Swain, Courtney Gains and many others.

CHAPTER ONE

Venomous shrills rattled the long, dark corridor. Bitter hatred enveloped and consumed the air. From downstairs the onslaught ensued, intensified by the second.

A cold sweat permeated the boy's brow. His fragile heart hammered, and tiny limbs quivered for the unknown. A tentative step over plush bears and action figures lured him further to the doorway.

The episode from below was far from new. In fact, the ruthless, relentless aggression was as common place and dependable as beans and franks served for Tuesday night dinner. Yet even young, innocent Damien knew full well his parents arguing was progressing well beyond the safe or ordinary parameters of adult interaction. Danger lurked below. A thick sheen of sweat dampened his mat of hair. His pulse doubled and tripled. Raspy pants of breath escaped his tiny lungs threatening hyperventilation.

In the distance behind him a gentle snoring resumed. For a moment the boy envied and resented his sister Peggy, two years his elder. Perhaps she wasn't sleeping. Maybe, just maybe this was her coping mechanism.

Common sense would tell him on any other night to burrow beneath the blankets. Squeeze his eyes shut and pray for the pain and hatred to go away. Something was different tonight. Enough was enough.

Leaning towards the flimsy, press board door, he cocked his head. Damien grappled to subdue the tempo of his rapid heart. A creaky floorboard protested underneath his uncertain stance.

He froze in sheer terror. Immobilized by impending doom the boy refused to falter even a hint of movement. Silently, in his head he counted, not super-fast like they did on Sesame Street but in the concentrated, deliberate fashion Mommy taught him long ago. One Mississippi, Two Mississippi, Three…he chanted the mantra in his head with blue lips quivering over chattering teeth all the while.

Conjuring the bravery of all his comic book heroes, his Star Wars action figures and prime time television icons he reached for the rusty brass door knob. He exhaled slowly. It seemed right at that moment. Just like the way he'd seen Mommy breathe out so many times in her Yogi bear exercises.

Inch by fraction of an inch he twisted counter clockwise. The door's tumblers and pins resisted little as did his determination and tenacity. He twisted further and further before taking the plunge and pulling the door towards his ragged, tattered pajama bottoms.

"You are not my keeper. I am the man of this house," every syllable was enunciated with cheap department store china rattling on verge of shattering to dozens of pieces. "I'm the bread winner and if I want to have a few drinks and play a few cards on my time that is my god damned business!"

Wailing sobs and pleas of mercy retaliated to his maniacal declarations. Sickening claps of flesh on flesh reverberated off the desolate country walls. Damien flinched and shook violently. A fresh burst of panic and urgency possessed him. Tossing any grasp

of caution aside he barreled down the stairs. His tiny slippers nearly tripped him up on several leaps and bounds.

"You're hurting me! Please just stop. I told you I was sorry!"
Desperation shrieked from Mommy. He'd heard her cry far too
many times before, yet never quite like this.

"And you have the nerve to ride my ass about rent money?"
Thunderous booms ejected from father. He was past the point of
return. Frothing with seething rage, there would be no reasoning
with father tonight.

"I work my god damned ass to the bone lady, to the bone. Day
and night and night and day I slave for you bunch of good for nothing free loaders. And what thanks do I get? What about me Joy?
What about old Billy boy?"

Mercifully his volume lowered yet somehow his vicious tendencies dialed up a notch. Damien could hear every chilling word,
every horrifying letter around the corner, at the base of the bedroom stairs. Ordinarily the mere thought of father paralyzed him
in terror. Somehow, he knew if he didn't do something Mommy
just may not see the light of day.

"Huh, what about old Billy boy? You think I signed up for this
shit Princess?" No mistaking it, he'd now resorted to humiliation
and mockery. "Well, you worthless bitch, answer me!"

A whirling gust of wind followed by the sharpest of cracks
burst Damien into fresh bout of violent tremors. The sanctity of
the stair's seclusion could last no longer. Innocence of fragility be
damned, the boy stepped out into mayhem beyond.

The spectacle was enough to obliterate any grasp of innocence
beyond recollection. Against the splintered and worn kitchen
counter father had mother pinned by the throat. As she twisted,
squirmed and writhed in terror, her efforts remained futile as father eclipsed her entire frame with his trembling upper torso.

"We're going to get some things straight, you and I," he whispered with a guttural, forked tongue. "Before this night is through

even your little, itty bitty pea brain will know better than to defy the likes of me ever again." Father's verbal assault was blended with slurs, yet the message was loud and clear.

She flailed in desperate sobs beneath his rage. Tassels of flannel whisked back and forth against the linoleum counter. What remained of her nightgown was defiled of all dignity.

"So, what you're going to do princess is make your old man a fucking burger like you were told. What's a guy got to do around here for a half descent bite to eat, in his own god damned house no less?"

Damien shuffled out of the vestibule, past the porch door left recklessly ajar. The family barbeque, a rusted bucket of bolts and charred memories lay on its side. Remnants of charcoal, butane and grilling utensils scattered the worn floor boards. Yet another scene courtesy of father's drunken tirades.

"Do you hear me woman or do I have to slap some more sense into you? The things you make me do…"

"Enough!" A piercing shrill ignited the room, suspending all momentary lapse of realism.

The hulking monstrosity froze. A fresh cocktail of disbelief and annoyance quenched his actions further. By the grace of god, he released his quivering prisoner. Color slowly flowed back to her bludgeoned, tear strained cheeks. Purple indentations upon her throat; like whimsical tattoos served as reminder for days and weeks to come.

Suspended in time and surrealism, Damien looked on. Although his tiny figure convulsed in pure horror, he stood his ground, fortified his last stand. Father straightened his brooding six-foot six stature. Snake like tendons pulsed along his neck and forehead. If pure rage could ever be exceeded, father had burst through the flood gates of evil personified. He glared down at his offspring, eyes midnight black and void of soul.

"Well, well, well. Just look at what we have here, baby Damien has come and joined the party. Why am I not surprised," he flailed his arms in mocked astonishment. Beefy, rippling appendages whirled through the air that could crush bone and cartilage with one executed strike. The boy winched and flinched with every motion.

"Can never be too far from Mommy's tit is that right little boy? Once a free loader, always a god damned free loader..."

Although the precise context may not have been entirely understood, Damien knew full well father was out to hurt. Maybe not in hitting type of hurt at first; Then again, he always did start his hurt with words. Still the boy held his ground. His very fiber to the core vibrated in terror of what to come, how this could finally end. The two of them glared at one another, locked in genetic standoff.

Sweat continued to drizzle down the boy's brow. The air was dense with tension, faint charcoal and sour whiskey. Rapidly, relentlessly Damien's heart thundered on.

"Well, well, sonny boy. Clearly you have something on your mind. Enough what, you little shit? Enough what?" Father grit his teeth, grinding them as his jaw pulsated. He clenched his haymaker fists in rejuvenated fury.

"Damien honey, go back to bed. Mommy and Daddy, we're just..." she stammered from over father's shoulder. Maternal as her instincts were, her pleas lacked any sense of conviction.

The sound of Mother's voice inspired the boy once again. Like a slap in the face he stepped towards his adversity. The entire room began to swirl and whiz out of control. Buzzing and maniacal laughter shrouded the walls of the remote country home. A virtual midway had spawned flourishing insanity, depravity and chaos.

"How do you like that? Junior just decided to get up and his balls dropped in the middle of the night. Well congratulation son, aren't we so proud of you?" Spittle of contempt flew this way and that. "You really think you can disrespect your maker without the thrashing of your life? Seems like Mommy isn't the only one getting corrected tonight!"

Words had barely erupted from father's lips before Damien began to instinctively retreat. Back peddling towards the sanctuary of his bed, he wished to go back in time. What an awful, awful mistake! The site before him, undeniable hatred would haunt him for years to come.

"Bill please, he's just a boy, don't..."

"You shut your trap bitch.' He whirled around all too eager to release his venom upon fresh prey. "My food isn't exactly making itself. God damn it! I'm surrounded by insolents and halfwits. You two, no this entire household would drive any man, any man to drink!"

Damien's hasty retreat ended abruptly. The air whooshed out of his lungs. Over a pair of discarded sneakers, he'd tripped. Helplessly he lay there. His brief act of heroism thwarted faster than it had begun.

Then redemption found its home. Just like the countless times he'd seen on television's Lorne Greene's New Wilderness program with the untamed animals cornered by a relentless predator, he roared into life. There was only one word to describe father. Although he was supposed to be their protector, their provider, their father and husband he failed on all accounts. Coward. He may have worn the mask of a king, but he was a coward for torturing his wife and children.

The words exploded from Damien's cold lips before he'd realized they were even uttered.

"Coward!"

On impulse the boy clambered to gather the closest object to defend himself. A moment of synchronicity transpired that must've been born of complete fate. While father hell-bent on blood, released mother and charged for his son, the family cat TC had burst through the room in frenzied panic. Ordinarily a feral species, likely afraid to death of father he'd occasionally come into the house for food or momentary comfort. Tonight's behavior was beyond out of character. As the feline bolted across the room in resilient fashion only cats can comprise, he tripped up the mastodon's feet in mid charge.

Like the saying goes in countless tales, the bigger they are, the harder they fall, father did not disappoint. Damien screamed. Embracing all vulnerability, forgotten hope, abandoned love he screamed. Long into the night he screamed until he could scream no more.

Father spun his arms. His eyes bulged within his crimson mask of hate. Finality veiled his face in sudden epiphany. Impaled by a pointed barbeque fork he sputtered and screeched. A deafening schlocking sound filled the midnight air. Blood sprayed over Damien's resilient little fists. Sinewy strands of larynx and flesh flapped against his knuckles. His creator and dominant foe wheezed and sputtered for merciful release. Imprisoned to destiny he continued to clutch and claw for vengeance. Rolling back into his skull his soulless, black eyes succumbed as he whispered towards his descending demise.

"It's not over, it's not over."

Bursting into life, Damien screamed. His chest rose and fell in rapid succession. Drenched in a pool of icy cold sweat, he whipped the satin sheet off his naked body.

As he swung his legs off the side of the bed, he braced his head between his clammy palms. Taking a deep breath, he resigned to the notion of yet another sleepless night. For a moment he refrained from standing. This routine was all too familiar. Standing right now would prove a dreadful mistake paying credence to vertigo and despair. From the other side of the bed, a soft murmur of resistance ensued. He glanced over the bundle of comforters, sheets and far too many fluffy pillows. A gentle smile formed upon his haggard face. For a moment he resented his girlfriend Jade's ability to sleep soundlessly. Resentment lifted to a passing envy as he slowly rose to stand on shaky feet.

He crept towards the bathroom. Each step more cerebral than the last. He cared not to wake his love. For more selfish reasons than courtesy, Damien couldn't stand to admit to yet another nightmare. Clinging to the past had never been his style. After countless years of therapy, psychiatrists, medication and more therapy the young man couldn't bare admitting that he needed further help. Jade's intentions were always the best, but he'd rather blow his brains out than be coddled over something she clearly didn't understand.

Into the darkness of the washroom he stepped. The door creaked, its infernal moan in its hinges. He winced slightly, awaiting a full-blown interrogation of questions. Satisfied she'd not stirred, he leaned against the porcelain sink. Such a familiar stance, it felt soothing and cool against his sweat ladled skin. He sighed into the silent air. Twisting the rusty faucets, he waited for just the right temperature. As he cupped his palms he splashed repeatedly the osmosis over his disheveled face. The room was a cube of blackness, save for the sliver of neon light slicing its way in through blinds from the tireless urban life. Damien glanced into the mirror. His heart clenched in dismay. A silhouette, ominous yet undeniable shadowed his features. A face familiar, yet far from his own, whispered into the sheet of glass, "it's not over, it's not over."

CHAPTER TWO

Mornings were never Damien's strong suit, even in the greatest of times. Shuffling past the small but quaint living room he yawned and stretched reaching for an unattainable two more inches. Through the kitchen's threshold he paused.

A ghost of a smile formed upon his lips, the first in several days. Jade was busy at the stove top sizzling up one of her culinary specialties. Pancakes, bacon and eggs were stacked esthetically perfect onto two plates. He regarded the generous contour of her posterior. Languidly his eyes traced the hems of her briefs hugging her buttocks beneath her flimsy chinos. He adored the way her fiery auburn hair whisked back and forth just above her waist.

Reaching for a cup of coffee, he leaned in and tenderly kissed the nape of her neck. She flinched ever so slightly, startled.

"Morning Hun," she smiled as bright as July sunshine. "Better hurry and sit. You don't want to be late for work."

Into a porcelain Iron Maiden mug Damien poured his piping hot java. Extra strong for mornings like this was just the way he liked it. Still dressed in his sweats and t-shirt he yawned for the third time since rolling out of bed. While bending into the refrigerator he grunted and groaned, an utterance usually reserved for someone fifteen years his senior.

Jade glanced sideways at him over her bubbling skillet and spatula. Under her breath she sighed and shook her head. Onto his plate she flipped the last of his pancakes.

Silently the two pulled out the chairs from their thrift store dining room table. In near calculated synchronicity they dug into their breakfast meal. Damien offered his best obligatory smile and felt a pang of guilt for not demonstrating more of his appreciation. It seems like she was always mothering him. At times her intentions melted his distant heart. Then at others her nurturing drove him straight up the wall.

"Another sleepless night babe?" She cooed softly over the centerpiece of their scarred and misshapen table. It was difficult, yet she tried to keep it light, knowing full well too much concern would send her love straight over the deep end.

In abstract, distracted designs he traced his fork, this way and that. He offered no rebuttal, evidence of confirming Jade's suspicions.

"Hon-you've barely touched your food." She reached across the table and caressed his forearm. Somehow her touch always cut through whatever melancholy he was feeling.

"I'm sorry babe." Reaching for his mug he stopped after considering. He wanted not to demonstrate his nerves coming undone with a shaky hand. "I guess I just have a lot on my mind with the wedding and everything."

She offered a gentle squeeze of his arm. "You don't have to shut me out. I know cousin Danny's wedding is only part of it." There. It was out there suspended in mid conversation awaiting a verbal dissection of epic proportion.

The two of them knew full well what the true origin of unease was. With a couple as close as the two high school sweethearts were there was little need for verbal affirmation.

"It's been a long, long time since you've returned home."

Damien met her with a wild-eyed gaze through matted strands of proverbial bedhead. In less serious scenarios his expression would've been downright comical.

"Yeah, well Seagrave doesn't exactly hold a lot of cherished memories Jade. You know that." She sensed his immediate defensiveness as he stood and scuffed the chair's legs across the worn parquet flooring.

"I know, I know Hun," she whispered taking a gentler approach. Damien stood in the kitchen doorway his back towards her feeling absurd. The flooding of memories, the recollection of that fated night paralyzed him. He'd completely forgotten why he'd entered the room to begin with.

"Maybe a visit to your hometown will finally bring you some closure." She stood behind him, wrapping her arms around his waist. "Thirteen years is a long time. It doesn't always have a hold of you. Yet lately, lately you've become distant again." The grip around his torso tightened. Damien could feel her arms shaking. He turned suddenly feeling like a heel for spawning a bout of insecurity.

Her eyes welled up as a steady stream of tears trickled down her creamy complexion. Such sheer vulnerability in this beautiful creature just about broke his heart into thousands of pieces. Tenderly he caressed her cheek, wiping the sadness away.

"I know that was an awful time, worse than any person should ever have to experience. But Baby it's over now and it kills me to see you go there again." Damien squeezed her tighter and sobbed in shuttering quivers. He hated like hell to see her pain and know he was responsible for her despair. "And you know full well you don't have to do this alone. I'll be there with you each step of the way. We're a team now, you and I." She looked up and met his gaze trying her best at an optimistic smile. "But you can't shut me out. I get scared when you keep to yourself and suffer alone."

11

At times Jade made more sense than Damien could readily process. She was his confidante. She was the rock he always needed.

"Just how on earth did you get to be so wise?" The two laughed in unison. "You remind me of a sexy little Buddha, you know that?" For the first time in days, perhaps weeks the two laughed heartily with complete reckless abandon.

"So, no more nightmares?" Seductively she whisked her perky cups back and forth against his mid-drift. "You could always wake me up and I'd be more than happy to distract you or at least wear you out."

"Now how could any red-blooded male refuse?" Damien smirked and felt himself stiffen. Come to think of it we do have at least twenty minutes before work." He glanced up at the microwave's digital face. "Eighteen minutes more than I'll need I'm sure."

Jade shrieked in submission as he hoisted her by a double grip of her haunches. Around his hips she wrapped her legs in approval. Leaning in she kissed his lips with a sense of urgency near desperation.

"I love you Damien Galligher, you sleepless twit."

"I love you too twit."

Into the bedroom he carried her and proceeded to show her just exactly how much.

CHAPTER THREE

All the way to work Damien felt like a new man. It never ceased to amaze him the power of a little pep talk, not to mention some early morning nookie. Such rekindled spirit even prompted him to roll down the car's windows and crank his favorite radio station. This day in age it wasn't easy to find anywhere that played Judas Priest, Motley Crue and Finger Eleven. At times he felt like a dinosaur musically then others he just wished to be buried face down so the entire world could kiss his ass.

Into the hazy summer air, the infectious beat ensued. Damien thumped his fingers onto the steering wheel. His endorphins burst free, conquering all his negative woes, he even cared not he was already cut off twice in traffic and the PT cruiser before him crept like it was senior's Sunday.

For a twenty-year-old man, freshly graduated from college, Damien did have a pretty sweet gig. He'd studied social work at community college. Upon completion he'd hoped to counsel abused and troubled teens. After his own ordeal and learning of Jade's personal survivor tale he vowed to boldly step out into the working world and save it, one soul at a time. Sadly, it didn't pan out quite as expected. There was little need for a male counsellor in such areas, so he had to take what he could get. Instead Damien's vocation found him at a local community center advising the long term unemployed. Essentially, he got those who hadn't worked back on their feet again. It was rewarding to make a difference. For the first six months he worked on an internship and they were so impressed with his ethic hired him on in a two-year contract. Forty thousand a year for a twenty-year-old was nothing to sneeze at either. Got to love government funded jobs.

He looked forward to embracing the day, even combatting downtown traffic in Toronto and thirty dollars a day parking. Not much could phase his triumphant spirit. As he swigged on his second coffee of the day, Damien clicked on his turning signal to merge off the parkway.

A piercing shrill burst through the stereo speakers. He'd flinched so violently he nearly spilled coffee onto his suit pants. The shrieking persisted, refusing to relent. This wasn't the ending he'd recalled to such an obscure yes, but otherwise perfectly in tuned Type O Negative song. Blindly he reached for the radio dial, all the while squinting against the infuriating pitch. Any longer he'd be positive all the windows and windshield would shatter in protest.

Then a sound so eerily familiar yet inconceivable reverberated from beyond the dissipating shrills. It resembled laughter from a formidable distance. An infernal second that seemed like eternity passed as the baying grew louder, more confident, more dominant. Its bass rattled the rear window. The next declaration so real, so possessed nearly caused Damien to collide with the guard rail on the off ramp. Scores of following vehicles blasted their horns in fury.

On pure instinct alone, he pulled over to the side of the road and slammed the gear into park. Hyperventilating he buried his face into his hands and rocked back and forth. His mind could not process the continuous chant from the radio, "It's not over. It's not over."

CHAPTER FOUR

It was closer to nine thirty by the time Damien had managed to pull himself together enough to enter the Queen Street office. Never a single blemish of tardiness on his record, a fresh wave of anxiety washed over him. With intense wide strides he rushed towards the reception desk. His briefcase fell and swooped in large dizzying arches.

"Good morning Mr. Galligher, kind of you to join us." Cheryl the office secretary was a pleasant, twenty-five-year-old Latina lady. Ordinarily the two had an inseparable rapport. A comical misunderstanding that originated from another consultant, Chitra's famous match making prowess had secretively asked Cheryl if she'd go out with Damien. One lazy Thursday afternoon after submitting his expense reports he was mortified to hear a heartfelt if not sincere rejection from Cheryl. The two laughed every chance they'd gotten after deciphering that indeed it was Chitra the perpetual cupid that figured Damien could use a nice, sweet girl to fatten him up and Cheryl could use a nice guy on the rise to success to take care of her. Apparently, she'd neglected to factor that each of the coworkers had intimate partners exceeding five years a piece.

Shuffling through papers in frenzied, shaking hands at last he replied, "Hmm, what was that Cheryl?"

She slid her glasses down the bridge of her nose. A gesture such as this was indication to back off, she meant business. Taking a deep sigh, she resigned.

"I said good of you to join us. It's after nine thirty and the monthly budget meeting started twenty minutes ago. I sent you a reminder email and wrote it in your planner yesterday. Did you forget?"

"Shit, shit, shit, shit!" Damien dropped his briefcase onto the lobby's cobblestone floor.

"Sweet talk all you will, but Mr. Chan isn't going to like this." Cheryl already retreated to opening one file or another and scanning the pages with a red pen.

"You're not helping Cheryl. Just grab me a cup of coffee and wish me luck that my ass isn't grass." Damien bolted towards the boardroom's corridor. He grappled to shake the horrific images from his mind in the past twenty-four hours.

"I wouldn't bother Mr. Galligher. You know how much they hate to be interrupted during a budget meeting." She offered that nurturing expression from across the lobby. This was likely one of the attributes Chitra saw in her in evaluating her compatibility with young, oblivious Damien. "Why not go to your desk and I'll cut Mr. Chan off at the pass when they come out. I'll let him know you had an emergency monitoring session that ran a little late."

Ah Cheryl she was always thinking on her feet. This excuse may just work. Consultants within the office did make regular company visits to check upon their newly recruited employees. Because the program was government funded, random, spontaneous visits were not uncommon. If a company was suspect of misappropriating government funds it was always best to investigate further under the guise of a checkup.

"Great ok, thanks Cheryl." He returned a smile rich with warmth and sincerity. "Listen. I'm sorry if I was short with you. Just a lot on my mind I guess." He turned the opposite direction to ascend the stairs towards his office.

"No worries Mr. Galligher. But do it again and you'll owe me lunch next time." She shook a mocking finger in his direction. "Do we understand each other?"

"Loud and clear dear." At ease once again, he smiled and straightened his tie.

"And don't worry about this weekend. Weddings are always over before you know it. Just stick to the bar and it'll all be a blur."

"Yeah, that's what I'm afraid of." The two laughed in unison as Damien retreated to his post at last.

Cheryl smoothed her skirt before returning to the leather seat behind reception. She shook her head and silently wondered what it would be like to escort Mr. Galligher to such affairs. The image made her smile. Chitra would be proud.

Once settling in Damien checked his voice mail, reviewed some expenditure requests and drafted a first copy for a pending training plan. Despite physically rolling up his sleeves and grabbing yet a third cup of coffee he couldn't focus on the task at hand. The disturbing images and memories that haunted his psyche were threatening to slay his very well being. Perhaps he'd make a phone call to his adolescent psychiatrist Dr. Rhys later today. He hadn't seen him regularly since he was seventeen. Yet the good doctor did manage to get him through a world of emotional and psychological unbalance. He was more like a friend, answering calls off the clock and addressing concerns. Dr. Rhys never needed reminder of Damien's case and always seemed up to speed with what was going on in his life.

Tapping his pen out of rhythm he decided yes, a phone call to the good doctor was exactly what he'd do later. Maybe he even had some good strategies or exercises to deploy prior to returning to his old stomping grounds. God only knew whatever feedback he had couldn't possibly hurt.

For a large portion of the day Damien did his best to avoid his superior, Mr. Chan. Although he was always receptive to constructive criticism and didn't consider himself to be insolent by any stretch of the imagination, he really wasn't up for a confrontation. Concentrating on the mundane and trivial was challenge enough for today. He was just about home free, excusing himself for lunch when he heard the electronic burping of his office phone.

At first, he was going to ignore it letting it go to voice mail. Against his better judgment curiosity reigned supreme. He lurched across his desk, knocking over a mesh canister of pens and pencils in the process. Retracting the receiver, he idly rubbed his ribs.

"Galligher," he'd always answered his phone that way much to the disapproval of his coworkers, friends and even family alike.

"Yes, yes Damien. Peter Chan here, I'd like to see you in my office before you go to lunch." In his thick Cantonese accent his boss's request came out more like 'rike and 'runch'. Damien stifled a snicker at his verbal faux pas and told him he'd be right there. Squinting he rubbed his temples feeling a migraine come on.

"So much for an early retreat," he offered to no one.

Anticipation left little to the imagination while walking the long hallway to Mr. Chan's office. How exactly does one prepare for a reprimand? The obvious choice would be to take the discipline with stride, maturity. After all, Damien had not been exactly offering one hundred percent at his job as of late. Still he resented the notion of being scolded like a child. He knew he wasn't producing results. He knew the core cause. If he could just get through this weekend in one piece, physically, psychologically and emotionally he could get back on track again.

On jelly legs he looked down at his feet. He wiped the sweat from his palms, took a deep breath and prepared to knock on his superior's door. At that precise moment calamity ensued. Mr.

Chan whisked the door in ward and Damien's raised fist nearly collided with his forehead.

After several moments of awkward grunts, groans and make shift apologies, he gestured him inside. Swiftly he closed the door behind them. As he walked around the perimeter of the seating area it seemed to Damien that Chan was deliberately prolonging his agony.

"Damien, please take a seat." He smiled his best reassuring, obligatory smile. A guy couldn't resent his boss for trying. Yet the whole charade seemed a little over the top.

Under the buzzing fluorescent lights, Chan removed his thick bifocals and proceeded to scrub them vigorously. Perhaps he too was as apprehensive as his junior consultant. The glaring overhead tubes did damn little to alleviate the migraine forming behind Damien's eyes.

"This morning we had our monthly budget meeting. As you know we meet every thirty days as information sharing. We like to see how everyone is doing, pass around ideas and mold the future of the company. When someone is absent Mr. Galligher it is not very becoming of our team's success." Throughout his banter Chan refused to connect with direct eye contact. When Damien had first met his boss, he thought it was a sign of weakness. Cheryl explained it was a cultural mannerism, a gesture of politeness. In a way Damien was grateful for small favors. He had an awful habit of staring at the bizarre three-inch strand of hair that perpetually dangled from a mole in his neck. Once again Cheryl mentioned it was a cultural token, a sign of good luck and fortune. Damien thought it was ridiculously hideous.

"Mr. Chan, please...' he swallowed fighting for the right words. "Let me explain."

He held up a solitary hand. Seemingly in disdain he shook his head. Perhaps he was just as insulted at being interrupted as he was by his staff's absence.

"Mr. Galligher. You are fine, dedicated consultant." For emphasis he stood and began to pace around the confined quarters. "As the youngest consultant in the program's history, your numbers of recruitment far exceed our quota and your efforts do not go unrecognized."

"Well, thank you. I mean that is a good thing, right?" Damien stammered while trying to follow his wandering lecture.

"Yet past two weeks your work is on steady decline. Contracts are late, signatures missing. Monitoring reports with miscalculations, once Cheryl saw you sleeping at your desk and it was only ten o'clock!"

He had little to say in return. Frankly he was startled at just how much the nightmares were taking over his everyday waking life. His pulse quickened fearing the inevitable pink slip to be passed along his way. Losing his job right now would be catastrophic. He had never made this kind of money before and was planning on renovating the very modest apartment he shared with Jade. He wanted to give his love a taste of something more.

"You're tired, distracted and unable to commit one hundred percent like we need you."

The two of them finally met one another's gaze. A horrific episode began to unfold directly before Damien's eyes. He gasped, clapping one hand over his mouth.

A shadow running from the ceiling had clouded over Mr. Chan's expression. It continued to run ominously unto the carpeting below. From his brow, cheek bones, nose and lips his face had morphed into the sinister profile of his father. He sneered, a reflection powered with contempt laced with internal loathing.

Damien nearly flipped his chair back head over heels. He clutched his chest, glaring at the floor with bulging pupils. Desperately he grappled to subdue his rising and falling chest.

The infuriating lights from above sizzled and popped, shooting sparks of rain. Flames licked and danced at the cheap wall paper, roaring into life on stacks of contracts, file folders and memos. From the ceiling's tiles, strands of clotted blood stretched, drizzling into blackness below.

Somehow, he conquered the terror of looking up once again at the risk of succumbing to complete madness. The metamorphosis remained the same grinning defiantly through rotted, chipped teeth. With the cerebral gesture of a solitary hand, the figure before him placed a translucent thumb upon his throat. Shrieks of metal on metal invaded Damien's ears. From his Adam's apple a tidal wave of crimson rushed through soaking all in its path. The desk, stationary, award plagues and Damien's entire body drenched in blood.

He clenched his fists and opened his mouth about to scream the most terror filled, primal screams in existence. Just as he looked up the room was one and the same as he'd walked in. A nervous expression now was predominant upon Chan's face. Reluctantly he held a glass of water nearly spilling it several times.

"You're not well Damien. Why, you're covered in sweat." He sighed placing his hands upon his hips. "Get your stuff together and call it a day. Go home early, get some rest and Monday is another day."

Exhaling slowly, Damien fought to clear his throat. He didn't know what exactly inspired this decision but would take the early departure in a heartbeat.

"Thank you Mr. Chan. Thank you. I'll return completely refreshed Monday morning."

He moved towards the door and offered something entirely out of character. With a tentative hand he placed it upon Damien's shoulder. He seemed to grapple with just the right wisdom or maybe the right translation.

"Not for everyone Damien. You are exceptional, and we need you exceptional again. Consider this warning. Miss a meeting again and it's bye-bye. Understand?" He waved a pointed finger in his direction for emphasis.

He managed a nervous smile in return. "Yes sir, understood."

Walking back down the corridor, he had to stop to collect himself. As he leaned against the wall he squeezed his eyes shut in vain attempt to erase the graphic hallucination that just unfolded. With a glance at his watch he wondered if a drive to Seagrave was conceivable in the next couple of hours. It didn't take long to consider as Damien was already grabbing his car keys and belongings to embark upon a midday road trip.

CHAPTER FIVE

While walking to the parking garage, Damien felt a rejuvenated sense of purpose. Sure, Chan had scolded him in his own roundabout way and forced him to go home when it was barely noon. On the other hand, who would possibly protest such a decision? It never made any sense to him. Even as a rebellious adolescent, skipping school always led to a three-day suspension from classes. That'll show them. Give them exactly what they want; Brilliant deterrent. Yet he felt for his boss and didn't want to give mediocre or lack luster performances in the future. He liked his job a great deal and it offered tremendous autonomy and independence. Now was not the time to screw it up.

As he twirled his key ring over and over along his index finger, he almost forgot where he'd parked. The little things were starting to slip. If he couldn't function in regular everyday life because of sleep deprivation, nightmares or god forbid waking hallucinations then he may as well commit himself to the rubber room right now.

Retracting the Cavalier's locks his mind drifted back to Jade. His heart fluttered and skipped a beat at the recognition of her devotion. She could read him like an open book. Getting into their relationship, even in high school she knew he came with baggage. A lesser woman would toss him to the curb and never look back. The pep talks she gave him this morning followed by the ravenous love made him grin from ear to ear again. As he turned the key in the ignition he felt like a complete prick for keeping this impromptu journey from her. Somehow, he knew she just wouldn't understand. She'd try and talk him out of it. Now in this instance more than ever Damien knew he had to confront his most paralyzing fears. He knew it was time to go home.

If the visions continued to persist in everyday circumstances, there would be little room for argument. He'd be committed, like it or not. A man should be able to drive to work or have a brief conversation with his boss without coming completely undone. Seeing the old house where it all began seemed crucial. The evil that consumed the very foundation, walls and plaster had to stop. If he could see it for his own eyes and dismiss memories as nothing more than tragedy and misfortune, then he could bury all of this and move on. The house was merely a symbol, a decrepit, old structure surely incapable of conceiving evil. If he could see that for his own eyes, then closure was inevitable.

Cruising eastbound on Queen Street, past the streetcars, sidewalk cafes and afternoon freaks, Damien reached for the radio then just as quickly resigned. Last thing he needed was another debilitating episode while in midst of congested traffic. Just some deep breathing exercises, like Dr. Rhys had shown him would be suffice. Who knows? Maybe he'd even enjoy the countryside and reminisce a little over the good times that began a little later in life. He made a mental note to call the good doctor as soon as he was in the neighborhood. It probably wasn't a good idea to just drift into town without anyone knowing his whereabouts. Besides Dr. Rhys would be livid if he knew he was around and didn't at least drop in and say hello.

Merging off the congested parkway and onto highway 401 was like a weight lifted off his shoulders. The breathing exercises may be to thank. Steady inhaling and exhaling while imagining all the negative energy expunged was beyond conceiving just how effective it was. He wondered briefly why he'd ever stopped. It always seemed the positive rituals we instill are the first to abandon. Yet bad habits and destructive behavior we return to again and again. Why were people so infatuated with their own demise?

Damien had become so relaxed in his near hypnotic state that he barely recalled driving through Pickering, Ajax, Whitby and finally Oshawa. The rural countryside, although somewhat diminished since his youth was a welcome, esthetic treat. Some peace and tranquility could be found here. He wondered if he could ever pick up and move with Jade back to their roots and away from the city's hustle and bustle. It wasn't completely out of the question to marry one day and start a family out there. This seemed a far better environment to raise children.

Engulfed in thoughts of marital bliss, white picket fences and so forth just about made Damien swerve into the collector's lane. A tractor trailer blared its horn causing him to jerk back to where he belonged. Through his rear-view mirror, he spotted the Peterbilt signal and merge into the lane next to him. He likely annoyed the trucker causing him to pass. No one needed a road hog when you're hauling tons of whatever kind of merchandise.

While the truck shifted gears it bounded into life closer and closer to the Cavalier's rear bumper. Aside from the incessant indicator blinking there was no motion of the transport going anywhere but directly towards Damien. He cursed and tromped on the accelerator. What was this asshole doing anyway?

Anger sparked and sizzled at his veins over being unceremoniously interrupted from his relaxation exercises. He pressed the gas further causing the pistons to thrust and pump into frenzy. His RPM was closing in on the red. Agitated, Damien rolled down his window and motioned the aggressive trucker to pass and ideally fuck off.

Wouldn't that be positively anti-climactic to get into a road side accident en route to piecing his crumbling life back together?

The further he pressed his defiant beater, the further the transport barreled after him. If he didn't do something fast he'd surely be rear ended and run right off the highway. An express highway such as this could spell ultimate doom with vehicles often whizzing by at an excess of one hundred and forty kilometers an hour. Plenty of fatalities occurred on this very stretch of asphalt every year. The notion ignited a fresh bout of rapid heartbeats within his chest. His mouth, dry as a Sahara Desert offered little consolation.

His vision blurred then doubled. No matter how hard he tried he couldn't catch his breath. A full-blown anxiety attack had spawned as he sped further and further towards a long winding curve up ahead.

At last by god's good mercy or some other divine intervention, the truck glided into the adjacent lane. As it approached Damien's side he looked up to see what kind of mug lay before such a twisted, juvenile creep. Some people never knew when to call it quits.

Through the corner of his eye he could not believe the spectacle before him. Sinewy strands of plasma gelatin hung like slabs of butchered meat from the trucker's face. Blood oozed from every orifice, his eye sockets, ears, nose and mouth. He grinned defiantly and reached towards the ceiling. Strands of intestines wrapped up in a chord dangled. He pulled and tugged, harder and faster. Not a horn sounded but a hellacious unworldly squeal like the sound of a thousand animals slaughtered all at once.

Damien opened his mouth to scream, but silence stole the air from his lungs as he swerved off the highway and launched into a desolate field below.

CHAPTER SIX

It could have been an eternity that had passed for all he knew. Lifting his head off the steering wheel felt like two hundred pounds of smashed granite and rubble. Into the mid-afternoon sun he moaned, rubbing the back of his neck. He didn't think anything was broken but he was incredibly stiff. Caked on blood below his neck indicated an enthusiastic nose bleed. The notion of getting out of the car to assess the damage consumed him with dread.

The airbags hadn't deployed. Somehow a slight chuckle erupted from his swollen lips. His chuckling progressed to full blown belly laughter then a fit of hysterics. Just east of Oshawa, a General Motors town if there ever was one and his car had managed to crash without any safety provisions such as airbags. A blind man could see the irony in that. Rolling out of the driver's door more than walking or stumbling he struggled to stand on sea legs. He braced against the hood of the car and wretched his coffee into the tall weeds and shrubbery. After one solid stream a series of dry heaving ensued tying knots in his stomach. Reminiscing about the good old days reminded him of his partying youth. More nights than he could count ended precisely this way but at least he had the bonus of being buzzed. Now Damien was simply disoriented, disillusioned and on verge of defeat.

The images and hallucinations, the nightmares and horrific interludes simply had to stop before he arrived home in a body bag. This last soiree with death was enough to make a personal inner pact to get some closure and get the hell out of dodge as they say. He retrieved a handful of napkins from his back pocket, wiped his lips dry and patted his moist brow.

From the corner of his eye he peered at the front half of the Cavalier. Nothing too out of sorts, the front corner panel was a little worse for wear, but it was undoubtedly still drivable. Placing his hand upon the roof of the car he took a slow, methodical walk around. Remarkably nothing was too damaged at all. Damien was awestruck at how he'd managed a high-speed crash coming out pretty much unscathed.

As he took a deep breath he retreated to the driver's seat once again. Now was as good as any time to call the good doctor. He only hoped Dr. Rhys wouldn't be able to detect the unease in his tone.

Even though the two only talked now around the holidays, exchanging pleasantries and well wishes he had the psychiatrist's number in his contact list. Dialing, he cursed, hit end and realized he still had to dial one prior to the remaining digits for a long-distance exchange. It seemed the most monetary of tasks required more thought and effort than he was capable of these days.

Resuming his relaxation techniques, he dialed the number again, exhaling. A slight twinge of pain shot out as he rubbed his side. After several chirps he thought the call would go to voice mail.

"Dr. Rhys's office, may I help you?" Caroline, the ever-faithful receptionist had answered. Damien always adored her no-nonsense attitude and professional demeanor. He wasn't in the mood for chit chat right now.

"Afternoon Caroline," he cleared his throat realizing how raspy he sounded. "Is Dr. Rhys busy?"

"Damien, is that you? Good heavens! What a surprise. He just finished with a patient." After a brief pause she added. "You know he's never too busy for you."

He smiled at her sincere offering even though he winced and cradled his forehead in his free palm.

"How are you keeping these days?" She barely took a breath before moving right along. "I hear your cousin Danny is getting married. Will you be in town for a while?"

"I am, I mean I'm going to be," Damien swiftly retracted. He didn't need to raise any red flags about his impromptu early afternoon road trip. "The wedding's tomorrow and we have rehearsal this evening. Jade's looking forward to it, but you know how I am with this town."

"I'm sure the two of you will have a lovely time. Speaking of which, planning on making an honest woman out of that girlfriend of yours anytime soon young man?"

Damien laughed heartily at this. The sudden jiggling and jolting seized his neck and shoulders. Leave it to a no nonsense gal like Caroline to choose now for a little bit of whimsical banter.

"You'll be the first to know Caroline. That I guarantee." He was proud of himself for volleying such mindless jibber jabber. Social exchanges such as this usually made him want to vomit.

"And you drop by the office sometime soon. It's been too long Damien. I'll get the doctor for you, take care sweetie."

"Thanks Caroline, I'll see you soon, promise."

On the steering wheel he drummed his fingers. As of late it seemed fidgeting mannerisms became his trademark. For a moment he considered hanging up, regretting making the call. Such a spineless gesture would not sit well with Dr. Rhys.

"Damien! Is that really you?"

"Hi Doc, yeah it's me. Did I catch you at a bad time?"

"For you son, there never is a bad time. How's life treating you?"

"Pretty decent, no complaints,' he cringed a little over his bold-faced lie. "That's not entirely true. Things haven't gotten a light chaotic as of late."

"Oh, please go on."

"I know I'm not really your patient anymore and haven't been for a few years but…"

"Now, now son, you know better. You're like family to me. If it weren't for that wealthy real estate mogul Dublin snatching up your mother and marrying her, you'd be calling me Dad about now."

The two laughed at the recollection. A brief intimate relationship did indeed include mother Galligher and Dr. Rhys. It was getting relatively serious despite an obvious conflict of interest for a doctor/patient's family relationship. In the end the two parted as friends amicably. Overall Damien's need for therapy far superseded their passion for one another.

"Think about that all the time, it's funny you mention family too. The nightmares are back, Doc and they're far worse than ever before. I feel like I'm coming undone, going crazy."

"Well you have been through a world of turmoil son. Post-traumatic stress disorder sadly does not just disappear over-night. It's something that needs to be addressed and revisited regularly. You've made leaps and bounds in terms of coping. A decent career, a loving girlfriend and making amends with extended family…"

"No, I know all that Doc and thank you for saying so." Damien gripped the steering wheel and shifted in his seat. "It's just that something remains incomplete, like I have to put this behind me once and for all. I guess coming into town for the wedding has been playing on my mind since the announcement."

"That's perfectly natural. In your subconscious you've been becoming anxious and ambivalent about facing a symbol of your personal tragedy. It's like opening old wounds and pouring in the proverbial salt if you will."

A brief lapse of silence followed that wasn't awkward and felt somehow necessary.

"If you like I can schedule a weekend appointment for you, just casually of course and we can discuss it a little further."

"That's really nice of you Doc. I may take you up on it yet but don't think it's necessary." He took a deep breath hoping courage would restore his intentions before pressing on. "I'm going to the house Doc. I need to see it for my own eyes and bury this once and for all."

"Oh, Damien, son, I don't know. This could have a potentially dangerous affect. At first glance, of course I advocate fear aversion therapy one hundred percent. I suggest that if you must absolutely insist, then to go with someone. A scene such as this may trigger a series of delusions, anxiety, hysteria, not to mention any number of possible physical ramifications."

He swallowed, hard but refused to repent. In his mind he scoffed the doctor attempting to interfere. For a moment he wondered if his intentions were always pure or if he had some sort of ulterior motives himself.

"I'm going regardless Doc. I just wanted your feedback. I'll let you know how it goes."

"Damien, promise me you won't go alone. And above all else do not I repeat do not forget to call me immediately after."

He flushed furiously, ashamed for his suspicion of the doctor and friend. Yes, that was the most adequate label, Dr. Rhys was his friend. He cleared his throat once again.

"I won't let you down Doc and thank you."

He terminated the call before any further distraction. Gazing through the windshield past a horizon of grassy fields and a midday blazing sun, Damien turned the ignition. The engine roared into life as he crept back towards the highway and his new-found destiny.

CHAPTER SEVEN

Speaking with Dr. Rhys seemed to restore Damien's sense of strength and conviction. Even though a tender age of twenty was merely a child in some circles, he felt the need to accept responsibility for his own circumstances. He couldn't rely upon parents to shelter under or sit around unemployed on the system or slink into an abysmal pool of medication and ignore the world around him continued to exist. No, Damien had plans and be damned if he'd allow his past to constantly interfere.

He even turned the radio back on and was relieved there was not a single out of place tone, noise, sound or note. The front end of the Cavalier shook ever so slightly approaching an excess of eighty clicks, but it wasn't a big issue. He may even get it serviced while the wedding was in procession. If anything, Seagrave had a multitude of mechanics and many were friends or acquaintances from high school. Don't sweat the small stuff he told himself. He laughed at the memory, another scroll of wit from the good doctor. The simple phrase was his mantra in junior high school and towards being a senior as well. If you couldn't readily change it, chances are it wasn't worth worrying about. He was on route to change the very thing that paralyzed him in recent days. Chock this one up to another victory. Damien was coming home and even Satan himself couldn't stop him now.

Getting off the frantic four lane freeway was a blessing. Now the true countryside rolled past as he left Brooklyn in the dust and quickly approached Port Perry. He didn't recall each of the small villas developing so rapidly. It looked as though his alma mater now boasted a Tim Horton's, Dairy Queen and McDonalds.

A small pang of resentment lingered as he couldn't help but wonder what growing up with these amenities would have been like. Instead his clique of degenerate friends resided at a local smoky pool hall. The facility was as shady as they'd come. Drugs, booze, teenage sex, weapons and all out brawls were the Friday night flavor for Funland. In hindsight he supposed he wouldn't have changed much those formative years. Still the whole debacle made him feel like an outsider looking in on the rest of the world. Almost subconsciously he tromped upon the gas apprehensive about leaving the spectacle behind.

It was now one forty-five according to the digital clock's face below the dashboard. He was a little surprised he'd made such great time all the way from downtown Toronto on Friday afternoon. Smiling to himself he surrendered to the notion he just may pull this off yet. There was plenty of time to see the old place, do what he had to do, get back on the road for home, pick up Jade, quick change of clothes and be back with time to spare for the wedding rehearsal.

Still, for the life of him, he couldn't fathom why he had to attend the damn thing anyway. He supposed his Aunt's wishes for him to be an usher at his oldest cousin's wedding was cut and all that. If he knew Danny at all, he'd guessed he couldn't care less. Guys so rarely do with these sorts of things, but he supposed his bride to be had to have her story book wedding, so whatever. He thoroughly planned on getting good and sloshed once this was all over and enjoying himself at the reception. For the love of God, he certainly deserved it.

Pulling off the main highway and crawling up the gravel roads made his heart skipped a beat. He was only minutes away now. There'd be no turning back.

A drive through the countryside was about as therapeutic as it was going to get. Acres and acres of rolling green hills filled the horizon. Majestic horses ran in packs, seemingly frolicking in the balmy air. Cattle grazed by the dozens, languidly shuffling about without a solitary care in the world. Damien envied such a basic, primal mentality. He strived for normality. His new-found obsession was erasing the past. This was far from the life that was intended for him. Every waking moment of his existence since the tender age of seven has lead up to this point. Come hell or high water he was going to close this chapter once and for all and burn the book from within it contained. Perhaps he'd even scatter the ashes in several different continents.

Along the dusty road the Cavalier's tires gripped and spat chunks of aggregate. He was cautious not to speed on such questionable terrain. Last thing he needed was another fender bender. He wasn't sure if he had the strength to crawl out of another one.

A wave of recollection provoked his nerves. His heart hammered in his bruised chest. Each of his limbs tensed like spindle chords on verge of snapping. Clearly within view was the Galligher home. Damien depressed the brake pedal. He couldn't even wait to thrust the gear into park. Clambering, he shouldered the driver's door open and spewed profusely. The nausea refused to relent. More and more streams of clear, mucous fluid flooded from his throat. A trickle of blood formed at his lips. He pushed away the possibility of internal injuries. Stubborn resilience conquered all rational thought. Onto the dirt road he sputtered, once, twice then after a moment a third time to be sure it was done.

Blindly, he shimmied into his back pocket for more napkins. He sighed in frustration, realizing he used his last supply after his previous episode. From the darker recesses of his mind a voice cackled in maniacal laughter. If he'd only invested some stock in a tissue company he'd either be saving a bundle about now or earning a fortune.

Taking a deep breath, he slowly concentrated his gaze upon the spectacle before him. He wasn't sure if he trusted his faculties yet. A glance above the dash was sufficient. If only he'd packed some cool water or even a soda to rid of the raunchy barf aftertaste.

It was difficult, next to impossible, to get a clear view of the Galligher home. Blades of grass and a bevy of varying weeds grew at least three feet high throughout the entire lot. The shingles upon the two-story were weathered, peeled and in many cases completely gone. Siding, if you could still call it that was deteriorated beyond recollection. It was obvious whomever the home owner was had taken the liberty of boarding up the windows and doors. In a small village like Seagrave, gossip travelled faster than an infectious disease in a Texas whorehouse. No one wanted to live where a murder had taken place. No one in their right mind wanted to lay their head where blood was shed.

After a few moments of symptomatic inventory, Damien stepped out onto the roadside. Going the rest of the way on foot seemed to make sense. There was no point in trying to wrestle with a rusty gate and drive his car over a glorified bush trail. The driveway hadn't been tended to in thirteen years. The path to despair had been as equally neglected as the Mammon of shattered dreams beyond.

Almost on instinct, a reflex of sorts, Damien resorted to his deep breathing exercises again. He was a lot of things, but one could not accuse him of lacking repetition. Towards the disheveled fence he walked. Within his mind he begged for sweet release he so longed for.

A moan of protest cut through the eerily silent air. He wasn't sure if his footing would hold as he stepped onto a sagging mesh rung. Bending at the knee he hoisted his free leg towards the clearance, careful not to round house kick the waterlogged post above. On verge of swinging his leg over the flimsy rung, it burst, sending him plummeting chest first onto the top of the fence.

With the air smashed out of his lungs, tears streamed down his eyes. If he hadn't bruised or fractured a couple of ribs prior to this, he'd clearly done so now. As he dangled on top of the fence his legs commenced an absurd rocking motion between torso and hindquarters. The lunatic laughter resumed in his mind as he was reminded of those plastic birds that dipped closer and closer to a reservoir of water in jerking, bobbing and swaying motions. Hysteria seemed his only god send as he flipped head over heels onto the driveway below.

A burst of indigo, blue and violet spread across his field of vision. Speckles of blackness danced around his eyes before gradually dissipating one by one. As he laid there staring up at the sky Damien wondered if it were so bad if it all just ended right now. Sure, there'd be his loved ones, his family and of course Jade that would be devastated at first. But how does one ever truly control their own demise? We really don't get to choose when our time is up. He closed his eyes perfectly comfortable with the notion. It'd been a pretty decent run, not the life he'd have chosen for himself. Somehow it was comforting to know all the failures, heartaches and pain would simply wash away like torrential rain off an eroded structure. In time all would be forgotten, even Damien Galligher. He sighed at warmth of submission, feeling a tingling sensation in his neck steadily rise to his cranium and back again. Into the sweet abyss of unconsciousness, he descended, the corners of his mouth twitching into a crazed smile of satisfaction.

CHAPTER EIGHT

There was no way of knowing just how long he was out for. By the time he managed to open his eye lids, the darkness that was within was comparable to the sky above. Sometime around dusk, the clouds seemed painted with purple veins dipped in blood red. This little spur of the moment encounter would prove to get him in hot water with many parties. Jade would be livid being abandoned on such an important evening for such intimate reasons. His family would be outraged for missing the ceremony's rehearsal. Of course, Dr. Rhys would scold him until this side of Tuesday for disobeying his advice.

Somehow, he managed to push aside all the interpersonal ramifications. They'd get over it. It was about fine time he'd stopped worrying over everyone and concentrate on him. What about Damien? What about him god damn it?

Would everyone prefer he just up and had a complete mental breakdown in front of them, at his cousin's wedding no less? Oh, that'd be rich. He'd be the talk of the family tree for years to come as the cousin that went right off his crackers for apparently no reason at all. No one wanted to associate a joyous event like a wedding with something like that. He nodded to himself, seemingly approving to such an honorable gesture as saving his family from his own horrific indignity.

As he placed one unsteady hand through weeds, stones and grit, he winced. Somehow it felt like he'd aged twenty years in the past twenty-four hours. Once this was over it may just be fine time for an extended vacation. Preferably the holiday could be someplace tropical and not an environment called the Shady Acres Ranch or some damned thing where the mattresses where on the walls and all the apparel was white and did up from the back. Uh, no thanks, submitting to insanity was not an option. This was precisely why he was here right now.

Just when he thought there was no fight in him left, Damien found himself vertical. A little woozy at first, he steadied his gaze upon his target. The house before him looked more ominous and ethereal before the setting sun.

He stumbled and limped towards the front door. Brushing past strands of dry foliage, he wondered what kind of creepy crawlies lurked in the midst. He wasn't a fan of snakes. Granted he was entirely afraid of them either. Right now, did not seem the best opportunity to have a choice encounter. His one phobia, one true irrational fear was of rodents. A shivering sensation rose from his feet and straight up his spine. He'd just about lose it if a rat or even a field mouse were to run across his path. Something about their beady little eyes, gnashing and gnawing, yellowing teeth and slippery, slithering tail was enough to through him into a fit of near cardiac arrest. Deep within his subconscious he knew full well he had his father to blame for this irrational fear, among countless other things. Somehow, he repressed the memory and refused to recognize it willingly.

He glanced around the yard and gasped in surprise to see the old tire swing was still intact. Just off to the side was a huge maple tree. His father had tied a rope and suspended a tire in its center, probably from one of his many rusty heaps he collected in the back yard. He used to take him out and swing him high into the air for hours on end. In his young, impressionable mind he thought he was Superman. He could fly through the sky with the greatest of ease. Father would push him higher and higher getting closer to the clouds each time. He encouraged him to reach further, and further. Next time, he'd collect a puff of sticky whiteness like cotton candy to enjoy inside later. He remembered laughing until he could laugh no more, and Father was laughing alongside with him.

Something chirped within the distance. It slapped Damien back to present reality. A grasshopper ensued its nightly sonnet of seduction.

Distracted from his initial path, in curious strides he gravitated towards the tire swing. He caressed its worn surface. The dank scent of musty mildew and rubber filled his breath.

From the shelter of the Maple's massive canopy he gazed into the back yard. A remnant of an old rusted over Volkswagen Beetle peered up defiantly above the weeds. This was yet another of Father's pet projects that was never fully nurtured.

A foggy reminiscence drifted back to him. He remembered a drizzly afternoon when it was just him and Father home. The two men of the house and he was ecstatic at being alone with him. He wanted him to play but was too frightened to ask, fearing he'd think it was silly. Instead it was as though he'd read his son's boredom and decided to bring him out back to see 'the beast.'

Young child like Damien could see the floor drifting further and further away from him. He reached for protective purchase and was delighted to find it was wrapped around Daddy's neck. With new found pride he was being paraded about by this giant of a man, to show him real man like stuff. It would be way cool, keener than neat and Daddy wanted him to be a part of it.

He remembered the air rushing into his lungs as he cooed excitedly, "Wow Daddy it looks like a spaceship." To his infant perception, it did look exactly like an interplanetary space craft. Bubble in shape with dramatic contours, curves and convex exteriors, the German engineering seemed like an obvious prototype for galactic travel.

"Yep, it's something else, isn't it son?" A thunderous bellow rolled into his tiny ear, filling it with bass and bourbon. "Want to have a look inside?"

Father depressed some sort of gadgetry or another and opened the vessel's entrance way. The interior was no disappointment either. Inside there was all kinds of mesmerizing knobs, switches and buttons. It'd take a real genius of a pilot to operate this thing.

Into the cockpit Father sat, strapping himself in. All kinds of shiny chrome surfaces were touched, caressed and flipped. At last he produced some sort of jingling device and dangled it before Damien's wide glassy blue eyes.

"What do you say, want to fire it up?"

"Oh Boy! Really? Can we Daddy?"

"Of course, we can, but just for a minute. I have to make a few minor adjustments here and there before its road worthy." He regarded his son for a moment then offered. "Why don't you do the honors co-pilot? I don't think it'd be a true mission if my co-pilot couldn't start the ship, now do you?"

"Wow! No way, can I really?"

"Of course, you can. Now when I say, ready take off, you turn this key away from you okay? Not a moment before and not a second after, understand?"

This had to be the most exhilarating, thrilling moment of any one's life ever.

The truly amazing thing was Daddy was just has emerged in the excitement as him. Together they chanted in unison, father and son, man and offspring, senior and junior.

"Ten," they shouted in the rustic, old Volks tuning the remainder of the world out.

"Nine," Damien shivered in pure bliss, hearing his giant of a keeper below above his tiny ears.

"Eight, Seven, Six," they chanted on. Father squeezed him tighter.

"Five, Four, Three,' each shouted on verge of drying out their chords. Damien tensed in complete wonderment.

"Two," Daddy and Damien held their breath synomonously. It was amazing their ability to be so in tuned, seemingly reading one another's minds.

"One!" Damien charged into life reaching for the chrome ignition. With shaking hands, he twisted and turned. The pilot did not disappoint, tromping his foot to the gas. For just a brief second the engine sputtered then roared into life. As a bonus Daddy pressed the gas further, releasing, further then releasing again. The desired affect was like a sleeping leviathan awakened and roaring an earth shattering utterance enough to crumble a rocky coastline into oblivion.

Damien squealed and clapped with delight. Up and down he bounced in carefree enchantment upon father's lap. He too laughed and tickled his son's sides. Once they'd finally subsided the initial thrill, Father added.

"All this will be yours one-day son. We'll restore her together and when you're all grown up and a man too, this will be your vehicle. You can pilot it anywhere you want to be. You'll never have to feel trapped and you can go on an adventure and journey anytime you feel like it." The speech even to a young five-year-old seemed a little deep but monumental. He had no idea what a milestone was at this tender age, yet this was it. Father was passing along wisdom and even more monumental passing a torch of sorts they'd bond over this activity surely.

In present day reality Damien stared, unblinking. Darkness had begun to ascend. He quaked to the bone at the recollection he wasn't a monster after all, at least all the time. Father was a human being, had a heart and good intentions. Into the brisk air, he uttered aloud, "Just what in the hell happened to him?"

Tears flooded his eyes, spilling down haggard five o'clock shadowed cheeks. Confusion had never been as predominant as now. Had he made a terrible mistake by coming here? Was everything just a modified, altered version of what really happened? Guilt washed over his psyche evolving into sorrow and desperation.

No this was essential in learning the truth, accepting the past and moving on. He'd have been a blubbering mess, a shadow of a man if he hadn't faced the truth. Piece by piece it was all making sense. Onward he strode towards the structure and prepared to walk inside.

Getting past the boards and nails would be no easy feat. The rapidly diminishing light would be an extra added obstacle he cared not to admit to. As he assessed the crisscrossed planks he tentatively tugged on one. It had a little give, but likely due to being rotted over time and neglect. He considered retreating to his car for a tire iron and sighed at the thought of taking the stroll back to where he'd began and over the fence again. On verge of giving up, the nails at last surrendered and let loose of their respective pockets. Damien nearly sprawled onto his ass from the unexpected force.

"Gentlemen, I do believe we have clearance," he proclaimed to no one in particular, caring not that he'd picked up his nervous habit of talking to himself once again. He'd worked diligently with Jade's encouragement and incessant nagging to drop the habit. Now it seemed to fit like a glove, his anti-social behavior. Here he could be himself away from the microscope of everyday judgement. Here he could do as he pleased without fear of failing someone, without ultimately disappointing everyone.

Taking the loosened board in both hands, he used the business end of the wood to jimmy it up into the remaining barricade.

He grunted against the strain, growled against the resistance. At last, a couple of deteriorated nails clinked onto the cement steps and he had a second board free. Eventually a third would be loosened, followed by a fourth and fifth.

He was grateful at least enough light was available to see through to the door. As he contorted his arm, he grunted once again. With ample cussing and further screaming he reached the corroded door knob and turned counter clock wise. The motion flashed a sinister memory that saturated his dreams repeatedly as of late. The turning of the knob was the beginning of the end thirteen years ago when he'd taken the plunge from bedroom to kitchen to confront his screaming parents.

Deeply he sobbed, his lungs incapable of breath, he nearly passed out from hyperventilating. The door pushed in at last. A cloud of dust, cobwebs and age-old stench swirled around. While climbing through the opening he coughed a whooping wail, uncontrollably. His face turned crimson while red splashed before his eyes. Just when he thought he'd never subdue his hacking, he was in and standing on the front porch.

All the Galligher family's articles remained just as they were left. The barbeque lay on its side, busted, dented and discarded. Paint cans, tools and shop memorabilia scattered in shadows of abandonment.

Access to the remainder of the house was much easier. Somehow, he couldn't deny the feeling of being a zombie from Night of the Living Dead eternally clawing and scratching to gain entry inside no matter how dismal the possibility looked. He searched his pockets for a lighter hoping he wouldn't have to take this walk through in complete blackness.

Retrieving a small lighter, he clicked the flint into life. He held the red depressor, careful not to brush his skin against the steel. Towards his right he ventured first. The vestibule just off the porch door where his mother, father and three sisters had stored their footwear and jackets seemed much smaller than he'd recalled. Just beyond was the ill-fated doorway to the attic where he and his sister Peggy has shared a bedroom. It didn't seem that important to take that leap right now, he'd possibly explore that later.

He walked back to his left and embraced the apprehension that lied within the kitchen area. It too seemed far smaller than he'd remembered. The wall paper had long ago peeled and lay in tattered strands. Even the kitchen table remained off kilter. One leg was missing while its surface was coated in countless layers of dust and decay.

A faint echo of screams tickled his ear drums. Cries of desperation, pleas of submission filled his head. He had to brace himself, dangerously close to collapse. The imagery eclipsed of his parent's final encounter bombarded his mind, dominating every sensory perception. He screamed in frustration beating his head repeatedly against soggy drywall. Into the mix he tossed his fists overhead, beating chunks of rotted beginnings out of the structure repeatedly. Losing complete control did little to suppress his rage, it fueled further as he shrilled obscenities, kicking deteriorated unions into obliteration. Chunks of splintered wood, moldy insulation and debris scattered before his feet. His existence wasn't worth the dry rot he stood. Life as Damien knew it was a farce, a shamble and complete waste. Into a heap he collapsed on the floor. Curling his knees into his chest he wept silently. For the first time in weeks he cried and cried caring not to stop until he was good and ready.

CHAPTER NINE

Silence had at last prevailed. The piercing shrills, demonic like whispers, taunts and torments was more than enough for any sane man to take. A nagging suspicion refused to relent with Damien. Somehow, he knew in his heart of hearts this was it. There would be no returning this normal life as he'd known it. He couldn't envision carrying on. He couldn't forgive himself for what he'd done to his father. He couldn't forget and cope in everyday society just like everyone else. In this day in age everywhere you looked cultures were filled with sociopaths. One thing the Galligher parents managed to do was instill a conscience within the boy. He wasn't entirely sure if they deserved the credit for that, but he would grant them this one small thing.

In the pitch blackness of the kitchen he found himself rocking back and forth. A gentle swaying back and forth, back and forth used to be a defense mechanism for when he was younger. Physicians were concerned he may have been mildly autistic, carrying several other traits and symptoms of behavior that are found within the afflicted. A battery of tests came back inconclusive however. This was simply an adaptive behavior. Now Damien didn't even realize he was doing it. It had been over ten years since he'd regressed back to this near catatonic state.

His aggressive onslaught did considerable damage to his hands and forehead. In rhythm to his uneven pulse, each of his hands throbbed, swelling further by the minute. A gash had opened just above his puffy eyebrow. There a solitary droplet of clotted crimson had formed, suspended in midair and threatened to plunge below with each swaying motion.

The air had become cold now. A slight shiver tingled along his spine. It'd been hours since the sun had set. His family would be frantically calling one another. Jade would be beside herself with worry. The discarded cell phone in the Cavalier was likely buzzing across the floor on verge of draining its last bit of battery power with dozens of messages. He'd wondered if anyone really knew him well enough to know where he was, what he'd gotten up to. Sure Dr. Rhys knew what his eventual intentions were. It could be days or weeks before anyone had pieced together the information to track him down.

He'd felt suddenly very alone, more so than ever. It would be so easy to just up and disappear, vanish and the rest of the world would carry on without him. It was beyond humbling to consider that not only would he not be horribly missed, but he really didn't think many would notice. It was like his adolescence and teenaged years all over again. Damien wondered what had even changed. He was virtually invisible, insignificant and inconsequential. He knew his parents never married, were pretty much just shacking up in this rented dump of a hole in the wall. It was one small step up from trailer park living and now more than ever he'd realized he was simply an accident. The bastard that should not be was not a triumphant beginning to anyone's life. As a mutt or human mongrel among a society of thoroughbreds what chance did he really have anyway?

Damien sobbed into his lap as the strand of drying blood spiraled to the linoleum tile below.

Never had he exactly considered himself to be a man of the world having only been out of Ontario twice in his life. He'd never had a chance to go overseas or even visit the state of California. For if he had, Damien would have had a firsthand account or recollection of what an earthquake feels like. Beneath his rocking stance the entire house rumbled and shook. Light fixtures in the ceiling, long ago defunct of any electrical juice running through them, popped, shards of glass rained through each room. Chunks of plaster collapsed around him. From the home's very foundation, the room quaked and shook out of control. If he'd been standing, he'd have fallen instantly.

From the base of a kickboard across the kitchen a splitting crack had formed. The sound of a dozen phone books being torn had permeated the room. By the second the crack grew wider and ran in frenzied zig-zag motions straight for where Damien was seated. Tiles of linoleum peeled inward then slipped altogether into the rapidly gaping hole.

Within several heartbeats, a crater the size of a sinkhole had consumed most of the room. As catatonic as he was, Damien at last sprung into life shuffling his feet beneath him, clambering for purchase. His treads conformed to the rest of his efforts and luck of the day, refusing to grip. Even his figurative grip matched his emotional and psychological predicament in completely coming undone.

The sinkhole widened, moaned and stretched beyond earthly proportions. Its dark abyss unleashed a pungent odor of waste and despair. The tiles continued to buckle in as there was simply nothing more to balance on. Into the hole he dove, twirling helplessly this way and that. The entire thing happened so fast his mind could not grasp what was happening. He had not the presence of mind to protest or even brace his inevitable collision.

Onto a mound of rotted decay, bones and excrement he land-ed. The air rushed out of his lungs as he bellowed an undeniable, "Ooof." Strands of slippery, slimy like plasma enveloped his arms and hands. He struggled for purchase, trying to rise and confining his movements further with each wasted effort.

His heart jack hammered while he panicked; thrashing this way and that. The more he struggled the more he sank into the grotesque pool of muck. At least he was appreciative of the dark-ness, caring not to know what exactly he had landed in.

From beyond the shadows a voice had beckoned, making Damien seize up, chilled to the bone.

"My, my, my, just look at what the cat's dragged in." Face first down in the mulch and goo, Damien did not need to see what lurked behind him to recognize from whom the voice had originated.

"Come, come now son. Let's get you on your feet. I was be-ginning to think you'd never arrive." The temperature seemed to plummet twenty degrees. He continued to squirm and twist regardless of his lack of success. Now he couldn't stop from con-vulsing from his inner core to his fingertips. A rolling fog had descended upon the pits floor. A stench so hideous and all empow-ering emitted from the ground. It smothered Damien's face and he struggled to breathe. Just when he thought he'd surely pass out he was yanked to his feet.

Clumps of gelatin hung from his limbs hindering any type of movement. He was shoved into a bumpy, unforgiving wall while his feet dangled inches from the floor. At last he gasped, coughed and wheezed. Sweet air at last found its mark into his chest. As he sputtered and panted back to consciousness, Damien looked up through the murky horizon.

Methodically, languidly a silhouette, a formation stepped towards him. The very presence wreaked of death and decay. If he had the air within his lungs, Damien would have screamed in pure terror.

The entity before him was purely skeletal except for a black-ened heart thumping inside a cage of bones. Its face donned strips of tissue and flesh, veins dangled with nonchalance. Worms slithered and squirmed from the thing's eye sockets. Brown and black teeth chattered on through non-existent lips.

With a single bony finger, he caressed Damien's tear and blood-stained cheek. The thing regarded him for a moment, cocking its grimy cranium sideways. An eternity could have passed yet it was merely seconds of unbridled horror.

"So glad you could make it. We have so much to catch up on. So much to see" The skeleton tossed back its scrawny skull, nearly snapping right off its rotted vertebrae. A banshee like wail possessed the cavern as his evil laughter dwelled into the very recesses of Damien's dark existence.

The entity he'd known as his father for a few short years of his tender life continued to stare into his very core. Through black bottomless pits resembling his eyes he fixated upon his kin. Damien writhed and wriggled, grappling for any kind of release. The fleshy restraints continued to tighten threatening to cut off his circulation. As he fought to speak, to lash out at this abomination, the gelatin in his mouth thickened and seemingly multiplied.

"There's no use in fighting dear boy,' the figure before him declared. "Resistance is futile as they say." He cackled, clearly amused with his maniacal banter. All laws of physics, every grasp of reality violated in this pit of despair The Galligher family once called home. The entity drifted and hovered off the ground, retreating into the shadows.

"You've become a shell of a man, a miserable disappointment unhampered by failure and mediocrity. I had such high hopes for you. We had a destiny, you and I and you murdered our fate the day you impaled my throat with that skewer."

Damien's eyes bulged impossibly by his father's brutal recollection. Sheer terror chilled his bones. It was a true marvel his heart hadn't ceased to beat from what unfolded before him.

"Come, come now this is no way to greet your dear old Da now is it?" The entity now sat perched upon some sort of make shift seat, a throne of sorts. He couldn't tell from his vantage point, yet somehow, he suspected his was sitting on a chair fashioned of bones. "One may suspect I would be angry or upset for you ending my life so abruptly, so unceremoniously,' a gust of wind accompanied by the stench of the dead seeped from his cavernous teeth. "I do not hold you accountable, nor do I blame you for altering our life's purpose. I simply consider this a momentary stumbling block, an intermission of the greatest spectacle unto life itself, yet."

At last Damien relented on his feeble resistance. The fleshy binds loosened ever so slightly, the plasma like goo liquefied within his gullet. Tears of disbelief began to shower down his grimy cheeks.

"I've been watching you from afar these years. One cannot argue that someone of your caliber requires a guardian of sorts. Thirteen years is plenty of time to embark upon a wayward path."

Rapidly he blinked against the pit's darkness and surroundings. The very walls within the cellar appeared to have a life of their own breathing in synch with each of father's crazed ramblings. This had to be a dream he couldn't wake up from. Somehow, he slept passed his alarm and Jade would shake him back to consciousness. He had to wake up, wake up and forget all about this dreadful horror.

"I assure you son this is no dream. Understandably I've taken for granted how this may be a little difficult to digest.' Father read his mind like an open book. The being breathed in, sucking all the life out of the room, making everything flutter and whither. "Allow me to remind you that trapped within purgatory for thirteen years at times, can be a touch difficult to digest as well." His last words thundered against Damien's chest rattling every molecule, every fiber in his being.

His skeletal father exhaled again. A stench so smothering, and overwhelming raped his lungs of any form of breath. "I do appreciate why even a tender boy of seven would do as you'd done on that ill-fated night. I'm not so certain if I were in your shoes if I would have done the exact same thing. You showed courage beyond your years. You may not believe this Damien, but I was most proud of your actions. But as I digress I need remind you, you severed our true greatness just as you had severed my life."

A red mist began to blanket the realm of their meeting. Grimy and constant its coppery scent forced Damien to gag and wretch repeatedly. Everything he'd become accustomed to grasping, realizing and understanding in life was suddenly challenged before him. In the few minutes since his spiral into darkness, he second guessed even the basic concepts of sensibility. This was no dream. He must have finally and completely lost his mind.

"We have certain...gifts...you and I." The entity moaned; an uneasy resignation. "The time was at hand for me to intervene or the alternative of your wayward path will be utterly catastrophic."

Just when he thought he could take no more, the fleshy restraints around his wrists and ankles blackened. Each receded, withered and crumbled into dust. Into a heap Damien collapsed onto the filthy floor. He wretched once again, fighting for air and wrestling with any rational explanation for what unfolded around him.

He wiped the gunk from his mouth, eyes and every orifice his face had harbored. A new-found sensation began to swirl within his very center. Trembling uncontrollably, he gritted his teeth and suppressed a primal scream from within. Unto his feet he bounded, adrenaline near blinding him with rage.

"How dare you invade my life, my every thought, dreams and rob me of any normal kind of interaction?" His face flushed beat red as he convulsed. Spittle flew from his lips as his voice heightened with each syllable. "I won't stand here and apologize for becoming your minion of mediocrity. My entire youth was deduced to a laughing stock, target for ridicule." Fearless he stood tall, his hands thrusted onto his hips. "Do you have any idea what it's like living with no father, no male figure to look up to?" He paced back and forth, every moment of his tortured years leading up to this confrontation. "Do you have any idea what it's like to have no one to go to advice for, no encouragement, no guidance? Say goodbye to learning the ways of a normal, breathing, functional, capable human being." If looks could kill the undead, Damien shot an icy glare before his father.

"I had no sense of comradery. How humiliating is it to admit to your friends that you have no idea how to bait a god damned hook when they try and take you fishing? How emasculating is it to admit to the love of your life that you have no idea how to put a simple book shelf together? Never mind having no fucking clue what the difference between a carburetor and a fuel pump is. I couldn't give a shit if the Maple Leafs won the Stanley cup, the Blue Jays won the World Series or if they all played grab ass and scratched their crotches until high noon and I'm Canadian! Every red-blooded man from twelve to ninety-nine lives, breathes, eats and shits sports and you robbed me of that Daddy dearest, you stole any hope in having a bond for me. Even beyond the grave you ruined any glimmer of hope for me." He now frothed with carnal madness. Storming towards his perch he screamed unrelenting. With an accusatory finger he thrust it repeatedly towards the decayed skull before him. "So, forgive me if I don't shed a tear for being unable to be the apple of your eye." It was now son's turn to don the mask of lunacy. "The years and years of self-loathing, rejection and heart break. The god damned suicidal thoughts and attempts, good God let's not forget about all the botched attempts...' He shook his head in uncontrollable disbelief. ". couldn't even get that right. All the endless humiliation from women deducing I could never been liked to let alone loved. I never knew how to approach anyone, communicate or act around women. Gee, a guy might think a father could lend some words of wisdom or give a kid some confidence. It'd sure be nicer than slitting your wrists."

In an illustration epitomizing defiance, he glared nose to nose, living to dead, breathing to expired. "All of these things,' he virtually whispered. 'these limitations, personal defeats, inept, inadequate, impotent philosophies forced upon my upbringing is because of you Daddy dearest and it's exactly the reason for the way I am. Next time you want a scapegoat for inability to spurt out a thoroughbred from your sickly, shrunken up ball sack maybe have a look at yourself. Maybe, just maybe your lack of devotion and commitment to marrying the mother of your children is just evidence and indication my entire existence has been a farce, a cruel miscalculation and nothing but one big, fat lie." He stared on, blind with contempt and disgust. "So, what do you have to say for yourself to a living, breathing thing that never should have been?"

A piercing shrill emitted from his paternal foe. "I would say there is the intestinal fortitude I've been waiting for and time is of the essence. Like I said before, come. I have such sights to unveil."

CHAPTER TEN

Tension had blanketed the room. The humble but quaint apartment on Thorncliffe Park was far too quiet for Jade's preference. It was now almost six o'clock. This was an all-time first.

While the clear coat on the parquet flooring had virtually worn out she continued to pace. What exactly was going on? It was unheard of for Damien to be so late especially on a Friday afternoon. Even on the remaining days of the week he usually ducked out around four and was home well before six. On Fridays this was far from the norm. It was par for the course to plan a spot check monitoring session with one of his clients just after lunch hour and be well on his way home by three o'clock regardless of where he was in the city. They'd made previous arrangements to try to be home by four o'clock at the latest. There was still her dress and his suit to pick up from the dry cleaners. A mountain of packing had to be done. She'd hoped they'd be on the road now to Seagrave, so they could be early and settle in before the wedding rehearsal. Now she was beginning to doubt they'd make it on time, period.

Years ago, Jade's mother had gone to extravagant lengths to ensure she'd quit her nervous habit of nail biting. Arguably it was a nasty, unsanitary habit that closely followed behind picking your nose. Instead of expensive therapy and harmful toxins to paint upon her nails she'd resorted to the school of hard knocks. She simply scolded and slapped her hand whenever observing her daughter's behavior. Let's just say Jade's mother was from the old country school of thought.

Over five years later she paced back and forth, back and forth while one of her digits dangled precariously from her teeth. This feeling of utter helplessness was all consuming. She hated having to rely upon the obvious unreliable. Her mind whirled into a neurotic frenzy. Of course, they'd be late if they made it at all. The whole Galligher family, Damien's mother, his aunt and cousins would be polite enough but would secretively blame Jade. She never understood his family. They always presented themselves one way and then gossiped behind one another's backs. This wasn't family honor. It was deceit and lying. If there was one thing Jade could not stand, it was a liar.

Supper had long ago been ruined. It wasn't as if she considered herself a culinary wizard or anything. Being of Asian descent the stereotype was naturally that she could whip up any kind of sweet and sour chicken, stir fry or some rice dish or another. Instead she put spaghetti on the stove long ago. The noodles were now water logged and the meatballs were burnt beyond being edible. Damien never complained about her kitchen skills. He was always as equally supportive. He even pitched in and made some mean dishes himself. She sighed into the air, missing him horribly now.

As she sat upon their rickety sofa, adjusting a stack of phone books that supported one side, she sprang to her feet just as quickly. She couldn't contain herself. Last thing she wanted was to cater to thinking something dreadful would've happened. What if he was in a car accident? Her stomach lurched at the possibility. What if he was just stuck in traffic? Facial muscles relaxed ever so slightly as this seemed a more viable cause. After all it was a beginning of a long weekend, a Friday afternoon no less. Toronto streets and highways were insane with vehicular insanity at the best of times. Throw in another day off into the equation and you had an asphalt carnival of madness. But why wouldn't he call?

She refused to appear like an overbearing, compulsive girl-friend that was insecure. Careful not to develop such misconceptions she simply called him three times. In fifteen-minute intervals beginning at five o'clock she had called his cell. It instantly went to his voice mail which was indication his phone was off.

As she chomped upon her second then third finger her rapid thoughts soared into the realm of no return. Could it be? Was her high school sweetheart capable of such inexcusable, unforgivable conduct? Is it possible Damien Galligher was having an affair?

She giggled to herself, shuddering at how mad she sounded in the quiet room. Of course, that was insane. Damien loved her and knew full well she loved him. Sure, he'd been having some problems as of late, coping with his past and what not. Good God who wouldn't? And they did have some rather fabulous horizontal time earlier this morning. She'd mentally noted to play with him a little about the jealousy thing, keeping it light of course when he finally did arrive home. It'd be the necessary tension breaker they would need about then.

Sighing into the air once again she gazed out the living room window. For some retrospective or insight, she opened the balcony door and stepped outside. From a stack of weathering beer cases she lifted one side and swiftly retracted a package of Du Maurier cigarettes. With shaky hands she lit one with the lighter concealed inside. It was another vice unquestionably far more disgusting than nail biting. She hid them there for moments of stress when she thought she could take no more. They were few and far between mind you, but Damien would kill her.

He had a heart affliction he was born with called aortic stenosis or something like that. Evidently his aortic valve had a defect in which it did not close entirely. As year's progressed and annual visits to a cardiologist evolved to bi-annual visits the valve was dilating at an accelerated rate. Surgery would be inevitable one day. If he knew she was engaging in something so reckless and haphazard as smoking while being perfectly healthy he'd say little but be defeated with disappointment. After all he wasn't asked to be born that way and had little patience for people that didn't value the health they were graced with.

So, she kept it to herself even though she felt horribly guilty. With trembling, raw fingers she rolled the rusty flint over again and again. In the breeze the lighter refused to catch then just when she was about to give up it sparked the dry tobacco into life.

Languidly she inhaled listening to the tiny whips of stems and leaves crackle between her lips. In a swirling gust she exhaled. A radiance of surrogate comfort permeated her from scalp to toes. She tapped her filter three times regardless of being no ash. Smokers always had the most obsessive-compulsive mannerisms about their nasty little habit. In other times it fascinated Jade to no end.

There were the pack smack and packers. You know the ones that incessantly rap their packages off their hands or a counter top. Jade supposed it was learned behavior or they'd been leading to believe they're packing the tobacco more rigidly toward the filter. She thought it was an empty gesture, executing nothing and making one look like a buffoon. She laughed into the pre-dusk air at last relaxing a little for the first time in hours. Then there were the pinch and roll smokers that held their cigarette like it was a joint. This made just as little sense to Jade as she often wondered what it was they thought they were achieving? Sure, maybe the nicotine stains would not tattoo across the telltale first and index fingers. Does having yellowish-brown finger tips and thumbs make any difference?

She took and drag again and shook her head. The whole torrid soiree of smoking was ridiculous. She'd made a silent vow to herself, she'd quit this time come hell or high water. Just bring Damien home safe and she'd never light a solitary smoke again. Flicking the filter off the balcony, she watched it spiral end over end down the twenty some odd floors to the rear parking lot below. Her head swam now, the combination of stress, withdrawal and toxins were an overpowering cocktail in her brain.

"Please just come home honey. I don't care about any silly wedding." She leaned against the iron railing and waited.

CHAPTER ELEVEN

"So, let me get this straight, you have such sights to unveil?" He shook his head and thrust his hands into his pockets. "Is that, about right? Because you sound like a broken record and a cheap horror flick with no special effects." He took another step towards his decayed perch. "What's to stop me from grabbing the biggest, hardest rock in this shithole and smashing your filthy, useless bones into dust?"

"Silence!" The room bellowed and shook. Squeals and skittering of unseen creatures scattered this way and that. "We can just as quickly resign to my vines of woe once again until you manage to get control of yourself." Legions of slithering tentacles came to life, wiggling and idling, awaiting a command of finality.

"You will not disrespect me further. I understand your indifference, indecision and even your hostility. But you will not address me further in this matter. In the end I am still your father Damien." A stillness bound each father and son in a match of wits. They continued to measure one another, relenting not a single blink in the interim. "The choice is yours. You see I, for one have an eternity. Nothing will phase me. You on the other hand,' he waved a gnarled fissure towards his face. "Are another matter altogether. Time is of the essence for your fate, dear boy."

"Okay, alright so time is of the essence.' A sharpened tongue exchanged yet he was cautious not to invite disrespectful tones. "What does all of this mean exactly? I mean you must see it from my point of view. I'm here talking to my dead father; a bag of rotted bones and organs and you expect me to believe I'm not drooling all over myself in the Whitby psych ward?" He smacked his dry lips against his teeth. "Obviously Dr. Rhys had no other alternative than to finally commit me and I don't even know it. "I mean I've gone completely around the bend."

"Oh yes and how is the good doctor these days. He did a fabulous job of taking care of you and your mother, now hasn't he?" The entity before him mocked before unleashing a gust of unbridled laughter.

"You don't get to talk about him or my Mom. Not then, not now, not ever. You were the one that beat and tortured her, remember? You were the one that made this mess and never cleaned it up or took any responsibility. Death was way too good for you and you know it."

"Perhaps, yes perhaps you are right." Damien was shocked to hear the spectacle before him become so compliant, so agreeable. "What if I were to say what you are about to experience will make you challenge everything you've been lead and mislead to believe your entire life? What if you can have a good hard look at the past, even before your past and see there is another entirely different perspective to our life history? And Damien, my good boy, what if I gave you the key to alter every miserable consequence that has unfolded since your very conception?"

The bony hand reached and caressed his arm, gripping upon his shoulder with tenderness and not at all in any harmful way. He was stunned to feel an icy calmness soar through his veins. Contempt and hatred washed away, drained from his every pore.

"I'd say, go on…"

"Excellent," Father slithered. "Look into my eyes, deep into my eyes and breathe deeply. As your lungs become full of air, expel them slowly, releasing your body of any negative energy. Your eyes have become heavy. You may feel like closing them, taking a little rest, just for a little while."

"Heavy,' Damien droned. "So, so heavy."

"Good, good. Now you're going down further but very aware and alert of my voice. I'm right there with you Damien, right there with you."

CHAPTER TWELVE

Even if he'd walked through the door by some miraculous divine intervention and left that instant they'd still be late. It was easily an hour and a half's drive to Seagrave and Jade wasn't even certain if the rehearsal was or if it was in one of the neighboring towns. He'd have to have some sort of unbelievable excuse for leaving her in this mess. Now she didn't care what it was. It was quarter to seven.

While watching the sun set over the city's skyline she'd somehow smoked another two cigarettes and chomped three of her nails down to stubs. She only hoped there was a manicurist that could take her tomorrow morning on short notice. Otherwise she'd look like a hillbilly all dressed up and nowhere to go. Jade made mental note to ask one of Damien's sisters once they finally arrived.

Drumming her numb fingers along the railing she refused to submit to what had to be done. While biting her lip she quickly reviewed in her mind of what to say. As she retracted her cell phone from her hip pocket she cursed indignation.

There was something about Joy Galligher, Damien's mother she could not stand. From day one they'd never hit it off and in more than one private conversation had agreed for boyfriend and son's sake they were civil with one another. They saw eye to eye on pretty much nothing but could agree that his happiness was all that mattered.

She had to terminate the dialing sequence three times before hitting send. It wasn't often she called the number. If there was any reason she remembered it at all was because she called so often during the dating phase of their high school union. Mrs. Galligher was intolerable then, a real bitch of bitches. She'd never be good enough in Mommy's eyes. To her she was just holding her son back, a burden and a slut. Jade cursed again and hit send.

It rang several times and continued to ring. Deep in the country, despite her husband Leonard's massive wealth she still refused to subscribe to modern amenities such as voice mail. Jade thought she was an old coot, off her rocker. It continued to ring and ring. Just when she was about to hang up herself a tentative, despondent voice began.

"Hello? Hello?"

Just like mother Galligher, keep uttering gibberish with no opportunity for response.

"Umm Mrs. Galligher? It's me'

"Hello?' a brief pause. "Hello?"

It was just like her to pretend not to know who she was. She could be so damn pretentious and condescending. "Mrs. Galligher. This is Jade." She raised her voice to quash any shred of inability to hear her.

"Well for heaven's sake child. You don't have to shout. I'm not as old and decrepit as you think you know. I mean I'm sure you'd just love to see me in a home somewhere but…"

"Mrs. Galligher! Please!" Jade squeezed her eyes shut, rubbing her temples. All of twenty seconds into a conversation and they were off to a bad start. "I don't mean to be rude, but this is important."

"Well what on earth could be so important now? Are you calling from one of those fancy new cell phonies? They're the devil's gadgets they are. Nothing but evil and pornography comes out of those."

"What?" Jade laughed despite herself. Damien's mother had never ceased to amaze her. "Well yes I'm on my cell but…"

"Then good you kids must be close. Are you going to come home before the rehearsal? We can all go in one car. There's no point in wasting your gas dear."

"That's the thing is we're not there yet. We're not in town."

"You're not in town yet? Well, where are you? Time is running out dear."

Jade could hear commotion in the background. A feeble attempt at covering the telephone receiver was apparent. Mother Galligher was catching her husband up to speed. Her voice echoed throughout the estate as clearly, she was conveying the information from one room to another. Jade could swear she heard her say something about being late and it was all 'that little oriental hussy's' fault.

Deciding to hold her composure, she exhaled before responding. "Mrs. Galligher, have you heard from Damien? He hasn't returned from work yet and it's getting late. He's always home hours before now. I was wondering if maybe he called you?"

"No dear! Oh heaven's no. I haven't heard from him. I don't really know why you'd think he'd call here. I mean I pretty much have to beg him to call once a month and I'm lucky if I get that."

"Never mind, I was just hoping…"

"Well you don't have to get all snippy. I'm sure there's a perfectly logical explanation as to where he is. I mean you kids and your Nintendo video games, fancy computers and taking the marijuana. Young lady you do not have my son using the marijuana, again do you?"

"Of course not. Look if he calls or if for some reason goes to the rehearsal alone can you please get him to call me?"

"Oh. Well. Of course,' a glimmer of hope could be heard in mother's voice. "You two aren't having issues these days, now are you?"

"You'll be tickled to know we're doing just fine, Mom."

"Oh, isn't that wonderful." She gritted her teeth at term of endearment used so recklessly without permission. "Well once he arrives you'll be the first to know and if he happens to check in with you be a doll and give us a ring to will you?"

"I will." Jade terminated the call without a single good bye. She felt, filthy and grimy, in desperate need of a shower. Interaction with that woman always made her feel violated. Perhaps a shower was just what the doctor had ordered. Walking down the hall to the bathroom she set her cell on the vanity in case anyone called.

She recited a silent prayer once again, just wishing the weekend could get on its way. Somehow, she still needed to broach a very important topic with her beloved. In all his haste this morning, the compounded stress she never even had the chance to tell him about the tiny life growing inside her.

CHAPTER THIRTEEN

"Whoa, what's going on?" Damien rubbed the back of his neck, rising to his feet. "Where am I?"

"Let's just say I took some precautions to attain full enlightenment."

After rubbing his eyes, he still felt foggy, as though suspended in slow motion. He looked to his left. The sight before him had to have been an illusion.

A tall, slender man, clean cut with dark short hair stood before him and smiled. His teeth dazzled in close rivalry to his sparkling, crystal blue eyes. With the physique of a Greek God and a tan of a bronzed warrior he reached out his arms. An orb of light illuminating and divine shined behind him. Rapidly it expanded nearly blinding out everything else.

"Dad?" was all he managed to stammer. The tranquility of his hypnotic state suppressed any form of aggression.

"Yes, it's me son."

For the first time he could remember, the two embraced.

"I had to start our journey a little further back for you to really understand."

"But the pit below the house, the snakes, goo...." He relented for a second unsure of how to proceed. "You were a skeleton and now...now...you're not!" Clapping his father on the shoulder heartily he bounced up and down in complete unchained bliss.

"It was rather essential for you to get the big picture."

"There are so many things I want to ask you. So many, many things I need to know Dad."

".... In all due time son, in all due time. But first you must understand that life as you know it has been dramatically distorted. You've been deceived I'm afraid. The truth has been hidden from you and we need to act before it's too late. I'm afraid it may already be too late."

"But, what do you mean?' he was pouting now, almost whining. It was the closest to anger he could express in this mesmerized state. "You keep talking in riddles and circles. Just tell me what's on your mind and we'll go from there."

"Your mother and sisters are not the people they appear to be. Your mother is a witch and a con-artist and uses her trickery to her own advantage. She's a soul sucking leech and a gold digging jezebel. Once something is within her sights she'll stop at nothing to get it. She's hundreds of years old, perhaps more and she plans on opening the very flood gates of hell."

"What?" Damien scoffed at his father's outburst. "What have you been smoking in the afterlife?" He began to laugh nervously, continuously then on verge of utter hysterically.

"It is true. She'd cast countless spells of illusion upon you as she charms the hearts of each of her predecessors. Once your gifts had become apparent she vowed to keep us apart even if it meant tricking you into defending her honor. She simply could not terminate me as you see Damien I can read minds. It is stronger at times than others. I can also communicate with my mind. It does pose more of a challenge with fewer and fewer responsive recipients."

"This is all just a little too far out, it sounds like some sort of campy drive-inn movie don't you think?"

"I understand it may be overwhelming to take in. This is the best way for you to truly appreciate the trickery and sleight of hand before your eyes. Now hush son and just watch we can see but will remain unseen."

Together they regarded a shimmering sheet of glass along the wall. From floor to ceiling it had no borders and an oasis lied just beyond. Every wish, wonderment and conceivable enchantment lied just beyond its threshold. With a massive, meaty palm, father reached for him. He nodded a gesture of finality and secured his grip. Through the vortex beyond they stepped into the past.

⇒‖↔⇐

"You over there, young man, oh young man." The svelte lady in the orange summer dress beckoned. "Could you give me some assistance please?"

"Right away Madam…" crouched over one of the gas pumps the giant of a man stood up, clutching the small of his back. Turned away from her he rolled his yes. Tourist season was in full bloom and there was nothing more he detested than a hoity toity know it all with her ass end turned all around and backwards.

"I seemed to have gotten all turned around in this cute little town of yours. Could you direct me to the Imperial Country Club?"

"Wow, who's the babe?" Damien elbowed his father.

"That's your mother, or eventually will become your mother."

Damien cringed at his awkward epiphany.

"I will give her that she was easy on the eyes."

The gas attendant, with grease stained coveralls leaned down to the beige Cadillac's power window. He smiled, a haggard yet not completely unpleasant smile. All the sudden he felt at ease and relaxed around this woman. Her gaze transfixed him. Conjuring all the coolness he could muster he slicked back his black coif.

The driver seemed to be taken with the attendant as well. Laughing and tossing her hair back she brushed her hand against his arm. The sensation of flesh on flesh was like kinetic energy unleashed. A spark of metaphorical and figurative proportion ignited. The grease monkey staggered backwards a step and laughed it off.

"Now why would a pretty lady like you want to go and hob knobble with a bunch of snobs at the Imperial?"

"Oh, the things you say, mister...."

"Bill, just call me Bill."

"Joy. Pleased to meet you Bill." The two swam in one another's eyes.

"You see I'm going to a wedding there. My date, the crumb that he was went and stood me up. So now I must go solo and everything. It's not for a few hours yet but I like to be early."

"I don't want to speak out of line, darlin' but seems any guy would have to be a crumb to stand you up."

"Oh stop," she giggled onward, blushing and fidgeting. "I hope this doesn't sound too, too forward Bill..."

"Oh lady, you can ask me anything."

Damien and his father looked on at the spectacle before them. He'd seen that goofy expression of unrelenting lust before. Looking up he frowned the said, "That's you, isn't it?"

His father responded with a solitary finger placed over his lips.

"I was wondering if you...that is if you're not busy later or anything...if you could accompany me to the wedding?"

"Well I'd love to but...."

"Oh, it was a foolish idea. You must take me for a real hussy. It's just that you seem so nice and dreadfully handsome."

"Joy. I was just going to say that I work until five. I'd be happy to take you then, that is if you'll allow me the honor that is."

"Wonderful. I'll pick you up here at five then?"

"It's a date." He rapped the hood of the car and whisked back to the gas pump.

Joy did up her window onto the highway with an undeniable smirk upon her lips.

⥥ ⥤

"That didn't seem so out of the ordinary to me. I thought you two met in a coffee shop. Somehow I don't think it's a crime against humanity to meet at a gas station though is it?"

"She put a spell on me, some sort of potion or other."

"It was no spell from where I was sitting. I mean the two of you were attracted to one another." He regarded the reanimated, younger version of his father. "I believe that is what they call chemistry. Although this is different from the stories I've heard about you two meeting I'd hardly say that is a distortion of reality."

The flesh upon the reanimated Bill began to ripple and bubble. Spheres the size of golf balls formed upon his face reddened and puss began to ooze from their centers. His eyes rolled back into his head while clumps of hair upon brow twirled to the ground.

"Oh gross, what the hell is going on here?"

In an instant there was a thunderous cracking sound. All was serene once again. Bill even smiled to offer reassurance.

"Forgive me, a tiny hiccup in our visual journey. Now, wait for it…" He held up a rippling, muscular arm. The entire landscape before them began to smolder and peel. The edges of their vision began to buckle and peel. A flame ignited at the focal point of the horizon. Inward everything around them smoldered and scorched into obliteration. A dizzying wave threw Damien to his knees.

"Oh, God I think I'm going to be sick." He clutched his belly as he collided face first into the grassy underbrush. A nauseating heat sent him into convulsion. Rapidly he breathed on verge of hyperventilation.

"Behold, rise and soak in the sights before you."

Slowly he opened his eyes. Dirt and grass clung to his forehead in rebellious clusters. He raised his head, careful not to stir a bout of vertigo once again.

"What gives? We're just still at the gas station again. I mean for a time traveler or illusionist or whatever it is you are, this is kind of uninspired."

"Sarcastic ingrate,' father muttered beneath his breath. "Look…"

Damien did as his father commanded over to the gas pumps and the cargo doors of the service center.

"Hey it's you!" He pointed unable to mask his enthusiasm. "Wow that's some get up. Really a baby blue tuxedo?!" He clamped one hand over his mouth feigning ignorance.

"Come on now do you really believe a humble gas attendant could afford anything more?" He joined in on his son's good cheer smirking at the super imposed memory.

Together they watched on as young Bill wandered back and forth across the gas station's parking lot. Several times he checked his wrist-watch and looked out towards the long highway. He stared that way for what seemed like an eternity then walked back to the gas pumps.

"So, where's Mom? I mean Joy? She always did seem to have this thing about being fashionably late."

"Fashionably?" He smacked his lips and rolled his eyes. "Is that what you call it?"

"Wait a second. She stood you up didn't she? You mean after all that flirting and teasing, asking you out. You went home, got ready and came back. She never made it did she?"

"Boy you do catch on fast don't you?" He clapped his shoulder in congratulations.

"So, what happened then? Obviously, you got together somehow."

Before the words barely escaped his lips, the ground began to rumble and quake once again.

⇒+ +⇐

"After waiting over an hour and a half for your mother I decided to take the high road. I was just going to go home, thinking some attractive dame had managed to get the better of me and was having fun at my expense. I was just about to call Jimmy, the local tow truck driver for a lift home when something just kind of snapped inside."

"Snapped? Snapped, like how?"

"Although I was an above average looking young man, polite, descent with a good sense of humor and a heart of gold I wasn't exactly what you'd call rich or one of those high society country club sorts."

Damien looked on regarding his father with genuine fascination.

"I was a good dancer at the time, brilliant in fact, really light on my feet. Your mother had been rather sheltered from such activity from her socialite parents. I decided to take her under my wing, teach her how to dance."

A frown of confusion spread across Damien's face. His eyes searched for shred of comprehension. He opened his mouth then closed it again. "Wait a second, that sounds an awful lot like that film, what's it called...."

Bill slapped his side with lightning fast reflexes. Birds scattered nearby trees in flocks while critters fled for the hills through long grass and dense brush. "I'm just shitting you son. And you thought they had no sense of humor in hell." He laughed and laughed while his flesh glowed, became transparent then whole again. It felt like decades had passed until he stifled his epic cackling.

"No, I decided I wasn't going to be that guy. I wasn't about to be made a fool out of. Maybe I wasn't some sort of rich man about town. I was aware of my psychic abilities then and knew even without that I was something special damn it."

"So, what did you do?"

"I got on the side of the road, stuck out my thumb and hitch-hiked to the club."

"Wow so rather than admit to defeat, and be shown up, you decided to confront her on her own turf. Nice..."

"Yes well, is it any wonder where you'd gotten your courage from?"

"So, what happened next?"

"It took some time to get a lift, to actually get there. Something about a six-foot six Teamster in a baby blue tuxedo don't like right on the side of the road."

The two exchanged glances without uttering a sound. At once they broke into simultaneous laughter.

"I guess that is one fork in the road, sure."

"If I'd knew then, what I know now, I'd be best off to head the exact opposite direction and get that temptress Joy Vander Lee out of my mind once and for all.

Damien looked down to the illusionary ground and shuffled his foot. It didn't take a genius to realize the ramifications of his comments. If fate presented a different twist he wouldn't cease to exist period. At times embedded in his sorrow he'd wished for this precise notion yet when he realized how close the possibility was it made him ache inside.

"But if I had never pursued that cold shoulder and walked off with my pride intact, there never would have been you."

Despite his tortured history and darkened memories, he couldn't help but beam with pride.

Onto a nearby rock Bill sat resting his arms on his thighs. He stared off into the distance, collecting his thoughts. Idly he plucked a blade of grass from the ground and began to pluck it.

"So, I made it to the Imperial. What a fine sight that was. I had to argue with the apes at the front doors and nearly got into a brawl with the one clown. Someone came over to see what all the commotion was about. I could see through the entrance, what a huge affair it was. Hundreds of people danced, drank champagne and shot their too good for everything noses into the air. Scores of people gawked out the foyer to get a good look at the sideshow that showed up and laugh their pretty little faces off. Some even out-right pointed and stared. I was made a real laughing stock, the butt of everyone's joke because of one woman's cruel sense of humor."

By now Damien had joined in on a nearby rock of his own, leaning back and taking in his father's recollection.

"So, what happened next, where does mom come into the picture?"

"I think its best you saw for yourself." With a grand sweeping gesture of his arm once again Bill unveiled their nature huddle unto the Imperial Country Club.

—=+ +=—

"Just what is going on here? We've paid perfectly handsome money for this exclusive affair. Is your job so difficult that you need it spelled out for you? Any bum that walks off the street is not per-mitted inside. There's no need to check the list when you have a humanoid like this standing before you. Do I make myself clear?"

"Ah, yes sir, it's just that Mr. Galligher here has stated he was invited and..."

"Howard where on earth have you gotten off to, they're just about to cut the cake." The striking vixen Damien had recognized as Joy, his mother sauntered to the doorway, slurring with cham-pagne glass in hand.

"There ask her yourself, she's the one that invited me here not three hours ago." Disheveled and distraught Bill had shot back. The doormen had to wrestle on either side to keep him in check.

"I don't know what your angle is sir, but I strongly advise you leave the premises immediately before the authorities have you escorted."

"That woman, right there invited me here from Rosco's Gas down highway fifty-seven and said her date stood her up."

"If it's money you're looking for,' he reached into his jacket pocket and produced a stack of hundreds, name your price sir so we may return to our celebration."

"My goodness what sort of heathen is raising all this fuss outside?"

The man shot back towards the swaggering Joy and waved into her face. "You know your place woman, now back inside before I show you what a heathen truly is."

This was all young Bill had to see and grabbed his opposition by the shoulder. Howard spun around throwing a round house south paw. He easily ducked his inebriated punch and landed a swift upper cut in return. A sound of dozens of walnuts being crunched cut the air between them. Like a ton of bricks Howard collided smack dab in the middle of the doorway. A half a dozen shrieks emitted from timid, impressionable trophy wives.

It wasn't long before the authorities did show up. Damien and Bill watched on from a far as the blue and red sirens twirled into the night taking a man in handcuffs away. As the commotion gradually subsided there was one woman that could barely conceal the leering sneer upon her face.

CHAPTER FOURTEEN

I t was amazing how a long hot shower can do wonders for the soul. In the living room Jade somehow managed to make the best of an anxious situation. She'd even turned on the stereo and bopping around the room to one of Damien's Motley Crue CD's. Donned in nothing but a flimsy towel around her waist and another bound tightly turban style wound around her head, she retrieved a couple suitcases from the front closet.

As she organized enough clothes for a week neatly into piles, she refused to acknowledge they'd only be out of town a day or two at most. Stacks of denim jeans and t-shirts to the right, she folded her cotton panties, socks and Damien's boxers to the left. Swiveling her hips and dipping at the knees she belted out the chorus to Same Old Situation. It was an anthem for precarious situations such as these. Perhaps she'd chosen it based upon subconscious but still smiled at the irony it had induced. With a less than graceful pirouette she bounded into the bathroom and wiped the steam covered mirror.

Into the glass she grimaced and tilted her head this way and that. As she expelled a copious amount of toothpaste onto her brush she continued to hum the tune's harmonies. Vigorously brushing this way and that a new-found sense of relief comforted her.

She cared not if they'd missed the rehearsal. Damien did express on numerous occasions how he felt it was ridiculous to be an usher at his cousin's wedding. He wasn't close at all to Danny. After all he was fourteen years his junior and had next to nothing in common with him. After much conversation the two had deduced that this was merely another example of familial obligation, something to keep the seniors happy while their collective offspring suffered in silence.

As she spat into the sink and prepared to rinse she didn't think it'd be the end of the world to miss the ceremony entirely. They could still take a leisurely drive, have a few drinks and check into a nearby hotel. Tomorrow was a new day. Surely they'd still make the ceremony and reception. Port Perry, the next closest town had become quite a hotspot for cottagers and would be a welcome retreat from their everyday hectic urban lifestyle. Maybe they could even take in some time at the beach and relax on Sunday before coming home.

She didn't blame her love's ambivalence over returning to a town that haunted him with bad memories. A little giggle expelled her belly as she made note to pack her new collection of Victoria's Secrets. She vowed to make some pleasurable memories to replace the unsavory. Then they could have a romantic dinner and discuss the arrival of a plus one to their immediate household. Nothing was for certain yet. But if anything was reliable it was Jade's womanly clock. She could pinpoint the hour let alone date and she'd never been three weeks late before.

Unleashing her towel and ruffling her hair she virtually glowed with pride. Damien would make a sensational father. He would be all the miraculous things a man should be to his son that he was completely robbed of in his own youth. She was positive as she'd ever been in anything in life that he'd be just as excited if not more so than her.

They hadn't talked about the actual wedding a whole lot in detail. She cringed at the possibility of sharing a table with Mother Galligher. It would be dreadful to have to sit at separate tables considering Damien was an usher and all. Who else would be at the ceremony? It was obvious his older sister Peggy and half-sisters Kassandra and Kaitlin would be in attendance. She seemed to remember there being four cousins in total. Danny had three younger sisters, the flipside to the chronological makeup of Damien's immediate family. There was the one aunt and uncle of course, proud parents of the groom to be. She knew nothing of the bride's side, but it didn't seem to be of consequence. Would there be any childhood friends there?

Jade and Damien of course had been together since the tenth grade but there were friends and relationships of course that had begun several years prior. Would there be any ex-girlfriends there? The thought made her shiver as she unraveled her towel, her nipples puckering in the chill. As gooseflesh spread across her damp torso and hips she had to reject the unthinkable. Had Mother Galligher conspired to set up an old flame with her son? It was certainly not beneath her. She began to sob softly thinking she'd been made a fool out of. This was crazy thinking, irrational and nothing good could come of it.

Then she remembered the doctor, Reese was his name or Rhys? He was a lifetime friend of the family. He must be going. Maybe she could call him and see if he'd heard anything from Damien. It wasn't so far-fetched for someone to call their psychiatrist given the fact he'd become a friend for some advice before returning to a very emotional location. Pulling on a pair of shorts and camisole she dashed into the kitchen with new found hope in mind.

Damien and Jade were just as retentive as the other in terms of organization and kept all their phone contacts in a rolodex beneath their landline telephone. She was certain his number would be in there and was not remotely hesitant upon calling him.

After clumsily shifting through "P's" and half way through "S's" she darted back to "R's" and found the card she was looking for, Dr. David Rhys. Water Street, Port Perry. In a new found rejuvenated spirit, she pressed the buttons on dial pad and shifted back and forth listening to the digital chirps.

"Dr. Rhys's office, may I help you?"

A sigh of relief spilled out from her lips.

"Yes, this is Jade, Damien Galligher's better half."

"Oh, good evening Jade. How are you? I thought I'd recognized the number. I hear you two lovebirds are coming into town. Has Damien changed his mind and decided to make an appointment for tomorrow?"

"Changed his mind..." Suddenly the floor began to swirl beneath her. "You mean he's already called there?"

"Why yes earlier this afternoon. In fact, we talked in length about the two of you and I believe the doctor even suggested making an appointment. He didn't approve of our boy wonder going to his old house alone, so it only seemed natural to set up an appointment."

An icy chill stole the air from Jade's lungs.

"Honey, are you still there."

She croaked into the receiver then cleared her throat. "Yes, yes sorry," she tried to laugh off her horrific instinct. "He hasn't made it home from work yet. I'm getting a little worried. Please don't think I'm crazy. I'm all the way here in Toronto but is there any way you can send someone over to his old house and see if everything's alright?"

"Oh, crazy isn't a term we use a whole lot in our field sweetie, but I catch your drift. I'm sure it's nothing but if it sets your mind at ease I'd be more than happy to drive by the old place on my way home. Not much an old bird like me does on Friday nights anymore. Just between us girls I was looking forward to snuggling up on the sofa with a good Eric Shelman novel."

"Would you really? Thank you so much. I'm sure it's nothing but it's just a hunch I have."

"Think nothing of it. That boy is family to us which makes you family by association. I'll give you a ring the second I pull up there, how's that sound?"

"Thanks again. I'll wait by the phone."

"Very good, I'm sure we'll all have a good laugh in no time. You know boys will be boys."

"Okay, you're probably right."

"I'll talk to you soon, good night now."

For the second time in mere hours, Jade hung up without a single good bye. She stared out the balcony window again. Now she'd wished she had more cigarettes.

CHAPTER FIFTEEN

The wind rustled blades of grass beneath Damien and his father's feet. He stared off into the distance attempting to absorb the scene that had transpired before him. As his genetic senior Bill had offered nothing but turmoil and chaos into his life. Now the very fabric of their relationship was in question. Another side of father was prevalent whether he welcomed it or not.

"I don't know exactly what to say." He trailed off scuffling his feet in the dirt. A sigh of resignation expelled from his lips.

"Does it matter that the man I'd cold clocked was your mother's first husband? He's the father of your half-sisters." The defeat in his tone was enough to make Damien shiver.

"But why on earth would she invite you to a reception,' he stammered on. "-a perfect stranger at a gas station," Looking up his eyes welled up with tears. "It" makes no sense. It's the sort of thing a cold hearted, manipulative bitch would do for theatrics and kicks. I just can't see Mom doing something like...."

A gentle hand soothed his shoulder. There was no use for any kind of empty words to be uttered. Nothing could be said to ease the impact of what had just unfolded.

"What possible motive…"

He was beginning to feel like blubbering, angry with himself for displaying such vulnerability.

"We still have much to see son." He grasped his shoulder tighter. "Perhaps its best we kept moving." With a solitary, fluent gesture he swept his arm across the landscape. The familiar visual buckle and rippling that had commenced from before ensued. A crack in the horizon formed, rippled, peeled.

Instant nausea gripped his stomach as his eye lids fluttered beyond control. His knees trembled and dipped. For a moment he was certain his bowels would burst into oblivion. A tinny sound ignited across the sky as clouds, rays of sunshine and tree tops spiraled into the prominent crack before them. The ground quivered and quaked and was vacuumed into the vortex in the distance. Just as he was bound on vomiting profusely until food became bile and bile became blood the scenery eclipsed as different as night and day.

A dank, sour odor of sweat, booze and defeat enveloped the air. Darkness confined any resemblance of hope for the inhabitants within the steel bars. Moans of despair consumed the captives.

An authoritative clicking assumed along the corridor. The footfalls echoed increasing in intensity with each passing step. A slight pause would seem like an eternity for any of the caged convictions looking on. Grunting, rasping and snorting ensued.

Retracting his nightstick, deputy Ray Traynor rapped the business end along the steel. Back and forth, back and forth the sound was enough to split the cranium of any criminal headache or not. As he whistled in singsong mockery he spewed into the air.

"Rise and shine, Muhammed Ali, looks like someone sprung bail, slugger."

Inside the cell a groan of incoherent proportion repelled.

In the shadows, invisible to all else, Damien tugged upon his illusionary travel guide. Father attempted to brush him aside, a futile attempt to shush his inquiries.

"Shake and bake tough, guy. Come on let's get a move on." The deputy bellowed so loudly it threw him into a fit of coughing hysterics.

Damien and father watched on as the rotund cop's face turned beat red. He doubled over coughing and wheezing all the while. The boy wondered momentarily if this guy thought he was keeping the streets safe at night.

"Get your ass in gear or stay, makes no difference to me. But you've got the count of five to haul on out of here. I ain't got all day."

The boy whispered up towards his father's ear, "This is where they locked you up? You were just defending yourself against those pretentious pricks. Jesus..."

Needing not another invitation the prisoner leapt to his feet off the decrepit cot. It took only three swift strides to make it to the bars. His eyes were practically swollen shut.

Deputy Traynor skipped past sequence counting aloud three.

"Well look who's joined the party Sugar Ray. Come to dance like a butterfly for us?" He cackled an obscene bellowing laughter. Rotted, yellowish brown teeth flashed in the dense air between them. "God only knows who'd pony up bail for a piece of trash like you." He looked him up and down, appraising his intimidating stature before him. His skeleton key penetrated the lock below. With a dramatic twist of the wrist he unlocked the door, running the door along its track. Concrete and steel clashed and clanged into the mildew and dust.

On shaky, sea legs the young, lanky version of Bill stepped out of the bars. He had to duck ever so slightly to avoid banging the top of his head against the perimeter. From the distance Damien's eyes bulged.

Deputy Traynor clenched Bill's arm and shoved him forward. Excessive force nearly caused him to collide with the floor below. Anyone could see it took tremendous restraint not to retaliate.

"I don't understand what happened in the meantime. I mean I saw…. we both saw the cops take you away, but it looks like you've been run over by a truck."

"Officers of the law in small towns are often uneducated and bored, son. Let's just say they used your dear old 'da as a punching bag to ease some stress once hauled here from the country club."

"My God, that's police brutality. Couldn't you have charged them?"

"Again, small town, small mentality, arrested for assault, who in their right mind would believe me…"

"So, this whole time, I mean even far before I was even born… it was like you were the victim." Sub consciously Damien clenched and unclenched his fists at his sides. As each second passed his gestures grew more rapid and fierce.

The towering figure beside him, peered down, uttering not a word.

From around the station's corner, into the dark corridor a figure had stood. Tension in the air could be cut with a knife. Even the regular cat calls and taunts from other prisoners were somehow subdued. The deputy and Bill froze in their tracks.

A slight nod of recognition was passed from the stranger to deputy. Instantly the officer released his grip upon Bill's arm. He coughed a submissive croak.

"Come along William. You're on my dime now and time is money as they say." It was evident who owned the voice at the end of the hall. "I'll catch you up to speed in the car. Chop, chop now we mustn't keep them waiting."

In complete disbelief, Damien looked on and for the first time in his entire life felt genuine contempt for his mother.

"As you can see Damien, things are not as exactly as they seem." He grasped each of his shoulders, turning him to face him. Eye to eye he regarded him and spoke with undeniable enunciation.

"Upon the final threshold of this journey, should you decide your opinion of me remains the same and wish not to alter the course of your destiny, then that is your decision son. Yet somehow, somehow, I believe that will not be the case. Regardless of your perception, I just wanted you to see the truth."

CHAPTER SIXTEEN

Dusk had settled hours before Caroline's decent into the winding country gravel roads. As a native of the Seagrave community, she knew these parts like the back of her hands. She didn't mind appeasing the young girl Jade's requests to check on the old Galligher place. Still an unshakeable sense of unease overpowered her. Her knuckles turned bone white around her grip on the steering wheel. Forever the cautious, she held her hands at ten and two o'clock, repeatedly checking her rear-view mirror. No, a solitary head light or any sign of life came into view.

She considered for a moment to put on the radio then just as quickly rejected the idea. There was no need for distractions. The faster she made it out to the old, run down house, the faster she'd be home. The thought of retiring for the evening on the sofa with a nice glass of chardonnay and Shelman's latest zombie novel in the Dead Hunger series delivered a flicker of a smile upon her lips. She enjoyed the little things to keep reality in check.

Having worked for Dr. David Rhys for over fifteen years, she was well versed in his case files. In a certain sense, she supposed she possessed the very same confidentiality that the doctor offered each of his patients. There was very little that surprised her anymore. Yet she recalled the first time translating Damien's sessions from audio into typed print and chilled her to the bone. The boy had been through hell and back. There was no wonder how the origin of all his horror in that condemned home would beckon him in his nightmares and every waking moment. Sometimes the only way to slay a dragon is to walk directly into its fiery bowels.

As the dip in the road gave way to a steep incline, Caroline knew she was approaching the vicinity. She clicked her high beams on caring not to collide with one of God's unforgiving creatures deciding on an impromptu road crossing. Chunks of aggregate crushed and flew beneath her tires as she braked and came to a steady crawl. She wasn't sure if the gate to the old driveway would be secured or not and prepared to park along the shoulder to avoid any unexpected surprises for the sporadic oncoming car.

Maneuvering her wheels to the right she nestled in as close to the ditch as possible. As she shifted the gear into park Caroline suddenly wished she'd had a flashlight and decided to check the trunk before going anywhere. Killing the headlights, she twisted the ignition off yet kept the keys in place. It wasn't as if she were in the Bronx or some damn thing. The likelihood of her car being jacked in the middle of nowhere was not exactly high. With her easy going, down home mentality she supposed she wouldn't even be that angry if her tiny Corolla was stolen. It'd be God's will that someone would need a viable means of transportation should they take her car. If they need go to all that effort it wouldn't be the end of the world.

She hoped a quick patrol around the perimeter would be sufficient to set Jade's mind at ease. Leaning towards the passenger seat, she clicked the glove box door and depressed the trunk's release. The cool, summer breeze lifted her spirits as she whistled a quaint tune to keep herself company.

Inside the trunk in all its meticulous glory, it didn't take long to find the flashlight she desired. With her cellphone safely stowed in her purse, she slammed the trunk and prepared to trek into the belly of the Galligher beast.

Thankful she had changed into loafers out of her high heels at the office, she strolled along the shoulder and dense under-brush. Sounds of the forest soothed her whereas she supposed a city dweller would be cringing in fear about now. The occasional howl, chirping or caw did not unnerve her. Nature's calls were just one of the many reasons she was so captivated with rural living.

Climbing the stony embankment, she made mental note to try and get more active. It seemed with each passing year she'd got-ten a little more winded than the next. Perhaps cutting out those late-night pastries would be a safe bet to longevity. But as a single, middle aged lady of the woods there wasn't anyone to impress and as they say old habits do die hard.

Upon reaching the driveway's entrance a sight before her was a little alarming. Just beyond the mouth of the road sat a parked car, a Cavalier by the looks of it. Although she'd never seen the vehicle she did recall the boy mentioning once in one of their many tele-phone chit chats that he'd just newly acquired a used car, a Chevy of some sort or other.

On impulse her hand retreated to hear purse and cell phone. This wasn't a good sign. If Damien was here, he'd have to have been here for quite some time. She didn't want to upset poor Jade, who was beside herself with worry already. After balancing the op-tions in her head, she decided to refrain from making any call yet. There was no real proof he was even here or if this was his car. She decided to wait to see if he was inside. The boy may be a little deli-cate at first and may even be embarrassed over being interrupted. She stood still contemplating a return to her own car and drive on home. It wasn't her place, but this parked car still meant nothing.

She sighed in frustration, knowing full well a promise was made on the phone and she always kept her promises.

Stepping further into the darkness she rested her hand on the hood of the car. It was still warm. That didn't necessarily mean anything either, the sun was rather hot earlier today. Then again whoever owned this vehicle didn't park it all that long ago.

She looked for a clasp or chain to unhinge the fence. With nothing in sight, she was a little aggravated it would take a little climbing to get over the fence. Loafers were one thing but in one of her nicest skirts was another matter altogether.

Incoherent gibberish slipped through her teeth, the closest the receptionist ever came to cursing. Thankfully she knew well enough to climb close to one of the posts where the rusted old rungs would be a little stronger, held more support. If she tore her nylons or messed up her skirt, rest assured Damien Galligher would be hearing all about it.

At last she wrestled her bony hips over the fence and dropped to the ground below. While adjusting her purse strap she clicked on her flash light waved its projectile beam along the driveway. Scores of milkweeds, dandelions and thistle brush dominated easy access.

Careful not to snag her apparel she scrimmaged around the foliage. The driveway wasn't long, not even a fraction of a mile yet it felt like an obstacle course of sorts, long ago abandoned. This was one rare moment she wished the whole thing could be excavated and turned into a shopping mall or some damn thing. Good riddance to bad rubbish she always said.

At last she reached the cusp of the house, a junkyard cemetery of shattered dreams and forgotten hope. Flashing the light along the tattered old siding she shook her head in disgust. How any normal, breathing human being could reside under that roof and four walls and inflict that kind of hell upon his wife and children was beyond her comprehension. Although she'd never uttered the words aloud she felt the fate that was served to Billy Galligher was far too generous. She'd only wished he rotted in jail for years before eventually hanging himself one day. Would serve him right to think about what he put everyone else through.

As she stepped around the side of the house she shined the light upon the front doorway. The sight before her made her gasp, nearly dropping the flashlight into the tall grass below. The boarded-up doorway had clearly been tampered with and no question recently. Shards of splintered two by fours lied discarded two and fro. A tiny swatch of fabric with what looked like a drop or two of blood whisked back and forth in the breeze, snagged in a sharpened splinter. Frantically she tore her purse off her shoulder and couldn't find her cellphone fast enough to fulfill her promised call.

CHAPTER SEVENTEEN

"So, you see son, I was brought up to always show your appreciation when someone offers a grand gesture."

While walking huddled together in sheer blackness, Damien scoffed.

"Yes, yes I know. If it weren't for your mother I wouldn't have ended up in that mess to begin with. I was a simple man, came from hardship. I earned a meager but honest living pumping gas. If I had to rely upon my own pocket to bail myself out. Well I'd likely still be there."

"Oh, come on Dad, that's a crock and you know it. She manipulated you and set you up. You looked like a damn fool and she laughed about it the whole time."

His grip tightened along his shoulder. Flashes and streaks of red light pulsed and danced around them. Their infinite darkness around them knew no bounds.

"Be that as it may, I still gave your mother a piece of my mind outside the police station that day. That infernal vixen! I tell you, she cast a spell on me. Every time she pulled a stunt like that, every time I began to protest or get angry it was like a cloud of ecstasy swirled around me. When I looked at your mother all I saw was love. Love in its purity and undying beauty. Her doe like eyes and vulnerable demeanor spoke to me and they told me to let go and to simply love."

A glimmer of light appeared in the distance, not entirely unlike a headlight at the end of a tunnel.

"So, you're telling me she brainwashed you or put a spell on you or whatever to always get her own way?"

"Exactly and whenever I thought I was coming to my senses and told myself Billy boy, just walk away, I just clammed up. Even when she told me about her scheme to use my itch, my touch or whatever you want to call it. I consider it a burden now, but when she discovered my intuition she made it crystal clear she needed me and would make us filthy rich. It was always all about the old mighty dollar with Joy. Sure, at first, she tried to tell me she was through with all the rich, snotty sorts and the limousines and worldly travel. She said she needed a good honest man with a strong back and even stronger heart. Later she'd trick me into taking her to the casinos or racetracks. She said my gifts could get me into the heads of the other competitors to find out their next moves. She said it wasn't cheating, it was strategy."

On their walk towards the distant light, Damien doubled over and began to wretch into the void. His stomach clenched to the point he thought he'd tear in two. Wiping frothy spittle from his lips, he at last stood.

"This is just more than I can really take right now. I mean my whole battered life has been pathetic but until now and only now I find out it's been a big fat paranormal lie. It is a bit to digest."

Something behind the layers of flesh pulsed and bubbled. The skin on Bill's face stretched and yawned beyond proportion. His eyes darted back and forth, quicker with each movement.

"She said she needed the money for her sister, her family. I guess she really meant her coven. They were planning a move from somewhere in Europe to join her. She always promised once they arrived she would be treated like a queen and I her king. I'd never have to worry or lift another finger in my life. She failed to mention her true, diabolical tendencies…."

Off in the distance the light intensified, glowed and sparkled.

"The crazy thing is Damien, is I actually believed her."

"What I don't get is you said you were from a decent upbringing and money and fancy things never got to you. So why the sudden enchantment, why get caught up in it all?"

"I am only human, and like I said in the beginning your mother had her way of captivating me. I only wanted to please her. I thought if I could only make her happy then the rest wouldn't matter. She was a vile woman at times, son. When she realized my talents were useless at such monetary gain she'd lash out at me for days on end. She'd throw every insult, put down and emasculated comment at me. When that didn't work she'd cut herself and threaten to kill herself. It didn't matter if her daughters witnessed it or not. She wanted them to know what a miserable failure their stepfather was and why they were doomed to a life of poverty. They were just emotional pawns to her and I was collateral damage. After locking herself in our room for days on end, I had to take care of the kids and somehow work at the gas station, double and even triple shifts at times."

"It still just isn't adding up. I mean if she was a witch and I do say if, then why wouldn't she just cast a spell on whoever the hell she damned pleased and get all the riches she desired. Doesn't that seem more plausible than all this dancing in riddles bullshit?"

"The ways of the witch are mysterious, no arguing that. I suppose if I had to fully understand it, they have their limitations the same as anyone else. They can't just walk up to somebody and sprinkle a bit of fairy dust and empty their pockets. I guess it's more intricate than that."

"It all just sounds like a really badly written novel or some made for TV movie."

"Look, its more complex than that. I think we've covered that, have we not?" Something demonic was resurfacing in father's tone. "If I understood it all don't you think I would've avoided this predicament we're in?"

"Yeah, I guess. I'm trying to understand. I mean I've got nothing else to lose." Except my freaking mind he whispered under his breath.

"When it seemed like the possibility of her sisters moving from Europe was getting further and further away the more ruthless he became. She once even threatened to sacrifice Kassandra claiming the blood offering to Satan would unite her with her coven. Can you believe she stood there with a handful of hair and a meat cleaver to her throat? I was mortified and still to this day can't believe I talked her down."

An eerie silence followed that halted each of them in their tracks.

"Believe me I know of the one everyone calls Satan. His lordship is nowhere near what society makes him out to be."

"What?"

"In terms you'd better understand, in the words of the late great Bon Scott: hell, ain't a bad place to be."

"You're out of your mind. This whole scene is just too messed up for anyone to take. I'm so out of here."

"Out of where Damien? If you haven't noticed there is nowhere to go. Life itself is an illusion. The only thing constant is the struggle between good and evil. Even the two adversaries have been catastrophically misrepresented."

In the midst of exchanging worldly philosophies father and son had stepped through the threshold of the light. They basked not in any form of tranquility or semblance. Throughout their infinite stroll of nothing they'd walked smack dab back into the pits of abyss in the Galligher home. Damien was surprised to see his father had not resumed the façade of his earlier demonic like appearance. His skin continued to buckle, writhe and crawl, yet it didn't give credence to his previous form.

Onto the dirt and grime floor he collapsed, exhausted from stretching the recesses of his mind. He propped his head upon his palms and bent his knees to his chest. Softly he cried. He just wanted it to all go away.

"I know son, I know."

"No, no you don't know. You can't even begin to know. All I ever wanted was to be normal, accepted and loved. Instead I've always been a freak on the outside looking in. It doesn't matter if you tell me now when I'm twenty years old that it wasn't what I thought it was. I still went through the same shitty life either way. Do you have any idea what it's like to go to bed as a teenager and praying night after night after night that you don't wake up in the morning? All the self-loathing and hatred you have that rules your soul, but you somehow don't have the guts to end it all? Oh God I've tried. Only heaven knows I've tried."

"Before the night is through, you will achieve full enlightenment...."

"No, no enough of your ridiculous parables and riddles. Enough of your over compensating and enough of your distorting the truth, unveiling the truth or whatever. What exactly did you expect to achieve out of all of this?" Snot and spittle trickled down his lips swimming with tears and dismay. "I don't even know what you are or how you're back. Whether my mother was an evil witch or not is irrelevant and it's doing precious little to save my sanity about now."

"I think it's time I showed you something a little different son..."

"And stop calling me that. You forfeited the right to ever call me that. I'm hanging on by a thread here, probably blubbering apple sauce off my face in a strait jacket somewhere for all I know and you're not helping. What's in this for you? Why are you so determined to show me the other side?"

"We're getting to that I promise you." Bill whispered into the gloom. He walked over to a web laced mahogany cabinet. Sliding one of the doors out, he gazed down with an expression of near nostalgia. Into his chest he held the book. "I think this is a far more effective trip down memory lane for you." He held out the offering, steadfast upon acceptance.

Damien stared in return and kicked bone debris with his heel. At times like this he felt like a spoiled brat throwing a tantrum. He just wished he could get one up without caving into someone else's demands for a change.

"Well it's not like I'm going anywhere," he yanked the book from his clutches. "So, what is it?"

"It's a scrapbook of course. Each photo and keep sake in there holds the truth behind the memory. Open it up, look inside and perhaps you'll attain the enlightenment you need without my interference."

"Why, where are you going? Back to hell?" Damien scoffed then couldn't help but laugh over how much he'd meant his query.

"Not exactly, but I will return. It seems this journey has taken its toll on my being more than I gave it credit for as well."

"So, when will you be back? When can I get out of here?"

"As I'm sure you'll notice the proof is within the pages that I know all and see all where you're concerned Damien. Since crossing over so to speak, that is. I will know when the time is right to return and discuss your discoveries."

Just as he barely finished hearing Bill's declaration he opened the scrap book on his lap. From within the very fiber of the paper the photos became fully animated, in motion. Clouds whisked by on distant horizons. Branches from trees swayed back and forth in the breeze. Children engaged in reckless abandon and fits of carefree laughter. Damien had only wished their laughter came from pure of heart.

CHAPTER EIGHTEEN

There was no clause in her contract with Dr. Rhys that stated she was ever required to squirm through a splintered hole late on a Friday night, searching for a previous patient. Nothing was holding Caroline to exploring the sinister Galligher home to any length. Any sane person would flee at that instant, at the first sign of danger.

Caroline was no ordinary woman. In fact, deep in her heart she cared for Dr. Rhys, his patients and of course the Galligher boy. She made a promise to Jade, to try and find Damien. Even at this moment she regretted the promise thinking she would simply be ruling out the possibilities of his whereabouts via process of elimination.

This new-found discovery of a tattered piece of fabric was gruesome. Bloody or not bloody, dangling precariously, it was something meant for police forensics, certainly not a mild-mannered receptionist. With quivering hands, she shuffled through her purse. It seemed infinitely deep and wide now with enough clutter for a self-storage unit let alone a simple accessory item. Her cellphone seemed as long lost a ship at sea and she clambered more frantic by the second. She felt herself on verge of hyperventilating and had to take deep, concentrated breaths. Inhaling and exhaling, Caroline grappled with getting herself under control. Years ago, Dr. Rhys had treated her for anxiety with medication. She gradually weaned herself off the regimen under his guidance and cared not to venture back to those nerve wracking days. The simple exercise restored her control, ability to focus.

Closing her eyes, she exhaled once again and fished the cellular out between her two fingers. Damn technology was making these gadgets smaller and smaller by the year. It was any wonder they even worked anymore. Caroline often joked with the good doctor that it'd only be a matter of time before people were wired with chips and no longer were slaves to their digital devices.

She laughed nervously to no one. Sometimes living alone could make a nervous Nelly out of just about anyone. Almost instantly she felt at ease with the front corner of the digital face peering through the zipper lining. Tapping the address app, she scrolled down to the last caller and hit send. With her free, shaking hand she held the flash light through the whole in the boards. From her vantage point she couldn't get a good view of what lied just beyond the doorway. Curiosity began to get the better of her.

"Damien, Damien, honey, are you in there..." she cried out, startled at the sound of her own voice. The incessant device in her left hand chirped on and on with no answer. Caroline felt suddenly absurd crying out in the darkness with no one around but God's creatures in the woods.

"Damien, it's Caroline. If you want to be alone I understand. We were just worried..." She waited for as long as she felt was humanly decent and attempted to jimmy her way on through the cracks. Extra cautious, she managed to avoid any of the shards that may have previously snagged the former entrant.

Onto the porch floor she collapsed in a heap. An audible whoosh of air from her lungs ricocheted off the walls. A minor phobia of spiders, earwigs or virtually any kind of creepy crawly was inspiration enough to make her leap to her feet. Dusting off her skirt and blouse she sighed as the flashlight beam created a strobe affect along the desolate corners of despair.

Through the second doorway she stepped. Each movement and gesture were more tentative than the last. Faint sounds in the distance of skittering and scratching brought a twinge of shiver from the base of her spine to the nape of her neck. She shuddered violently at the thought of any unknown creepy crawlies wiggling anywhere the eye could not detect.

In her left hand she looked down and was flabbergasted to see the call had been terminated. She'd realized her battery was low and thought perhaps it may also have been the result of being in a dead zone. Such a morbid thought it was to be trapped in any dead zone literal or otherwise.

Desperately she searched for any kind of surrogate comfort. A wall, a chair or something to brace herself with in case she felt the onset of another panic attack seemed crucial at this moment. It was too damned dark.

Caroline looked down at her cell once again and was relieved to see she had just enough juice left or reception to make the call. Hitting send had never felt more essential. As she lifted the phone to her ear she barely had enough time to hear it chirp again and was shocked beyond comprehension.

"My, oh my, don't we just look delicious enough to eat?" A maniacal laughter ensued like a thousand nails shrieking down a field of slate.

Caroline stretched her mouth to unleash the unholiest of screams. Sound had somehow eluded her, lodged in her throat. The cell fell to her side bouncing carelessly this way and that. If she'd held it a second longer she'd hear her recipient shout out in a frenzy, "Hello, hello, Caroline is that you?"

Razor laced tentacles lurched from the outer reaches of depravity. Stitched into her flesh upon her cheeks, shoulders, hips and thighs the mandibles synched. Convulsing and tweaking Caroline's skin tore from a dozen destinations. A rain of blood showered the walls and floor. Ravenous growls filled the receiver.

A lonely, middle aged receptionist's only crime against humanity was being a social recluse. Now Caroline drew in her final breaths. As her eyes glazed over, receding forever into the back of her head, her last thought was how she wished she'd just made it home for a quiet night of reading.

CHAPTER NINETEEN

The spiral bound scrapbook that held many Galligher family memories and early childhood mementos was something he was always aware of, but wasn't entirely sure if it was something he'd seen. It was just another one of those things he'd repressed in memory. Yet another item that was abandoned because of fleeing the structure that held so many reminders of pain and suffering.

In no time flat he was mesmerized with the book. It's dusty, worn surface and tattered corners did little to deter his interest. He'd thought he'd had just about enough of this whole bizarre façade. Somehow, he knew the answers he was looking for was somewhere between cover to cover. Momentarily he felt ashamed for losing his cool earlier with the apparition claiming to be his father. He hated like hell to be so damned vulnerable. The last thirteen years of his life he'd worked hard at putting up emotional barriers and letting anyone in. A defense mechanism that evolved to reflex, Damien now felt weakened that he'd enabled himself to be so exposed.

Upon the transparent covers over the pages, he caressed his thumb and forefinger. It was a sight to behold as the photographs beneath became their own boxed in show of wonderment. At the bottom of the first page his attention fixated upon a tiny, plastic bracelet. Through years of deterioration it was difficult to make out the lettering. Age had a tendency of eroding over paper, font and any memory attached to it. Damien had wished his own existence had managed to fade away with the same lack of fanfare.

He was gentle to peel back the cellophane, protective cover as to not disturb the layout of the remaining photos. At first it seemed a little absurd to be so delicate with items that clearly, he would associate with haunting experiences. But in his gut, it felt essential not to disturb the action sequences before him.

The cover peeled back with an audible tearing sound that made him move slower and more gingerly. Some remnants of the sticky background had managed to be lifted onto the plastic, making the endeavor more challenging. At last he peeled the top and bottom corners to the right-hand side of the page and ran his fingers over the hospital issued bracelet.

Squinting at the type writer print on yellowed paper he rubbed the pads of his thumb and finger along the surface in hopes of clearing a better view. It was evident from what he could make out his name, date of birth, weight and hospital name were enclosed upon the item. This is where it all had begun.

His hands began to glow, a vibrant light so prominent, the average viewer would surely scorch their corneas. Like a shadow from an airplane on an open field, the light grew like a sleeve upon his arm, forever radiating in varying colors. Fear did not possess him. Quite the contrary, Damien had felt an overpowering sensation of righteousness, peace and harmony.

As the sleeves spread he pinched the corner of the page turning it onto the book's cover. In the next section, another picture, easily aged and void of any of the resolution you see now in digital pixels lay before him. White sheets had crumpled and shifted beneath a young woman with a bob style hair cut that was mussed in wild tufts. Upon the bridge of her nose thick, black frames of glasses, the style that Buddy Holly would don, slid. The woman in the picture adjusted them with languid, exhausted movements. In the crook of her left arm a new born had slept. If it weren't for the occasional involuntary flailing of his arms and legs, one would be unable to tell if it were breathing or not.

A flash of light pulsed. All encompassing, Damien was forced to squeeze his eyelids shut. Certain blindness would follow if he had not reacted.

As he opened them once again, tentatively, uncertain at first, he looked around the room. Everything seemed dramatically out of proportion in comparison to what he was accustomed to. For as far as his eyes could see blue flannel had filled his field of vision. Along the trim of the fabric he saw a chin that was shaking, gently yet still shaking all the while.

Looking down he was astounded at what lied before him. Tiny appendages, almost purplish in color wriggled this way and that. He managed to deduce that these were indeed his arms even though he still possessed all the articulate thoughts of his usual processes.

His eyes darted to his left as his legs kicked in cycling motions. Damien felt the hold on his body stiffen. The gesture however felt empty of emotion. Cold and detached he sensed a sensation of tired obligation void of any love or nurturing.

To his side he spotted a makeshift desk or table. It was L shaped, configured to enable mobility on one side while maintaining structural integrity on the other. Upon its surface a stack of loose leaf pages was rapidly filling with blue ink in almost nondescript hand writing.

His fragile vision only enabled a few select words to be comprehended in the body of paragraphs. Incubus, living hell, failure, heart break and disappointment were among a few excerpts in the letter. Mother was clearly composing a letter but to whom exactly Damien could not conclude.

There was no warmth or sense of rejoice behind the composition. In fact, his mature capacities enabled him to feel utter contempt, hatred and rage. He began to buck and squirm and felt a sense of sheer unease rise from his tiny belly. Never so urgently, had he felt the need to wail out in complete sorrow.

Just as his thin reddened lips were about to burst the flood gates of ear piercing shrills a figure stepped into his sight. A presence so dominant, it eclipsed the fluorescent lights from above, it seemed to look down upon him with a sense of longing.

"Make yourself useful and take this heaving bundle of crap and puke." The voice, all-consuming demanded.

"Please Joy. Be gentle. The boy is tender and impressionable. Let me hold him."

"I just said, take the damn child. Honestly have you gone deaf or even further retarded?"

"He may not understand the words, but he feels your emotions. Look. You're upsetting him."

An uncomfortable silence blanketed the room.

"Oh, for heaven's sake never mind. Take this letter and get a stamp from the gift shop." She folded the letter with expert precision, with one hand. "Or is that too complicated for you?"

She thrust the letter at him. Damien heard a revolting grunt as the sheets were thrust into the figure's abdomen.

With his mature mind and delicate body, he managed to process the lack of love or devotion between the couple. There was nothing there but absolute repulsion. Their disdain for one another would be enough to make any well-adjusted child flee in tears and panic.

He swiped the letter with a gruff and turned to storm out of the room. An uncontrollable shriek had rumbled within the pits of his miniature belly. As he unleashed his cries of discomfort, the advanced mind knew full well the sounds were for lost love and not the immediate fixations one may suspect.

Joy closed her eyes and bit her lip. Ignoring shrills she fought to subdue the white-hot anger rising within.

From the corner of his teary eyes he saw a hunched over, shell of a man, battered and defeated. While his shoulders indicated gestures of bobbing and flinching he grew more engrossed with each second. Damien could not tell if father was tearing up the letter or crying. Somehow, he supposed it was a combination of the two.

⭇ ⭈

A sensation of being pulled startled him back to consciousness. It was almost like a feeling of thousands of magnets beckoning him from his vulnerable state. Weightlessness followed; an overpowering sense of floating.

He looked down at the delivery room. The hospital bed, sheets, pillows and of course an angst filled mother spiraled beneath him. Gazing down at his infant self he felt pity and sadness. The baby hadn't stood a chance from moment one. What could he possibly evolve to? How could one possibly grow emotionally, cognitively or spiritually with such bitter hatred between his guardians?

While enveloped in his floating form, he wished idly that he could've remained in this state. The sense of limbo would be a welcome change in comparison to absorbing all the pain and torment during the shambles of his life. An overpowering sense of peace permeated from him. The sadness resumed in stifling waves as he was propelled from the room into darkness once again.

As his weightless form tumbled and spun in abstract circles he glanced down. Beneath him another scene had begun to unfold. He'd recognized the photograph from what seemed eons ago.

A day filled with sunshine and bliss filled the borders of the photo. Most of the shot displayed mounds of moist earth, with the odd scattered patch of grass. In the top corner grey cement accented with vibrant yellow siding revealed it must have been the rear of the Galligher house, just outside the backyard.

A sinking feeling ensued. The feeling of being pulled through gravity, much like quick sand had interrupted his serenity. Warmth that could only be offered from persistent sunshine radiated along the bottoms of his tiny feet and legs.

He looked down at his bowlegged quads. Into the moist dirt his toes wiggled and clenched. A second more thorough appraisal revealed his attire to be a ridiculous sailor's singlet. His bottom felt bunched and pinched. Upon his delicate head a newspaper crafted into a hat had resided.

Crouching down into the dirt, he made enthusiastic sputtering sounds. In his clutches he navigated his favorite toy, a yellow Tonka truck fully equipped with dumpster bed and moveable tires. Little Damien was laboriously at work shoveling handfuls of mud, stones and grass into the bucket. Onto his knees he bent making the ever present sputtering sounds so important when mimicking any engines as a child.

The maturity still resided within his head. He was quite capable of registering sophisticated thoughts and complicated reasoning. It was baffling as to why he was all alone with no supervision. Yet he preferred it that way. The backyard was a fantasy sanctuary. Here a kid could be a kid and not have to worry about any of the madness inside the house.

Onward he sputtered tracing the wheels back and forth into the dirt and grit. His motor skills were alarmingly advanced for a two-year-old. Backing the truck, he lifted the bed to discard all the earth into strategically placed piles. His intent was on placing several piles then building a dirt castle, so he could keep all the meanies out and be a knight of his very own kingdom.

A sound in the distance made him jump from the activity at hand. The creaky screen door the moaned, before its aluminum shell collided with the side of the house. Stomping fueled with agitation graced the back deck.

"Oh, for God sake Kass, you're supposed to be watching Damien!" the voice screamed loud enough for the neighbor two miles over could hear. "It's not like Mom and Bill ever leave us alone. Now they never will for sure."

An onslaught of cursing and exasperation followed. The current mind of Damien, even though embedded in his infantile shell could easily register the possessor of the voice as his oldest half-sister Kaitlin. She'd become somewhat of a surrogate mother in later years much to her own distaste and resentment.

"Come on Kass, I can't be late for work again. I'm going to get fired over you, you know."

She continued to shout into the house with no response. Kaitlin had worked at the local donut shop a welcome retreat from the circus of the household.

Rapid pacing followed along the deck's surface. By now Damien had officially blown the whistle on quitting time for his excavation enterprise. He watched on, shaking in his ridiculous sailor's outfit knowing full well what was about to unfold.

"Jesus Christ," she expelled through reddened, peeled lips. She reefed on the screen door, smashing it against the wall once again. Pounding footsteps echoed through the windows into the boy's ears.

Although they were inside the house Damien could still hear every sound and syllable. Into the basement Kaitlin stormed beating each stair dramatically with a well calculated step. An eerie silence settled in the air. In the dirt pile Damien shifted with unease. He scoured the grounds for some sort of retreat. The violent fights between his sisters were at times worse than anything he witnessed from his parents.

The foundation and walls did precious little to muffle the exchange that transpired inside.

"Really Kassandra? Really smoking pot? How irresponsible can you be and with this loser? Go on Buddy time to make like a tree and leave."

"Who in the hell do you think you are?" a banshee like shrill retaliated. "You're not the boss of me. I can do whatever I want, whenever I want."

"You're supposed to be watching Damien and Peggy. I've got to go to work.' The voice trailed off. Damien could envision his older sister crossing her arms and tapping her foot impatiently.

"I am watching them. What's it to you? The little rug rats can run all over the fucking yard. They don't need to be chained down man."

"Yeah man, chill out,' a clearly inebriated Buddy had offered a futile attempt at mediator.

"Shut up Buddy and why are you still here?"

"You can't talk to him like that," Kassandra returned.

"Oh, I just did! So, what are you going to do about it?"

"You're just jealous you bitch. You want to screw him, and he can't stand the sight of your ugly face."

The primal screams always unnerved Damien and incapacitated him with fear. He eventually had to at least look on from a distance to make sure everything was alright. Deep inside, he cared for his sisters even though they'd be just as happy if he dropped off the face of the earth.

He crawled along the backyard to the back steps. It was a textbook case of defense mechanism that he always regressed back a phase or two when witnessing trauma. Along the deck he pounded his knees and tiny fists emulating his older sister from mere moments ago.

"I'll fucking kill you is what I'll do about it!"

A loud crash reverberated off the walls followed by a series of smashing and obscenities.

"Whoa, dude." Was the most the stoner known as Buddy could muster as he stood back and did nothing.

In a wild frenzy the two sisters grasped fistfuls of hair and swung mercilessly at one another. Under other pretenses their commotion would be near comical, resembling that of a Loony Tunes grapple of dust between cats. As nails slashed and flesh slapped upon flesh the two tumbled into anything and everything that lied within their path of destruction.

Chairs were knocked over, pictures fallen from the wall. End tables were smashed while dishes were thrown and shattered to pieces along the floor. The intensity of their battle fizzled not as they screamed blood curdling screams of hatred. Throats were clenched, eyes were raked. The two would make a formidable duo, if pitted against anyone. If they could ever get past their sworn loathing for one another.

Damien continued to crawl through the living room and kitchen. From upstairs he heard the bathroom door slam. Peggy had managed to barricade herself once again. Her only way of coping with their vicious violence was to lock herself in there and drown out the sound in the shower. She cried herself to sleep sometimes in the bathtub.

Sitting on top of the stairs the toddler was torn between sitting idle or somehow intervening. Subconsciously he began to rock back and forth, searching for retreat. He couldn't full well leave, knowing it'd be his fault if something happened to either of them.

The half-wit Buddy managed to separate the two gladiators. He didn't come completely unscathed. For his efforts he was furnished with a blind shot here and there.

"I hate your guts Kaitlin, you know that. And I could care less if that little shit Damien choked on his own spit and died in his sleep. It'd do us all a favor."

Each Kassandra, Buddy and Kaitlin jumped in unison. It was now their time to be shocked as the basement door was slammed behind the fleeing boy.

In the next instance it appears hours had passed. Father and mother were home and the dust had settled once again from the usual bout of mayhem. He didn't immediately understand why but Damien had the distinct, delicious taste of cold Tiger tail ice cream upon his tongue. He sat perched proudly upon Father's lap on the family's vinyl orange sofa. In conscious living he had not the memory of watching his favorite shows of Barney Miller and All in the Family. A thunderous, full belly laughter shook his whole body every few minutes. He couldn't fathom why he'd forgotten such a cherished experience.

⊶⊷

The familiar sensation of being propelled from his infant host returned once again. As he floated towards the ceiling he fought the inevitable. It'd be perfectly fine to abandon all the strife and heartache he felt growing up if he could just return to this memory, bask in its glory for just a few more minutes. He felt proud and complete showered with his monster of a father's affection. Nothing could compromise that, and nothing could change it. Now it was being stolen from him as he glanced down upon the spinning living room. The cheap, tacky shelves and chipped porcelain knick knacks seemed to taunt him as he drifted further and further away. Press board pine consoling upon their television glimmered as he succumbed to the vortex overhead. The screen flickered and faded away as he plummeted through the unknown.

Through tired, haggard eyes Damien absorbed the next photograph. A rare capture of each of his childhood cousins, Danny, Diane, Suzanne and Shelly sat bright eyed and bushy tailed around a massive sparkling Christmas tree. Tinsel, garland, ornaments and popcorn adorned the branches and needles with care. Stockings dangled and swayed filled to the brim with good tidings of joy. Balls and scores of crumpled wrapping paper among boxes lied like disposable heroes to dress upon awe inducing gifts of wonderment and enchantment.

Damien assessed his new-found host. Along his arms and chest was thick, itchy green and red wool. A sweater with a reindeer upon the front had been knitted by his Aunt Julia. It appears Joy was finally united with her sister after all. Yet the overall mood of the room did not suggest anything sinister or diabolical.

Mother was chain smoking her infernal Export green cigarettes while Father sat on the direct opposite side of the room. There were no possible routes of direct distance that could be anywhere further from apart. Damien considered it must have been morning judging from the rampant enthusiasm from the cousins. A quick glance to the roman numerals upon the den's clock confirmed precisely that.

Briefly he wondered where Peggy, Kaitln or Kassandra could've been while sitting cross legged, Indian style in his beige, corduroy slacks. The thought passed just as quickly as he busied himself with his plush Burt and Ernie dolls. He'd pause every now and again to wave thick clouds of blue smoke away from his bubble of fun.

He glanced over at mother and steadied his gaze upon her. Downing a mug full of something he'd never seen before made his nose burn. When draining her cup, she'd hold it at arm's length jiggling it vigorously. Apparently, she expected to be waited on hand and foot.

"Joy, honey, must you smoke so much on front of the children? It's like a cigar lounge in here." As a nervous after-thought Bill added from across the room, "You're going to stunt the boy's growth." He attempted to laugh off the request signaling his good nature. He scoffed and shook his head. "The poor child has a heart affliction because of your smoking. Will you not be satisfied until you kill him before your eyes?"

"You! You, sniveling worm, when you spit out a thirteen-pound baby out of your crotch then we'll discuss what I can and cannot do."

"Joy, for the love of God; it's Christmas."

"William darling, I'm aware of the calendar date. Now be a prince and quiet down. Fetch me a Spanish coffee." She wriggled her wrist and shook her empty mug towards the floor. "And bring back some wood for the fire. I'll catch my death in this cold."

Silently he stood and stormed over to where she sat. She took up an entire sofa to herself, propping her legs up beneath a knitted afghan. Danny and his sisters along with Damien had to sit on the floor to unwrap their gifts. Julia sat in an easy chair to her left. He looked down at her barely containing his disgust. She sat passive, refusing to meet his gaze or dignify his unease. With a grunt he snatched her wrist and clenched for all he was worth. Beneath his grasp Joy tensed and sucked air between her teeth.

"William, please not in front of the children." Julia intervened.

Darting his eyes to his sister in law he seemed to be sizing her up silently then nodded. He grabbed the mug and stomped off up the stairs. Even to the remaining children in the room, you could cut the tension with a knife.

"Honestly Joy, what do you see in that behemoth anyway? I swear he's the product of inbreeding."

"Oh, come now Julia we all need our minions now and again, now don't we?"

The sisters exchanged a cackling laughter that would surely sour milk and wilt plants all at the same time.

"Julia, we really must discuss more pressing matters, in more discreet quarters of course. The sisterhood is most disappointed with your lack of participation as of late."

A sigh of resignation was her reflexive response.

"This isn't the time or place Joy. I need not tell you the kind of betrayal I've sustained in recent years."

Through innocent bedazzled blue eyes, the boy sat and stared at his mother and aunt. His developed mind and reactions must've made his five-year-old body seem beyond ludicrous.

It didn't take long for his inquisitive nature to be detected among the origin of his spectacle.

"What are you looking at you little imp? Well? What's so damn fascinating?"

Young Damien jumped from his mother's outburst. He wanted to respond but was so shocked by her callous comments he didn't know if what he had to say would even make any sense.

"Go on and play in the laundry room, get out of my sight for more than five minutes, will you? Mother and Auntie are trying to talk like grownups."

Still imprisoned to his private world of plush dolls and drowning the adults out, he sat dumbfounded.

"Go on dear, you heard your father. Smoking isn't good for growing boys. Go and find Danny and the girls they've been playing in the laundry for hours," Julia offered feeling the necessity to lighten the blow.

On unsteady legs, adolescent Damien gathered his playthings, nearly tripping over the piles of cardboard and wrapping paper. He felt like crying all the sudden. It was one of the moments he wished he could just retreat into a room, bury his face into a pillow and dream of a better day.

He didn't want to look for his cousins. They were way older than him and didn't even seem to like him. Three out of four were girls, just like his sisters. Danny was over twelve years his senior, a teenager now and had no time for a little boy like him. This Christmas flat out sucked and he couldn't wait to get out of here.

Shuffling his feet, he walked around the den's bar and past the pool table. Since Auntie Julia had become what mother called a window or widow, something like that she had a lot of expensive stuff. Damien didn't care for any of it. It was useless if you were constantly being barked at by grownups not to touch any of it. So what good was it anyway?

Reluctantly, he grasped the collapsible doors leading to the laundry room. It wasn't a traditional place of washing and drying clothes mind you. It was a kid's game room and makeshift storage room. There was a pin pong table, fuse-ball table and all sorts of board games. Maybe he could talk Shelly or Suzanne into playing Candy land with him.

Once opening the shutter like doors, the child version of Damien had to exert his limited strength. It seemed near impossible to get the handle to cooperate. He was just about to give up then realized it would okay for now to set Burt and Ernie down, just for a second. They seemed like his only friends right about now, but he was sure they'd understand.

Squeezing through the makeshift frame he made for himself he reached down to retrieve his friends. Danny and his sisters scattered. Kaitlin, Kassandra and Peggy were there too nearly tripping over one another. It didn't take an adult to realize they were up to no good. Even a five-year-old could tell they were doing something that clearly shouldn't have been.

"Oh man it's just the squirt," Danny called in relief. "Whatcha doin' kid?" He reached down to rustle his hair. Damien flinched unaccustomed to impromptu gestures of affection. "So, are you in or are you out? If you're going to hang out with the big kids, you have to close the door."

He nodded displaying his understanding. Reaching down for his chums Burt and Ernie his actions were met with a round of infectious laughter. His face reddened instantly. Just when he was about to retreat out the doors, Danny enclosed him in laughing even harder.

"Aww look at little baby Damien playing with dollies. Hey Kaitlin, you never told me your little brother was actually a sister." He clapped his thigh over and over, thinking it was the most hysterical comment ever recited.

"Come on Damien, aren't you too old for that stuff?" His sister offered.

"Geez yeah, at least it could be a GI Joe or something like that. This stuffs for babies."

His wit was met with a further uproar of laughter. Damien felt like punching him straight in the nose. Who did he think he was anyway? He never asked to come here on Christmas and be treated like this.

"Did Santa Claus bring you these dollies or did your mommy give them to you?" He snatched Ernie out of his hands and dangled it above his head, tormenting him further. Cousin Danny could be a king-sized jerk when he wanted to be.

"Give it back!" Damien wailed trying to jump and save his friend. "That's not funny, give it back!"

"Aww what're you going to do Damien cry? Go on cry like a little baby!" He cackled relentlessly flashing braces and acne in his face.

The peanut gallery from behind engaged in further outbursts of juvenile giggling.

"I'm going to tell Mom, give it back Danny!" This time he did haul back and punted his shin.

"Ouch! Shit that hurt you little twerp," he danced on his good leg.

"Here! Take the doll. It's stupid anyway."

Damien snatched it from his grasp, ashamed at how upset he'd gotten so fast. Even with his adult mind concealed in his adolescent case he felt on the verge of crying hysterically. Why couldn't he just go home already?

"Well if you're going to stay in here at least do something for a change. Go and get us the Ouija Board. Mom keeps it stuffed all the way in the back in the crawlspace." Danny winced while rubbing his shin. "Mom says it's not for kids. I think she's just spooked since Pop died."

His afterthought seemed to induce a great deal of sympathy from Damien's sisters. Even brash and crass Kassandra rubbed his shoulders. While the girls comforted Danny, Damien stared at them in disbelief. He was grateful to be needed yet he knew he'd be doing something wrong. Deep down inside he just wanted to fit in and assessed the alternative of getting a spanking or worse.

"Come on! Are you going to be one of us or what?" Danny seemed to read his mind. "Or are you going to sit there and suck your thumb with your stupid dollies."

"Shut up dummy. I'll get your stupid wee-wee board." Damien was stunned that despite his articulate thought he was unable to control his response. Perhaps he was trapped in this memory as solely an observer after all.

"Now we're talking. Go on in the crawlspace. You'll find it once you get in there. We're all too big to get past all that junk."

Feeling ridiculous in his reindeer knitted sweater and cords he hugged his friends for strength. Maybe his cousins would finally accept him. His sisters would follow suit. He'd be the hero in their eyes for a change rather than the constant zero.

He looked around the game room trying to decide a safe place to set his friends down. Deciding there was nowhere comfortable he could entrust the care of his confidants, he shimmied over to the crawl space with one in each hand. They seemed to be talking to him at this moment, encouraging him, cheering him on.

After getting their precious board, he'd feel ten feet tall just like father. Then they'd see. They'd never poke fun at him again. Maybe they'd even ask him to join in.

"Go on. What are you waiting for a written invitation?" Danny bent at the waist taunting him further. Suzanne bashfully slapped his back. Diane and Shelly clapped their hands over their lips to conceal their laughter. Kassandra glared on indifferently while Kaitlin crossed her arms. Peggy seemed to wait patiently for her turn at the pinball game.

Cautiously Damien knelt on his knees. The space was no question very confined. He wasn't aware of any claustrophobia, but it did look awfully creepy in there.

As he took a deep breath he closed his eyes. It was now or never. He'd show them, just wait and see.

Lying down army style he wiggled on his forearms. His sweater morphed into a makeshift broom, sweeping all the dust in the vicinity. Damien didn't care. Dirt was far from a deterrent.

Piles and piles of boxes balanced in limbo. Each stack appeared to be on verge of a paper landslide smothering all in its path. Garden equipment and tools adorned the walls, hanging from their respective pegs.

Once in at waist level, he started to pull further. He never wanted to soil his friends, but felt it was a small sacrifice compared to leaving them behind. They never deserved the treatment they'd receive from Danny. Besides there were good luck charms, his talisman of sorts in this momentary dare of lunacy.

His slacks were filthy from the crawl as he attempted to brush them off before mother saw them. To his right a tower of boxes seemed to provoke him, threatening to teeter over at any given moment. He maneuvered himself delicately, so he wouldn't tempt fate.

Over bags of clothes and sporting equipment he stretched. This wasn't so bad. Maybe he'd be in and out of here before he knew it. It was no worse than listening to the slime ooze out of mother's mouth.

He was just about to holler out for instructions when Danny called from just behind the wall.

"You got it yet squirt?"

"Not yet," Damien croaked.

"Well come on, even a retard could find it by now. On the big bookshelf, you can't miss it."

Frustrated Damien wished he could sock his cousin again.

"Okay, give me a minute. I see it."

His response was half lie, but he made his way over to the bookshelf nonetheless.

There it was in all its glory. Upon stacks of withered forgotten Reader's Digests lied the holy trinity, the grail of his evermore acceptance. Mustering up all his courage he marched with chest out and head held high.

It was awfully high. The bookcase had to be at least seven feet high, a major feat in comparison to his two and half foot height. Ever so delicately he balanced Burt and Ernie on a hockey net, so they could see their friend achieve his challenge.

On one musty shelf he placed his tiny hand pushing down while reaching higher for the next. The towering structure groaned but showed no sign of budging. Bracing his sock feet on the baseboard he hoisted his step to where his hand was previously.

This wasn't so bad. It was kind of neat. He'd conquer this tower and bring the jewels to the village and make a fool out of the court jester Danny, yet.

Hand over hand he climbed, exhilarated and panting. After this conquest there was no telling what he'd do next. Today the wee-wee board, tomorrow the very skies.

One shelf passed, and another then another. He was just about eye level with the pile of board games. The very top of the bookcase was more cluttered than anything else. Even the piles made it difficult to find adequate grip anywhere.

While his eyes fixed upon the prize he never faltered his gaze. Blindly he scampered along the surface, searching for just the right grip. Then something entirely foreign brushed upon his inquisitive knuckles.

A moment in horrific synchronicity, he shrieked in total shock. Within his reach was a massive grey and brown rat. His swift movements startled the filthy vermin into reacting on defense. It sank its yellow teeth deep into Damien's thumb before dashing off the musty box tops.

The last sight Damien recalled after pin wheeling backwards off the tower was the fat, grimy tail slithering behind its owner back into the bowels of the unknown.

After falling three times his height onto the concrete floor, his eyes bulged out while the air swooshed out of his lungs. He clutched his chest as a stream of crimson ran down his hand. Rudolph looked more ridiculous than ever with a spatter of blood drizzled over his eyes and antlers. His sweater was ruined. Now he was going to get it. Worst of all he'd failed his mission and let all his subjects down. They'd never let him live it down.

He bucked and convulsed beneath the debris, fighting for air. His rational mature mind wrestled with getting him to relax. Still it was no use as he was simply there as an observer. At least he pushed away the thoughts of dying. For such a young child to have the wind knocked out of them he had no idea what the feeling would encompass.

An undeniable commotion commenced beyond the crawlspace entrance. Worse than being in trouble he supposed if the adults were privy all the siblings and cousins would be in for it too. After all the shouting and bickering an eerie silence ensued.

A prominent, authoritative voice beckoned. "Damien are you alright? Come here son." It was just the right blend of reassurance and no nonsense.

"Dad? I'm in here.' he rasped back. "I-I can't breathe." Obviously, his breath was slowly returning, or he wouldn't have been able to speak. Father seemed relieved.

Some further commotion took place followed by some whining and apologies.

"Let's get you out of there. Come on now."

As he rolled over he could see his eyes, large and dark awaiting any kind of movement. He crawled over to those eyes, a virtual porthole for comfort.

On verge of being completely spent, Damien felt himself tugged free of the crawlspace entrance/exit. He was hoisted high into the air and cradled in the nook of father's arms.

"You kids know better than to send your brother and cousin in there. I'll deal with you each later."

For the first time that fated Christmas day Damien did not feel completely useless. Perhaps not all was lost after all.

⧯ ⧮

Once again, the sensation of being propelled towards the sky returned. Even in his boyhood host he could have remained until his last dying day. The feeling of belonging and love had comforted his bones and soothed his soul. Nothing else mattered than that moment of being protected and shielded by father.

He was aware of his phobia concerning rodents. Time and again throughout his teens and even adulthood he suffered ridicule. Imagine a grown man wetting himself at the mere sight of a field mouse. It was enough to send even children into hysterical fits of laughter. Damien had done everything within his power to avoid such circumstances. Even when the household cats would deliver their trophies of prey unto the doorstep he would refuse to use that exit for days on end. Mother would give him more than a stern tongue lashing for climbing out the basement window. Somehow the memory didn't seem right. He'd always attributed the fear to a mishap involving his sister Peggy. Nearly touching the repulsive rat had been one and the same with a blind reach. But he always attributed the memory to searching for their change jar deep in the kitchen cupboard above the stove. The two were going to embark upon a Saturday morning adventure to the corner store in search of potato chips, soda and comic books. Flailing off the highchair he recalled colliding with the kitchen floor and knocking the wind out of himself. He'd always remembered his mother rubbing his back and whispering sweet songs of assurance until he subdued his panic attack.

Now it was as though a virtual tear had formed in his reality, ripping apart at his cognitive recollection. It seemed from what father had been showing him, black became white, night became day and everything he knew up until this point was persistently challenged.

He sighed as he drifted away from father's protective embrace. The top of his head skimmed the ceiling tiles within the game room. A gentle smile formed upon his translucent out of body being as he watched his boyhood image nestle his tiny cheek into the crook of his Dad's neck.

Piercing through the unknown and the aerial view of the last photograph he tumbled and spun. Blackness once again blanketed his freefalling spirit. The scent of cream soda, candy bars and cheap bubble gum filled his aura.

As he gazed down he saw a sheet of tarmac as far as the eye could see. Sand swept lines of white bordered the area where large pillars housed backboards and basketball nets. An overpowering sense of reckless freedom consumed the air.

He was looking down at his elementary school playground. The sounds of frenzy and flight could only signify one thing, recess time.

Children ran this way and that, rosy cheeked and bleary eyed. Some ran and hid while others pretended to bury their face in their arms against the closest oak tree. Others kicked around a soccer ball while others yet slapped around a tether ball watching in fascination is it twirled around on its destination.

Some of the girls sang in utter bliss as they twirled around their plastic skip rope. The lazy autumn sun beat down upon their dresses as they hopped and jumped.

Within Damien's advanced maturity he wondered how long their carefree bliss would last. He wondered how long it would take for their precious innocence to be ripped from their clutches. How many of these kids would even make it to adulthood? How many would become drunks, criminals or drug addicts? How many would realize their dreams and how many would stand along a street corner in peril if they'd make this month's rent or not?

"I get to be Luke and Jason gets to be Beau."

"No fair you always get to be Luke," Damien heard his high-pitched protest. Evidently the boys were about to engage in some emulation of the television series Dukes of Hazard. Jeff was placing dibs on being the lead protagonist or hero of the troop. They were his best friends, hell his only friends in kindergarten. Still it seemed like he was always the brunt end of their cruel jokes and mockery.

"I don't always get to be Luke." Jeff had hollered back defiantly. "Besides me and Jason are the strongest and fastest. It only makes sense why we get to be the Dukes." He inched closer to where Jason stood silently. "Who told you to play with us anyway? If you don't like it, go and play hopscotch with the rest of the girls."

Jason and the rest of the boys joined in with Jeff and the hyena pack's uproar in laughter. Some of the other boys snorted and pointed. Others made juvenile, mocking gestures.

"You can be Uncle Jessie, because you're slow and fat. Or you can be Boss Hog." Jeff clapped Jason upon the back over and over. "I still think you should be Daisy because you run and throw like a little girl."

The other boys circled young Damien, like predators among prey. One would motion to bolt towards him to make him flinch. The others would laugh and begin the cycle all over again.

"You are just like a little girl Damien. What kind of a sissy name is Damien anyhow?" Someone unknown had shouted. The remaining boys in the pack nodded or uttered grunts of, "Yeah" concurring.

"Take that back Jason, you don't even know what you're talking about dummy."

"Oh, what the little girl going to do; run home to mommy and cry?" Several boys began to rub their fists under their eyes and make over exaggerated boo-hoo sounds.

"Quiet down Jason! You don't want his witch of a mom to put a curse on us." Jeff shot back and his emulated Duke Brother. "You don't know if she'll turn us into a frog or something." The rest of the clan bellowed in laughter. Some had even started tossing handfuls of grass and dandelion tops at him.

"Yeah, you're right. You're a weirdo Galligher and your whole family is nuts. Who would want to play with you?"

In his adult mind, Damien could not distinguish the casual schoolyard chum he'd hung out with, and the vicious little twerp before him.

"I think the Dukes should run him out of town what do you think Luke?"

"I think you're right Beau, we don't need his kind around here."

Together Jeff and Jason mimicked getting into their prized General Lee. Making sputtering and roaring sounds they ran in circles, kicking up dirt and stones in Damien's direction. While one made a high-pitched whirling sounds the other would yell yee-haw. "Let's get this boot-legger out of town."

One by one, in unison, the boys would run behind Damien and shove their shoulders into the back of his neck and solar plexus. He couldn't believe what had just unfolded before him. Twice he nearly lost his footing, and hurled face first to the ground.

In near demonic, chaotic frenzy the boys sped up, yelling and screaming louder. Frantic with energy they'd buck, kick and push their way into Damien. One would push from the back while the other shoved from the front. Louder and louder they screamed and roared taunting and provoking him.

"Go on you dirty boot-legger! You're good for nothing and your Daddy's a drunk too." The children laughed and bayed in rejuvenated splendor. Each Jason, Jeff and cronies kicked, swung, spat and pushed. One hooked his heel behind Damien's knee forcing him to the ground.

Instinctively Damien rolled into a ball, covering his head and drawing his legs beneath him. His defense only egged the ravenous pack on further. They were hell bent on blood, sweat, tears and humiliation.

"Your Daddy's so slow he can't even hold a job pumping gas." The other kids whooped and clapped dancing around their fallen friend. Damien could not decipher if they were still in the Duke game or discharging genuine insults.

The words hurt nonetheless. He felt like a prisoner even at school. These boys were supposed to be his pupils, his friends when there was no one else to turn to. How could they turn on him so easily?

As each of the kids engaged in gratuitous aggression they cheered and chanted. They ran around him. Kicking and bucking they laughed whenever he flinched.

"It's no wonder why you're such a sissy with a Dad like that Sally-Gally-Grrr" They jeered and squealed with delight. It was just about all the boy could take.

As Jason whirled around to hoof his side, Damien lashed out. He grasped his ankle in mid strike. The other kids ran into his back, throwing his momentum completely out of whack. Damien tugged for all he was worth. His assailant shrieked in shock as he was thrust to the ground, the back of his head skidding along the dirt.

He lurched into life, frothing at the mouth and vibrating with rage. The other children looked petrified, dropping the clumps of dirt and grass and back peddling over their own heels. Two of the other kids had already high tailed it out of there.

"You want to play a little game Jeff?" He bellowed deep from his diaphragm. The sounds emitted resembled more of a demonic beast unleashed than a fallen victim. "Let's play the incredible hulk, ever played that one? Ever played that one?" He roared into his face with grasping his shirt collar. Shaking him like a rag doll, he spat venom into his eyes with each consonant and vowel. From the ground Jason was incapacitated with disbelief as his friend's feet swayed back and forth. His sneakers barely scuffed the blades of grass below.

"If you ever, and I mean ever, so much as breathe my father's name again. I'll kill you. Do you understand?" Damien grit his teeth through crimson cheeks.

Jeff nodded vigorously, tears streaming down his face. In the distance the recess bell rang. The chimes seemed to snap young Damien out of his trance. He dropped Jeff like yesterday's garbage and looked down, repulsed with his own hands.

"And get your funky ass Duke cousin out of here." He bellowed after them.

Somehow, he knew this was the last time anyone belittled his father again.

The afternoon did not continue as victoriously as the noon hour recess had transpired. Mrs. Talbot had delicately and discreetly walked over to where Damien was sitting crossed legged in the class circle. As she knelt to his side she whispered into his ear and held out her hand.

Damien reached out and allowed himself to be lead. They walked down the long hallway that seemed to go on forever. Mrs. Talbot's heels clip clopped along the tiles. He wondered if this is what the drum roll had sounded like on the way to the gallows.

Inevitably they'd ended up at the principal's office. Mr. Dean was a stern, emotionless administrator and simply would not tolerate any indiscretion in his institution. The adult mind of Damien knew full well why he was there, but he could offer damned little to suppress the violent shaking of his nervous boyhood host.

It wasn't so much that he was afraid of being in trouble. That wasn't it at all. His mature mind could process the ramifications of his actions. The thought that was utterly unbearable was being centered out once again. He hated being the focal point of shame. The episode on the playground was only the beginning. Just wait until his father found out.

He felt all about six inches high, sinking into the cheap vinyl sofa designated for visitors in the principal's den. The receptionist acted like he was invisible which was just fine by him. She fussed about her desk, steading papers that didn't need to be steadied and lingered over her phone like it was a telethon rather than an elementary school line.

The constant hordes of gawkers walking by the glass window is what unnerved him. It didn't take a genius to realize why someone would be waiting outside the principal's lair. Hell, it didn't even take a gifted child to realize how someone would end up there. The gossip mill would churn into overdrive forever fortifying a reputation for the boy before he even stepped inside. Young Damien could not help but sneer at the possibility of being considered a bad ass.

His new-found epiphany was thwarted short, just as aluminum knob turned and plexi-glass door creaked inwards. Stony faced and all business, Mr. Dean stood and silently gestured for him to come inside. He stood motionless until the boy obliged and walked in to meet his fate.

Every step felt like he was walking through water. His heart hammered inside his chest. There was no mistaking it. He knew the difference between right and wrong. He never did anything wrong, but couldn't shake the overwhelming sense that he was about to be persecuted.

Stepping past the pleated slacks and matching jacket with tie, he looked up and was greeted with utter astonishment. Both Jason and Jeff were sitting around Mr. Dean's desk. But they were not alone. Each was sitting with their mothers while Bill Galligher sat in the adjacent chair. He wore a rigid expression but subtly offered Damien a glimmer of a wink when he was certain no one else was watching.

Either of the mothers began to cluck and peck at the possessor of their sons' woes. Several times Mr. Dean had to intervene to get the ladies to calm down again. He expressed this was a serious situation and fighting could not and would not be tolerated at his school. His adapted the role of mediator, delicately and patiently listening to everyone's side of the story. Of course, the other boys' version had been grossly modified to accommodate their own innocence. He then allowed Damien his time on the floor. Satisfied that no one would own up to being at fault for causing the brouhaha, he suspended each three of the three boys two days off from school and a written essay on why they felt their actions were uncivilized. He dismissed each the parents and children one at a time.

Walking down the sidewalk to the curb where Bill had parked his beaten up old Volks Beetle young Damien anticipated utter doom. It didn't matter he'd been practically bludgeoned beyond movement. Even then he knew this was a phase that would pass. Within his adult mind he knew he was picked on regularly at school. He never recalled this memory. The way he'd recalled it, it would take several years for courage to conjure a way to stand up for himself. He'd frightened his former pals to a point that he should've felt ashamed. Yet this felt like a bona fide milestone. Even five-year-old Damien Galligher was not a doormat for anyone.

The sense of sheer dread he'd felt was what father would have to say in the privacy of their own company. His reputation for lack of diplomatic discipline was legendary. The tiny boy quivered at the thought of being physically punished once again.

Opening the passenger door for his son, he patiently waited for him to get inside. His movements seemed near cerebral as he stood motionless. Gently he closed the door behind him ensuring his legs were nestled inside.

The seconds it took for him to walk around the hood of the car seemed more like an eternity. Swallowing hard, he felt the back of his throat grow arid with anticipation. Even his little palms began to percolate sweat to match his dampened brow.

A rusty groan ensued as the driver's handle was lifted and pulled. Regardless of age or mental faculties, Damien was amazed such a giant could squeeze into a modest vehicle. Defying the odds, he stretched his legs and sank into the faux leather interior.

"Son I want you to realize what you had done today was wrong." He looked over at his offspring, seemingly rehearsing just the right delicate balance of wisdom and concern. "Sometimes it takes a braver man to walk away when faced with hostility." Bill gripped the steering wheel, caressing its surface. He stared off into the distance as equally distracted in thought. "But I also want you to know that I am incredibly proud of you for standing up for my honor." He reached across the console and engaged in an awkward but very tender embrace. "You will have to make many difficult decisions within your complex life. Standing up for honor is never something to be taken lightly. There may come a time again when you will be forced to decide if you should defend my honor and I trust you will make the right choice." His voice cracked ever so slightly from the sentiment as he let his son go.

Without another word he depressed the gas, pumping it before turning over the ignition. Turning out into the barren street, the two drove home in a comfortable silence.

<hr />

It seemed as though every page within the scrap book, every photo and keepsake were a detour in Damien's heightened suggestive state. Each and every memory he held prior to this twisted date was deconstructed, relocated and newly forged to imprint a completely different circumstance. How could one person's history be so misrepresented and so misunderstood?

On the car ride home Damien took solace in the cool autumn air and country landscape. The quantum sensation he was gradually becoming familiar with descended once again. It was as if a sunroof that knew no bounds had suddenly appeared, beckoning him towards the heavens.

He floated without resistance, knowing any defiance would be futile. Inviting the calming symptoms of warmth and peace he closed his eyes and allowed the drifting. It took some effort to remain in darkness, yet he cared not to look down upon his father and school aged self. The sense of abandoned reality saddened him, and he'd sustained just about enough sorrow for the time being. How life could've been different if he hadn't been numbed towards the truth.

Engulfed within the realm of infinite space and time he swirled. He contemplated on what the next possible memory would entail. The transcending porthole seemed not to last as long as previous odysseys. An aqua rippling pool shimmered just below him. A tentative dip into its surface unveiled the next landscape.

The photo was a familiar one. He'd seen the snapshot several times as a young and was surprised he remembered it in such vivid detail. Each of his sisters Peggy, Kassandra and Kaitlin were huddled in a group hug against a rustic looking fence. It appeared to be a petting zoo of sorts, but Damien remembered the excursion as the one from Marine land.

It wasn't news that his parents were far from well off, but the kids had pestered Mom and Dad to take them there. The persistent television ads luring children of all ages with their jingle of 'Everyone loves Marine land' was enough to captivate any impressionable mind. The opportunity to see Dolphins, Killer Whales and Sea lions was just a bonus.

The fashion in which the memory was recalled to him was indeed a little one sided. Mother had explained in illicit detail that Bill was flying high on prescription medication. After making a complete spectacle of himself he grew agitated, argumentative and forced the family to take the three-hour drive back home after being there a mere hour.

Something was amiss between Joy and Bill. They were at first very uncharacteristically affectionate with one another. Walking hand in hand they'd even engaged in occasional laughter. Even teenaged Kaitlin and Kassandra seemed to be having a ball, running ahead of the family then back again with reports of wonderful sights to see.

As an adult Damien remembered the television adds, and squirmed with discomfort whenever seeing them. He knew something awful had taken place that day but had somehow repressed the circumstance. What on earth could possibly go wrong in an amusement park and sea world combined? His family was getting along. The sun was shining. The day seemed like a direct transference of total childhood ecstasy.

The part of the commercial that had always gotten Damien was the chance to feed the baby deer. How cool was that? The closest he'd gotten to any wild life on previous occasion was the family cat TC and of course that hideous rat on Christmas day.

Getting a chance to feed a living creature would be nothing shy of extraordinary. Damien's out of body entity watched on as his family strolled by the petting zoo and of course the advertised deer. A burst of unbridled excitement unleashed from the boy as he jumped up and down. This was it. This was the spot and there was no way they could miss this!

Eager hands clenched and tugged upon each father and mother's pant legs. Childlike persistence was often admirable at times. So many lessons we can all learn from the youth.

At last Bill had crouched down so he could see eye to eye with his son. After engaging in whispered discussion, he ruffled his hair. Beaming with pride he shelled out the coins it took to get the pellet feed for the livestock.

Joy had seemed aloof and retreated to the faceless crowd. From the confines of the bustling crowd she stood with her arms crossed. She waited.

Father instructed his boy to carefully cup his hands, so he could hold the pile of feed. After reviewing with him verbally and getting him to repeat the instructions back to him he seemed satisfied Damien knew what to do. Depositing the kibble into his hands he stepped back and allowed the autonomy of a cherished moment to unfold.

It didn't take long for the pubescent does and bucks to saunter over to where they sensed their next meal was. Squealing in astonishment, the boy's eyes looked like royal blue saucers sparkling in the sun. He looked over at father for approval and to demonstrate is this cool or what?

Bill nodded, cautious not to take his eyes off his son. It was rather strange that Joy and the girls were nowhere in sight. Didn't they want to see their son and brother bask in all his glory?

Peach fuzzed snouts, snorting and trickling moisture nestled into his palm. He giggled and reached to pet their heads. These deer had been tamed some time ago and didn't flinch one iota. Damien seemed mesmerized with their lush, fuzzy coats.

A little disappointed the kibble had been devoured so quickly he went to stand back. He didn't want to upset his new friends. It'd only be proper if they were to remember him as fondly. A flash of the commercial unraveled in his mind. The boy that fed the deer on TV was certain to hold up his palms, signaling it was all gone.

Never much for photos, the boy decided this would make mother and father happy to create a cherished memory for them too. Smiling ear to ear he held up his hands high into the air. We looked over to find mother to see if she got the picture. His eyes scanned frantically, unable to find her. Father stood alone, just past the gate where the feed chute was.

Gasping, his pulse began to quicken. How could this happen? A perfect moment to be captured and his mom was nowhere to be found.

Little Damien held his hands high above his head, shaking them repeatedly. Maybe the repeat gesture would cause someone to get the signal. It was useless.

What the little boy did not anticipate was how hungry the deer had been. One rather large buck, still young but sizable nonetheless, reared up on its haunches. It merely meant to brace its front hooves on Damien's chest to get a better look at what he was concealing. The force was so formidable it caused the boy to go hurling head over heels into the dirt and manure behind him.

To any bystander or internet vulture scavenging for slapstick humor on YouTube, the scene would have been beyond hilarious. For Damien all time and reality had suspended. An innocent, beautiful brush with nature had been slashed to lying paralyzed and breathless in a heap of dirt and shit. Trapped on the base of his neck he kicked his legs. His arms lashed out for any purchase, anything at all.

Once again it was father that ran to his aid. Hoisting him high into the air, he brushed the sludge and grime from his eyes and nose. He shouted in state of panic to see if he was alright. As he ran back to the gates to see where his mother could have possibly gone, he froze. Looking frantically this way and that he seemed to lose control. Damien sensed his unease as his defeated sobs morphed into wails of travesty.

"Get that sniveling little brat away from me." Barks of violation caused patrons to rubber neck and gawk. "I'm dead serious William! Don't you dare embarrass me! You deal with him for a change."

Utter shock and dismay had washed over the shaken youth. Despite his capability to process sophisticated stimuli he was aghast and such brutal, callous detachment. Buried in his father's cradled comfort, he was suddenly grateful he didn't have to witness the expressions volleying back and forth between the parents.

A sense of abandonment left him naked and alone inside. He didn't know how long it took to be back in mother's company. This new found feeling of insignificance was devastating. Somehow, he knew the family's fun filled adventure was over for the day.

CHAPTER TWENTY

I nside St. Timothy's cathedral the mood was anxious. Danny paced the floor while shaking his head in disbelief. His sisters chatted among themselves, prattling on about the latest gossip no less.

Occasionally Leonard, Joy's husband would receive an abrupt elbow to the midsection. His choice in passing time with the local newspaper seemed as taboo as fornicating within God's house. Kaitlin, Kassandra and Peggy fussed over their husbands. Their efforts seemed useless as it wasn't a dress rehearsal, merely formalities to ensure no one was caught with egg on their faces the following morning.

Danny and his bride to be Elise seemed to be taking shifts shooting dagger like glares at Julia. Their efforts fell short as well. She sat in a pew next to her sister Joy and Leonard. Every five minutes or so, she'd sink her nails into her sister's arm.

"Are you certain Damien is coming, dear?" She pressed on through pop bottle glasses. "We're running nearly thirty minutes late." A razor of condescension would not be concealed in her tone.

"I mean Father O'Malley is a man of the cloth but I'm almost certain he has better things to do with his Friday evening than simply wait around and smile foolishly."

"For the last time Julia, please. My boy will be here. He doesn't take the responsibility of being an usher for Danny very lightly you know." She slapped her husband's arm. Leonard grunted but offered no defense. "It is a long drive from Toronto you know. We don't all have the luxury of stepping into our backyards."

Danny reflexively looked onto a wrist that was void of a watch for the thousandth time. Into his fiancé's ear he whispered. His wild gestures with his hands were not so subtle.

"Mother please, can we get started? The boys are taking me out on the town, and celebrate my last night of freedom." Danny's uncensored honesty was received with a round of applause and laughter. It was Elise's turn to smack her partner's arm. He winced from her velocity. "We won't be going at this rate," he muttered under his breath.

Father O'Malley rocked back and forth on his heels at the altar. It didn't appear as though the good father had a care in the world. He seemed relieved that anyone at all was inside the Cathedral. Silently he'd smile at each the cousin's, The Galligher siblings and their respective partners. He'd nod occasionally expressing warmth and unity.

"Julia, darling, please let's just give him another fifteen minutes. Your customs and traditions simply are something that not everyone is familiar with. I don't want him to get flustered and knock over the flowers or some damned thing tomorrow."

"My customs?" Julia smacked her lips. "What on earth is that supposed to mean?"

"Oh sweetie, take no offense please." She coddled her older sister with a pat on the thigh. "You have to take into consideration this is the twenty first century and not everyone is Catholic anymore."

"Well I never..." Julia leapt to her feet, knees popping all the while. She nearly sent a stack of new testaments spilling to the floor. "Let me tell you something Joy Galligher or whatever it is you're going by these days. It takes great devotion and inner depth to have faith. But I suppose you wouldn't know anything about that on husband number three and children from two different father's no less." For theatrical emphasis she gripped her abundant hips while bobbing her head side to side.

"You leave my kids out of this sister." It was now Joy's turn to lurch to her feet meeting her sibling's gaze. "They have the right to make their own choices in life and I never force fed them any brainwashing, propaganda or rituals, religious or otherwise. And I'll tell you another thing, there are so many pointless little exercises to this ceremony I don't want my boy to get confused with kneeling, standing, kneeling again and making some ridiculous cross gesture on his chest either. Who can keep track of all that?"

"Why don't you say what's really on your mind Joy? Why don't you stand up and tell everyone how green with envy and jealousy you are? It's because Danny's lovely bride is the rightful beneficiary of mother's ring?" Several gasps expelled around the church.

Joy pursed her lips, furrowing her brow.

"Lenny, are you going to allow her to speak to me this way?"

Her husband sat silently, pouting over his confiscated newspaper.

"This isn't the time or place dear Julia. But since you brought it up, you know full well that ring should be going to the youngest granddaughter of the youngest daughter. And here I thought you knew a thing or two about tradition." She folded her arms making no efforts to mask her huff.

"And if you knew anything about the faith or purity of heart dear sister you would know greed and envy are sins. Why don't you go ask Father O'Malley to go sit in confession? That'd be a bang-up way to kill a couple hours or so."

"Ladies, ladies please. It's getting close to nine o'clock." Father O'Malley at last intervened. He laced his fingers together then opened them again in a grand, sweeping gesture. "Why don't we get started and if the boy arrives in the meantime we can catch him up to speed?"

Joy and Julia stared off into opposing directions. At least there was plenty of beauty to beyond and keep one's attention distracted. The statues and stain glassed windows were breath taking and fit into a museum as easily as St. Timothy's.

After shuffling about nervously it was finally Joy who had broken the ice.

"I'm terribly sorry Julia. I suppose it's just nerves. I don't mean to rain on Danny's parade. If I can be completely honest with you I'm getting very worried. It's not like Damien to be so late. If that boy is anything he's always punctual."

"Oh, it's alright dear. Think nothing of it. I'm sorry too. I just want everything to go perfectly for my boy. I was beginning to think he would never settle down."

"They are a handsome couple, aren't they?" Joy had cooed in unrestrained wonder.

"Elise has been an absolute princess for him. She comes from a very good family as well. I think she'll instill a lot of family values that perhaps we had missed out on in recent years." Julia shuffled through her purse, retrieving a crumpled-up tissue. Dabbing her eyes, she tucked the moistened plies into the sleeve of her dress. "His father Kenneth would have been so proud."

"Yes, Danny is a lucky man. I hope he's good to her." Joy sighed, exasperated and perhaps a little over exaggerated.

"What is it Joy?"

"Oh, it's nothing…"

"Come on now, who knows you better than you know yourself? Out with it, now."

"It's just that little floozy of a girlfriend, Jade. I knew she was trouble for my boy from day one. Shacking up together and running around with all that devil's music, books and movies, it's just not natural. Did you know she doesn't even have a job? I suppose she just expects Damien to be a provider even though they're not married. She's a little hussy that dresses like a whore."

Julia had to conceal her mouth into her tissue once again. She didn't want to her sister to see she couldn't stop smirking. Talk about the kettle calling the pot black, what a hypocrite.

She cleared her throat then offered, "I'm sure if it's meant to be they'll make it. If she's truly trouble, Damien's a bright boy. He'll figure it all out."

"Come along now, places everyone." Father O'Malley clapped his hands and smiled his perpetual radiant smile.

Thank you, Joy had mouthed the words and reached to embrace her sister. Julia returned the gesture drawing her near.

"Thank God, there's a brew and a lap dance with Danny's name on it." Someone anonymous called out from beyond the pews. The air was filled with mixed contempt and laughter.

"Now the groom's men will line up and walk the aisle first..." Father O'Malley commenced.

For the first time in perhaps decades Joy gazed up at the savior's statue and silently prayed.

PART TWO

A World Without Heroes

CHAPTER ONE

Into the thick, humid air Jade sighed. Pressing send over and over into her cell phone was redundant and futile. The result was one and the same. Caroline's phone went directly to voice mail.

A deep furrowed embedded into her brow she vied to decipher what exactly all the commotion had meant. Getting Dr. Rhys's receptionist to run the fool's errand out to the old Galligher place felt like a lifetime ago. She never left her cellular out of arms reach. When it had chirped into life she was all too enthusiastic to answer it and find out what had become of Damien.

When the call was connected the truly bizarre and non-sensical had been unleashed. A barrage of banshee like squeals had nearly forced her to drop the phone on the floor. Calling Caroline's name over and over was no use. Something had gone dreadfully awry. As she recalled the unearthly wails projectile through the receiver icy finger tips danced up and down Jade's spine.

Had Caroline been in accident? Jade knew full well the old Galligher home hadn't been occupied in thirteen years. There stood an excellent chance the place was so deteriorated and

disheveled that Caroline had fallen and was lying alone, unconscious or worse.

She shuddered at the ominous combination of possibilities.

For the tenth dozen time of the evening she explored her lower
lip with her gnawed off finger nails. If anything had happened to
her.... No, she couldn't entertain such a horrible fate.

What now? This still didn't explain what happened to Damien.
She was no further ahead than when she placed the reluctant call
to Caroline. No question she was in even deeper now.

Over her shoulder she whisked her long, auburn hair and
paced the floor once again. Never could she recall a time in recent
memory when she'd felt so utterly helpless. Just when she was about
to resign to utter defeat she sat down to fire up the household
desktop computer.

In the search engine she was about to type in the Greyhound
bus site and search for scheduled fares running to Port Perry. It
would be an agonizing venture, but she had to know the truth.
She'd never forgive herself if something unspeakable had happened to Damien, Caroline or the Galligher family. If travelling
the three hours is what it took for some peace of mind than so be
it. It couldn't be any worse than this. There was no way she'd give
Joy Galligher the satisfaction of thinking she didn't care by just sitting back in Toronto and doing nothing.

Gritting her teeth, she cursed as the infernal swirling icon sig-
nified a snail's pace of achieved internet connection. Every other
second her knee nearly collided under the desk from her rapid,
jerky bouncing.

"Come on, come on. Damn you," she spewed into the air.

In a moment of astonishing synchronicity, the webpage engaged,
and the landline burst into foreign succession of bleeps and blurps.

Jade shrieked and just about tumbled out of the swivel chair.
Between Damien and herself they'd rarely used the landline for
anything anymore. Adapting to societal ways they became fixated

on their cellphones. They always meant to get around to cancelling the home service. It was just one of those many things people procrastinated about. Jade swiftly hoped in all her heart she would have the luxury to be able to procrastinate with Damien again. Remorse, take for granted, put things off for another day, Hell, take a trip to the North Pole and back again; if she had Damien by her side everything would be alright.

A little more aggressively than intended she clutched the receiver. Squabbling a mile, a minute into the mouthpiece she refused to relent or breathe.

"Damien, honey thank God."

"Where the hell have you been?"

"Do you have any idea…"

"You know your mother called and…."

Incoherent gibberish, countless incomplete thoughts shrilled into the phone. In Jade's excitement and enthusiasm, she failed completely to allow the caller the dignity of identifying himself.

At last her hysteria gave away to common sense and she let out an exasperated breath and waited.

"I beg your pardon Jade. Have I called at a bad time? This is Dr. Rhys, Damien's friend."

Her intestines seized up in anguished protest. A flash of pounding hammers slammed within her inner cortex. The whole room seemed to have opened to a midway ride forever spinning, picking up speed, dipping this way and that. Jade's tongue stuck to the roof of her mouth as she wrestled with the ability to speak.

"Hello? Hello…."

"Dr. Rhys," she croaked, a barely audible, feeble utterance. "Yes, it's me." Clearing her throat, she apologized and felt her complexion grow ten degrees warmer. "Excuse me. I'm afraid Damien's not home. In fact, he was due some time ago and is very late. Just an over protective fiancé I suppose." She cringed at how ludicrous her own attempt at laughter had sounded.

The good doctor moaned a distance retort. His baritone vocals although were exemplary in soothing distraught individuals he had conversed with, something in his musings gave segue to an undeniable concern.

"Not home you say?" He hummed another bar or two of distant, inner reasoning. Jade thought his silent calculations would be next to drive her bananas.

"Is there a message I can give him or help you with something doctor?" Jade winced at her own tone realizing how terse it had come out. She was losing patience with this game however.

"Oh. I'm sure it's nothing sweetie. I don't want to worry you further."

"Please Dr. Rhys if there is something on your mind, tell me. I'm next to beside myself with worry. Earlier and I feel awful about this…"

"Go, on my dear. I'm sure it's not half as bad as you may think."

Jade rubbed her temples and smirked at the psychiatrist's banter. Forever the professional, she wondered if it was reflex or if he was always consciously on.

"Damien and I were supposed to go to his cousin's wedding this weekend."

"Yes, his cousin Danny. It's been in all the papers. Damien himself, actually told me all about it." Just as swiftly as he'd said it, he abruptly went silent. Breach of confidentiality whether it was the past, patient and doctor relationship was equal to utter blasphemy. If Jade had detected his retreat into being mute she'd made no indication as such.

"He was going to come home straight from work and pick me up, so we could head to Seagrave for the rehearsal," releasing her anxiety aloud to another rational human being unleashed a steady wave of sobs. "That was hours ago, and he hasn't even called or anything." She sat up straight, and sniffled trying to compose herself. "I spoke with his mother. She even thinks I'm the reason he's not there. It's just not fair…"

On the other side of the line Dr. Rhys did his best not to chuckle at the bitter sweet ponderings of Ms. Joy Galligher. God love her, as he did too, but no one could argue she was a real handful from time to time.

"I understand my dear, perfectly in fact. We mustn't despair. There is a very simple explanation for all of this, I'm sure. I'm sure the lad will be calling any moment and we'll all have a good laugh."

Into the receiver Jade bellowed, an epic cry of pent up frustration and angst. "No, we won't! Why is everyone so convinced we'll all sit around and have a good old-fashioned side splitting laugh? Why is everyone humoring me?" She rubbed her temples, ashamed for losing control but figured what the hell there was no turning back now. "You know what I think? I think Damien's mother is behind all of this and convinced him to come alone to the wedding and set him up with one of his starry-eyed exes. That's what I think. Oh, she'd just love to have me out of the picture, so she could have her little boy back. Well she can go to hell if she thinks I'll just roll over and let him walk away."

Thankfully Dr. Rhys was more than prepared to deal with this line of perpetual paranoia.

"I certainly see why you feel that way. Let's have a look at this from all angles. What time did you say Damien would be home?"

"Oh, and that's another thing. I called your office to see if you'd heard from him and talked to Caroline for a minute. We both kind of think Damien may have done something reckless, like go to his old house. To put my mind at ease she agreed to go out there. I haven't heard from her since. She tried to call once but all I heard was loud screaming on the line then it went dead."

Dead silence.

If the doctor was attempting to emulate what had happened to the connection between Jade and Caroline, he was doing a smash up job.

"You say Caroline went out there?"

"Yes, and that was well over an hour ago too. This just keeps getting weirder and weirder."

"Jade can you be ready in ten to fifteen minutes?"

"Ready? What do you mean- "

"I was on my way through Toronto to Niagara for some leisurely weekend equestrian time. I'm nearly in Mississauga but I can back track again. I called, concerned for the very same reasons you and my receptionist have expressed." The doctor sighed as he unraveled his professional demeanor. "I can pick you up in less than fifteen minutes. I think it was best we got to the bottom of this together."

Without another word he terminated the call. For the first time this morning Jade felt relieved that something was finally going her way.

CHAPTER TWO

Involuntary shivering and shudders made the scrap book before him swim with a menagerie of full motion bafflement. Into his darkest recesses, Damien began to rock gently back and forth. Pinkish membranes on the floor pulsed and breathed and unsteady, unholy rhythm. The reprised version of his Marine land exploits fresh in his mind, he cringed at the ultimate ramifications of each of these new findings.

How could everything be so massive in their distortion? Everything he'd known and felt was a virtual lie, a fabrication on his very existence. He knew his mother and siblings even less than he'd known his father. An entire life has been challenged. From birth to infancy, adolescence and young adulthood Damien Galligher was an absolute stranger onto himself.

Racked with violent sobs and funneling rage, he scanned the basement of his formative years. Sinewy strands of clotted blood and tissue swayed and slithered from the walls and ceiling. Simple mold and decay would be a god send for his aromatic stimuli in comparison to the death, destruction and depravity that consumed the very air he breathed. The foundation crumbled with shards of bone, dust of abandoned hope.

Sighing into the stifling confinement he absently brushed his thumb and forefinger against the surface of the aged memorabilia.

What would become of his life from here on out? Would he be imprisoned in purgatory like limbo for eternity while his loved ones pondered his disappearance? What could the future possibly hold after everything he'd known and believed was the exact opposite?

A gentle, tranquil breeze stirred the hairs upon his forearms. Tucked within the lower half corner, a dog eared, crumpled Kodak photo diverted his attention. To an unassuming witness the picture would appear endearing, borderline humorous in fact. Before a modest bungalow home in the front lawn stood four youths straddling various bicycles and beaming with childlike, unaltered bliss. Even at age twenty Damien recalled the memory with impeccable clarity.

The two taller boys were Cameron and Roy. Each grasped the handlebars of their BMX bikes with such pride one may suspect they were under the impression they were Harley Davidson choppers. Peggy leaned against Roy with such transparent infatuation, the affection took on a life of its own. Sean leaned back in his smaller but equally tripped out ride on his banana seat. While Damien, red face and bleary eyed hovered inches off the ground in his three wheeled Big Wheel.

As the breeze in the image ruffled the children's hair and willow branches swayed this way and that, Damien pondered over how this cherished keepsake could possibly be thwarted. He was eight years old at the time, nearly nine. It was well over a year since Bill's untimely demise.

Damien often reflected on this time and considered it a passage in coming of age. Lord knows he had to grow up far too soon, experience things no living soul should have to endure let along a young boy.

Beams of lazy July sun glimmered off the bike's spokes and reflectors. Plastic and aluminum pedals spiraled seemingly in defiance against conformity. As far as Damien could remember this was a sacred day, a magical time. The five by seven image swirling into vivid life before him was a representation of a milestone. This was the day he finally learned to ride a bicycle. Without a father and a mother working three jobs to make ends meet there simply was no initiative to teach him the simple joy every boy should experience several years before.

Cameron and Sean were the Douglas's. Since mother had been working so much and Kaitlin was off to college that only left Kassandra. Let's face it Kassandra was, well Kassandra. Mother couldn't afford a babysitter, so Peggy and Damien often went over to the Douglas's after school and throughout the day during the summer months such as these.

Damien had held this day so close to his heart he often fantasized about being a father himself one day and teaching his own son to ride a bike. The complete and utter expression and thrill of achievement upon his would-be son's face would be priceless. These were the sort of memories that made life a glorious thing. There was no way such an eventful, joyous experience could be tainted.

Just as Damien combated with the inconceivable, a vortex of sparkling dots danced in frenzied waltz before him. A magnetic force gripped his cerebral, pulling and dragging with unseen hands. A coppery taste frothed over from his lips and his eyes peeled back into his head. A wave of vertigo dominated his core. Into the image his astral form glided in quest of a conclusion that pushed the very boundaries of his comprehension.

Like a dime store paratrooper swirling through the breeze in all its plastic splendor, like the Douglas's had chucked off the rooftop so many times before, astral Damien drifted towards his boyhood host.

The shell of a boy looked so nondescript, so oblivious to his surroundings. He busied himself with vigor pushing his Matchbox and Hot wheels cars through the sandy crevices between the sidewalk slates. In the distance a screen door creaked and clambered against its frame in percussion.

Much to the disdain of Wendy Douglas she hollered after her boys to either stay in or go to the park. Just as quickly she amended go to the park, they were giving her a migraine. Cameron and Roy voiced their obvious approval and had saddled their speed racers faster than she could say be back for dinner and take Damien with you. The last tad bit of instruction was retorted with a rebellious groan of disdain.

Pushing the black trans-am through ant hills and tufts of weeds Damien barely registered the slight. The boy would have been perfectly content engaged in high speed chases through granules and concrete for the remainder of the afternoon. Plus, there was a neat black Persian cat that would wander over to his quarters whenever the calamity finally died down with the insipid screen door slamming. The cat, that he nick- named Black Beard was his true friend and came to speak to him, shared all kinds of goodies that only he could understand. He thought maybe the feline was a runaway or what he heard the grownups call a stray. It didn't like other people, only Damien which made him special. He could share with the kitty with just his mind and no talking. The cat was wise and understood him. The cat knew he was lonely and felt bad but also told him how to survive with other people, how to fit in when he needed to.

"Oh, come on Mom. Do we really have to take the squirt?" Cameron hollered prior to letting the screen slam against the trim for the umpteenth time in the last fifteen minutes.

"Don't you dare smart mouth me young man. You take poor Damien, you could all use the exercise. Now get a move on. You're all making me crazy."

"But Mom. He's such a little creep."

"Cameron James Douglas! You better mind your mother if you don't want a lickin'. Now move."

At this indignity Cameron shoved the rickety shell of a door, nearly puncturing a hole in the mesh screen.

In an over exaggerated walk of defeat Cameron kicked at the dirt while walking up to the driveway where his speedster was laying on its side.

"Hey Chief, what's got into you?" Roy sat upon his plastic perch mimicking a revving motion on his handlebar grips. He was Cameron's senior by almost two years at fourteen. He was always the leader of the gang, with the most experience and tended to gravitate towards younger kids for the sense of dominance and importance. A natural born trouble maker, a trip to the park for Roy meant smoking cigarettes behind the gazebo and looking at girlie magazines under the slides that he stole from his father's secret stash.

"Lay off Roy. I'm not in the mood." Cameron kicked at his pedals a mask of frustration donned upon his face.

"Easy Pedro. Hey, I'm on your side." Roy held up his hands in mock surrender. As an afterthought, "We crusin' or what?"

"Or what." Cameron snapped a little more viciously than intended. "If we're going to the park we got to take Sean and the little bastard over there." To emphasize the humanity of the circumstance, Cameron gestured with his thumb over his shoulder.

"So, what gives? The little turd can't be any younger than Sean. The little snots will dizzy themselves on the swings while can just hang and be cool. No big deal, man."

"Yeah I guess." Cameron eased up a little. In an almost conspiracy type whisper, "He's just so, I don't know, weird you know?"

"You just leave it to Uncle Roy." He languidly swung one leg off his motocross and hunkered more than walked over to where Damien was at play. On the way he confirmed in a whisper of his own that Cameron had indeed scored the smokes. Cameron nodded the affirmative and showed the stash of five menthol cigarettes he lifted from his mother's pack earlier that morning.

In his best no nonsense, cool demeanor he swaggered over to Damien and squatted on his haunches, to the miniature demolition derby the boy had fabricated.

As a reassuring gesture he looked over his shoulder and winked back at his pal Cameron. He had this. No problem-o.

"Hey-ya rug rat. Whatcha doin' there?"

"None of your bees wax dummy." Damien giggled and slapped a hand over his mouth over his brazen reflexive retaliation.

"Why you little..." Roy flushed ruby red in his cheeks, clearly off guard.

In the back-ground Peggy and Sean, joining the fray had engaged in their own bouts of unchartered laughter.

Placing a tentative hand on the youth's shoulder, Roy pleaded. Last thing he needed was a little snot nosed brat invading their cool time.

"Easy now junior, Roy's on your side see?" Just like the he swiftly produced a rolled-up package of Big League chew bubble gum, the kind of long strands of shredded, pink sucrose filled bliss.

"Go on, it's yours." He held up the sugary offering with methodic precision. As Damien reached for it, he flinched and just as quickly reeled it back.

"On one condition. Uncie Roy doesn't give it up that easy."

Damien, already bored with this game just wished these other kids would leave so he could get back to his game. Within adult, lucid Damien's mind he remembered not any of these happenings. He had thought by now Roy, Cameron, Sean, Peggy and he were riding with the wind, all their troubles at their heels, tires spinning towards an infinite cycle of reckless abandon.

"Fine," he'd shrugged. "What is it?"

"Oh, you can have the gum kiddo. Just be a good little ragamuffin, make like a tree and leave when we get to the park. The cool kids Cameron, your darlin' little sister Peggy and I need some big kid time. Capice?"

A startled rustling in the bushes broke their inquisitive silence.

"Oh great. You big jerk. You just went and scared off Black Beard. Thanks a lot!"

Roy stood up now, wavering turned to Cameron, frowned and lifted his arms in defeat.

"You can keep your lousy gum too. Black beard told me what you get up to behind the gazebo. Smoking's bad for you and stealing's wrong. Your Daddy's going to give you a spanking when he finds out you're looking at his dirty pictures."

An eclipse of white hot rage had shadowed over Roy.

"You take that back you little punk. What the hell do you know anyway?"

Even Cameron had winced at his older buddy's anger unleashed. Peggy stepped to intervene, but Sean quickly grasped her pant leg. He didn't want to interrupt the show.

"I know enough not to steal from my parents and that smoking will kill you. How dumb are you anyway?"

If looks could kill, Roy's gaze would have shattered the boy into a thousand pieces. Like a tsunami, his inner turmoil washed away its path of destruction just as quickly as it had come on.

"Oh, I get it." An ear-piercing cackle ensued. "Oh, I get it. Cams, you old dog, you really had me going there. Hardy-har, har. You put the squirt up to this right?" For emphasis Roy slapped his thigh time and again. "You can't kid a kidder, but you almost had me. You know?" For a split-second Roy glanced up at his pal with an expression of what, pleading?

Cameron's sullen, placid expression failed to bail out his chum.

All the color had feigned, grinning drained from Roy's face. It took all his composure to avoid pin wheeling his arms as he took a step back and just about tripped over his own heels.

Peggy drew one hand over her mouth and pivoted away to avoid grand standing her laughter. Sean didn't know what to do with himself while Cameron grew antsier by the moment. Damien simply returned to his cavalcade of road demolition, tuning everyone out.

Everyone bolted in unison at the sudden disruption of awkward silence.

"Screw it Roy, let's just head over to the park. You heard 'Ma. She'll have my ass as grass if we don't make ourselves scarce."

Roy muttered something incoherent but nodded in agreement. Idly he adjusted the waist band of his jeans from the rear, evidently his secret storage compartment for his father's triple x fanfare.

"Yeah. I'm with you dude. Let's blow this scene." As though on cue, Sean and Peggy headed towards the garage to retrieve their own two wheeled spit fires. Cameron made an about face with Roy attempted with a little too much effort to swagger back to his ride.

"Wait, what about Damien?" Sean chimed in befuddlement.

Cameron and Roy rolled their eyes in impatient synchronicity.

"What about him?" Cameron piped, his voice unveiling pitchy pre-pubescence. "You heard 'Ma! We have to take him or we're in for a lickin'. Give him 'Ma's bike." Then under a conspirator whisper to Roy, "It's not like her fat ass ever uses it."

Peggy and Sean exchanged nervous expressions. Across the driveway, Damien zoned out the rest of the world resuming his sputtering sounds with his lips and explosion sounds with his inflated cheeks.

"It's not that," Sean glanced at Peggy for direction.

"Well what Sean? We don't have all friggin' day!"

"Damien doesn't know how to ride. That's what." There it was out there. Despite Sean's flushed face and refusal to meet anyone's eye contact, he was the bearer of unfortunate news. What was it they said, don't shoot the messenger?

"Oh, for Pete's sake!" Roy gritted his teeth and discarded his motocross horizontal onto the asphalt driveway. He could care less for the kick stand at this imposed revelation. He marched over to where the squirt was playing abandoning all urgency in looking cool or dapper with his swagger. Each stride was more exaggerated than the last. Each footfall pounded into the dirt sending clumps of dirt and grit flying this way and that. Without hesitation, he whipped one swinging leg over Damien's head and kicked the dinky cars into a spiraling chaos, bouncing down the driveway.

"Hey asshole!" Damien screamed and leapt to his feet. He spun around glaring at his assailant clearly two feet taller and nearly twice his age. Under other circumstances the scene as it began to unfold would have been outright comical.

Lucid, adult Damien could not remember one iota or fabric of these moments. Through bleary eyes he stared on at this poor excuse of being.

Roy crossed his arms over his chest and turned his head to the right, mocking and seemingly lost in thought. To emphasize his astonishment, he rocked back in forth on his heels, torturing his inquisitive junior before him. With methodical execution Roy leaned down inch by inch with his hands on his knees until his face was mere inches from young Damien's. Their noses near touched as Damien could smell the foul odor of baloney and cheese.

Through gritted teeth, Roy kept his proclamation to a murmur, so Mrs. Douglas wouldn't hear from inside and have a damn bird or something. Spittle formed at the corners of his mouth. A spidery webbed like vein formed on his forehead. The last time Damien was confronted like this from someone older and much larger it hadn't ended well. He doubted this would end pretty either

"You mean to tell me, you little freak that you can't even ride a bike?" On each syllable Roy's eyes darkened, seemingly conjuring funnel clouds of fury. "What kind of baby doesn't even know how to ride a bike and still plays with little itty bitty dinky cars?" Into Damien's scrawny little chest, he poked his finger harder and harder with each word.

Into the grimy soil and weeds Damien stared, his body beginning to tremble from the knees on up. Great, just great now I'm the center of attention because I'm such a loser I can't even do what the other kids do.

"Well?" Roy bellowed into Damien's face. The octaves startled everyone else out of their paralyzed disbelief. "What do you have to say for yourself you little punk? Or does the cat that tell you all its secrets got your tongue too huh?" Roy scanned the yard to meet Cameron's approval. He was on the curb by now waiting to flee the scene as well. He regarded his compadre with an all too knowing sneer.

"Leave him alone Roy. He's just a boy." Peggy interjected from the relative safety of the garage's doorway.

Roy whirled around on her and darted his finger at her interruption.

"You stay out of this missy. This is between me and the sissy here."

Something began to come over Damien at that moment. He felt a bubbling heat in the core of his belly, popping, sizzling and threatening to over boil. To his sides he clenched and unclenched his tiny fists over and over again, forever more rapidly. His whole body quivered, convulsed and trembled. Tears of humiliation pooled at the center of his eyes. For his first time since Father's demise he missed him terribly. He'd never allow for this to happen, this shameful spectacle. No sir. As nasty and awful as he'd been he would have taught him how to ride a bike long ago. He'd be pedaling circles around these chumps and that's for sure.

Roy cackled to himself getting further amused.

"Go on, you little turd. What're you going to do huh? Cry? Go on cry like a little baby so you can run along all the way home and have Mommy change your diaper huh?" Tiresome of his own taunting, Roy shoved the boy with one hand while standing up right and walked back over to where his bike was.

The world spun out of focus. Where the side of the house sat in his field of vision now escaped to unveil a brilliant blue sky while thick, fluffy cumulous clouds. For a brief second Damien pondered if lying back wasn't so bad. He could watch the white tufts form into nifty shapes. Then the rage of ridicule returned like a savage beast. Onto his feet he leapt, nipping up from back to feet. The momentum of his lunge just about sent him barreling over his shoes. Red hot tears streamed down his face and he wailed uncontrollably. How dare they make fun of him? How dare they banish him from clique and leave him on the outside looking in? How dare they reject him and label him insignificant, unimportant? His stomping tantrum initially lead him towards the screen door where he was going to tell. He was going to disclose all the horrible monstrosities to Mrs. Douglas at the hands of the evil Roy. She'd deal with him in a hurry and boy oh boy would he be in trouble. Then something snapped with the young boy.

Lucid, conscious, adult Damien just about smothered in all the adrenaline-fueled animosity. Enough. At the tender age of eight Damien would stand for this no longer. He dealt with father, he looked straight into the eyes of fear until fear was nothing but a bubbling dwindling coward. How dare someone with the likes of Roy treat him this way? He didn't know what he'd been through. He never felt the pain, the terror and the humiliation at the hands of his father. So why was he trying to make him feel this way? He should have been taking the time to teach him how to ride. Coach him, encourage him to learn something new. Stealing dirty magazines and cigarettes was for cowards who refused to see their own responsibilities. Damien would show him what he did with cowards. He'd show everyone.

Down the driveway the asphalt all about blazed with young Damien's propelled, rapid strides. His hands shook into fists and blurred beyond recognition to a hapless onlooker. From the depths of his shackled soul, he shrilled the most anguished of battle cries.

Throwing all caution to the wind and ejecting his own body into the unknown, Damien leapt off the curb with a resilience that would make any track and field high jumper rendered in awe. At the last second Roy turned his head, his eyes bulged from their sockets registering his impending doom. Shoulder first Damien collided with Roy's throat and spun him clean of his pedals. Their collision was explosive, Damien flung head over heels into a parked station wagon's front tire across the street. Roy's upper torso and head bounced off the paved rubble skidded to a violent stop just inches from the far side curb.

Like a banshee possessed Damien sprang into life charging Roy' incapacitated form. Bounding into the air he met his chest with both knees and clutched a handful of sweaty, blood ladled hair upon his head. Bashing the back of his head off the street time and again and screeched into his face, "Who doesn't know how to ride now, huh Roy? Who's a big cry baby that can't pedal his own two feet to the park huh?" He shoved his head one last time into the debris of the street.

Peggy, Sean and Cameron burst into action, at first dumbfounded into shock at the scene unfolded before them. Running and screaming in shock, they came to the aid of their friend, as volatile as he was at times. No one deserved this kind of onslaught no matter how much of a jerk they were.

In all the mayhem, Roy's concealed treasure had ejected from the back of his pants and lay face open on the lawn. Pages of perversity and raunchy acts of lewd conduct glared up at the sky for the whole world to see. Advertisements of eight hundred numbers followed by obscene declarations shimmied into view as the breeze turned the crumpled pages over and over.

Damien clutched the glossy rag by the center and bunched it into ball. His nails pierced images of buxom bevies in a kaleidoscope of contorted positions. If his heart wasn't jack hammering and his breath wheezing out of proportion he would have heard

Roy moan in semi-conscious debilitated state. Like an uncaged animal he pounced back over to his fallen prey. He shoved the pages into his face, smudging back and forth. Cameron raced faster thinking the brat was going to smother his friend to death.

"Get a good look Roy? Huh? Get a good look old chum? Well you better because this is the last time any woman will ever let you close to her again. You're way too young for this. You God damned pervert." Into the air young Damien tossed the intrusive obscenity and walked back over to the Douglas driveway and just about collapsed. By then Cameron, Sean and Peggy were checking over Roy. Mrs. Douglas waddled and bellowed down lawn with a cigarette dangling from her pasty lips and her hair in rollers. Damien didn't care. He looked for his disheveled toy trans-am and knew full well that the likes of Roy would never call him a baby again.

The photograph was correct. Roy was a little shaken up but still ok to go to the park. The kids still rode over and the incrimination evidence was promptly disposed of prior to Mrs. Douglas's appearance. Roy was forced to apologize, as was Damien. The boy didn't mind these types of formalities. The point was already made. Besides when he stood up for himself, Sean let him ride his glow in the dark green and black Big Wheel. It wasn't exactly a bike. It was a three-wheeler but still plenty rad to ride the two and a half blocks away to the park. Mrs. Douglas made the kids pose for that photo. In hindsight as the kids grew older they'd supposed she did things like that to document how good of a mother and babysitter she was. Whatever.

Damien felt his insides grow hollow as the skin on his arms begin to fade. His opaque appearance pulsed into translucency back and forth. A prevailing wind rushed up from seemingly nowhere and drifted his astral presence from the Big Wheel and beyond that fateful July sky. Into the unknown his spirit soared in search of the next destination to exhume his next forgotten memory.

Conscious thought bombarded Damien's essence into the here and now. Besides the most obvious disturbing elements of his journey through this is your life, something had dawned upon him. A paradox of epic proportion, something simply did not fit into the grander scheme of things. He was nestled into his childhood home. A home in which he hadn't stepped foot into for thirteen years. Sure, it was true enough the boyhood locale invaded his tortured slumber night after night in dreams yet how was it possible for a photograph to appear after his family's departure from this house? How was it even remotely comprehensible that a memento of any sort could find its way into the Galligher scrapbook when clearly none of them had been there? He had to get to the bottom of this. In the last few hours everything he'd known, learned and experienced had been challenged to the max. Right was wrong. Night was day. Black was white. The supernatural seemed as common place as the mundane. The unexplained was ordinary perception. Little of this knowledge did anything to comfort Damien.

He continued to drift and swirl through the vast astral unknown, swirling this way and that. The tranquility and peace were sheer Nirvana and he wondered if this is where people are beckoned to in that moment just before their earthly existence has expired. He wondered if the infamous light everyone sees is indeed a galactic type sky in which the soul floats in search of purpose. There was so much to learn, so many questions. With every breath he took, he became more relaxed, more at ease and at unity with himself. Nothing had seemed to matter except for the moment. The trials and tribulations in hindsight were far gone from conscious thought. Yet they seemed a necessary blue print a virtual payment of dues to prove one's worth in the great divide.

His eyes began to water, tears crystalized from the slits trickling this way and that floating with awe inducing clarity. They failed to fall, twirling this way and that like a cluster of precious gems scattered into an anti-gravity chamber. He wished not to close his eyes. A defiant gesture to avoid missing a solitary second of this miraculous sensation. Eventually even pure will submitted to a greater cause as he reluctantly closed his burdened eyes inhaling a deep breath of ecstasy.

In limbo he continued to drift with inconsequential speed, direction or urgency. He merely existed in soul charmed splendor and wanted to bask in its infinite glory. Somewhere in his mind he knew that this too, would not last and his journey was far from over. Just as the thought had registered he began a languid descent with increasing speed, plummeting towards his next destination.

The next moment Damien had opened his eyes a searing white light has blinded his vision with a piercing, throbbing head ache. He lifted his head unceremoniously from a cool, smooth yet very prominent surface. With rapid, blinking eyes he scanned his surroundings, trying to make sense of where he was. Before him a dust ladled blackness consumed most of the wall. Decorated in chalky white lettering and numbers, a calligraphy type script brandished its perimeter donning the alphabet. It was evident he was in a classroom.

Squinting off the intrusive, he pinched the bridge of his nose in vain attempt to bring objects and images into focus. A stirring snickering echoed off the walls coming from each direction bouncing this way and that. He lifted his head with uncertainty, his head feeling like it weighed of a sack of stones. The snickering picked up momentum, a harmonious chorus of ridicule and spite. Some incoherent jeers and giggling ensued as he grappled to attain full awareness.

Slightly adjacent to the blackboard stood a thin but not entirely unattractive young woman. Her wavy, dirty blonde hair beckoned a memory within adult, lucid Damien. Impatiently, she shifted her glasses on the bridge of delicate nose. With pursed lips she tapped a meter stick upon the blackened wall forcing a tornado of chalk dust into the air. Of course, this was Mrs. Breen, his third-grade teacher. Damien had always liked his instructor, a certifiable mentor of sorts in the formative years he'd endured after Bill's demise. In a couple of years after the Galligher family had fled the abomination of their lives, mother had remarried, a wealthy real estate mogul by the name of Leonard. It seemed irrelevant at the time, he was also her employer. As the years progressed, one could not help but question the merit of foundation in their relationship.

Mrs. Breen had been the first female to conjure foreign emotions within the boyhood psyche of young Damien Galligher. She was always attentive, supportive and encouraging. When it seemed like the boy was invisible, Mrs. Breen had given him praise and compliments, forever cheering him on. The woman had given him a sense of self-worth a self-esteem in a sea of sunken hope and drowned direction.

The scene as it was about to unfold before him was vastly different from what he could recall. At last he blinked away the last bit of grogginess and began to register his surroundings in conscious clarity. Although his adolescent host was developing rapidly, beyond a nine-year old's expectation his adult, lucid mind still lingered within the cerebral cortex.

"Mr. Galligher. How kind of you to join us once again." Across her chest Mrs. Breen folded her arms, a terse gesture of disapproval. In an uprising of acknowledgement, slight a siren of raucous laughter ensued. Surrounded by soul carcass, devouring hyenas Damien wondered and shuddered from the imagery. In formulated, symmetrical lines, rows of desks faced the blackened, dusty abyss known simply as the blackboard. The hyenas of course were just regular, ordinary students like him. Well, scratch that, not really like him at all, but just regular kids nonetheless. In unison they each cackled in laughter, pointing and sneering at red faced, oblivious Damien.

Clutching the meter stick as a talisman of sorts to harness the powers of superiority in a harsh universe she looked on, awaiting an answer.

"Now that I can see you are indeed awake. What is the answer Mr. Galligher?"

An undeniable silence had smothered the room. Each of the bright eyed and bushy tailed boys and girls stared in expectation. Their mouths practically salivated at the sight of their prey, watching, waiting, prowling for Damien's response. Anyone looked like they could have leapt into action at any second.

His tiny lips quivered yet failed to release any coherent response. Below the lacquered surface, between four steel legs his legs shifted nervously. He longed for the suspended sense of animation floating throughout existence. He wished that he could sink into the knotted pine of the chair beneath his bottom and dwell between the crevices, shielded from all this anguished ridicule.

"Um, ah, um," utter gibberish whirled around his throat emulating a humming sound from his lips.

A torrent of rapid gestures ensued from the predatory flock. Their collective hands gnarled and slapped against their chests in battle cry. Moans and groans imitating Damien's response swallowed the classroom. A sing-song chorus of laughter burst into a quaking revelation.

"That's enough children," Mrs. Breen mused while barely concealing a sly smile of her own. She licked her pearly white incisors through scarlet red lips. In adult, lucid Damien's mind the movement was not entirely with erotic pretense. The room gradually quieted down.

"Well, young man.' Methodically she prowled the perimeter of the desks homing in on her prey. Each step and stride were calculated, an execution of authority and all-encompassing power. The meter stick, ever present, lie to her side wavering in semi-circles along her grey-pleated skirt.

To divert his gruesome fate, the boy stared on at the blackboard jungle praying for a miracle, silently bartering with a higher force for the answer to come in rushing tides to him. The infinite blackness betrayed him however. Scores of numbers were pulled like a vortex into the addition and subtraction symbols and stirred all the figures like a humanary stew.

Tension in the air was thick, uncompromised. Certain doom lingered and threatened to be unleashed at any given moment. Mrs. Breen continued her ceremonial prowl forever closing in on his desk centered in the middle of the room.

A stillness unleashed without warning. Each of the pupils, study aids and inanimate objects froze in debilitated state. It was as if all time and existence failed to exist. Everything before him looked like a hideous wax formation in those B-rated House of Horror Vincent Price flicks we watched late at night.

In a thundering succession of unprecedented force, Mrs. Breen sent her talisman crashing against the surface of young Damien's desk. The whipping motion barely missed his wrist by inches. Damien flinched and scurried to the far side of the desk provoking a fresh onslaught of laughter and jeers from the flock.

Bending over to accentuate the severity of the situation Mrs. Breen leaned into her hapless prey. Damien absently thought she smelled a little like strawberries and apricot and his insides did topsy turvies. There was something strangely appealing to his instructor despite her obvious disapproval of his insolent behavior.

"Mr. Galligher,' she stood once again fastening a hardened hand upon her hip. "I appreciate you're new to this institution and haven't quite found your bearings yet. "You will do well to complete the mandatory assignments as required in our curriculum." Almost as a sense of tender after thought she mused. "I'm going to need you to stay behind at recess, so we may discuss the matter further. Understand?"

Damien fueled by sheer instinct alone looked up at his intimidating mentor and nodded vigorously.

"Good. Very well," gradually she backed away from her prey and ensued her path back to the front of the class. While her back was turned, a succession of crumbled up papers collided with the back of Damien's head. Spit balls clustered the side of his face. If Mrs. Breen was privy to the attack she offered no conscious acknowledgement.

"Now, for those of us who had completed their homework as instructed, who can answer the problem on the board?"

A series of frenzied echoes burst into the dense air. Most if not all the students jolted their right arms into the air flexing further and further towards Valhalla or whatever it was they were hoping to reach. Their pained cries of desired recognition were enough to force a whirlwind of nausea within young Damien's belly.

"Yes, very well Suzie. Please come up to the front and answer the question." A young, pert girl wearing all matching choreographed pink skipped proudly to the front of the class. Accepting the piece of white chalk from Mrs. Breen she stood on her tip toes and began her flourished font after the equal sign. Placing the writing stick back on the easel instead of Mrs. Breen's hand she clapped her hands together in swaying fashion and peered at Damien with a disgusted sneer.

"Excellent Suzie. You are correct…"

Before she could finish Suzie piped up and volleyed back.

"Thank you, Mrs. Breen. It was easy really. Anybody who isn't a dummy and did their homework should have been able to figure it out." Her candor was matched with an uproar of squeals and a round of applause. Mrs. Breen held a hand, feigning her appreciation of diminishment while pretending to have a sudden itch.

"That will do children. Let's quite down now. For the remaining half hour, I want you to turn to page fifty-seven in your textbooks and work on the problems. I want complete quiet before recess. Understood children?"

"Yes Mrs. Breen." The flock complied in such unity it made Damien cringe. He didn't belong here and he all the sudden felt like he'd do just about anything to bring father back. He hated this school and knew full well he wouldn't have to go to such a retched place like this if he never had to move in the first place. The only thing preventing him from breaking down in defeated sobs is he knew in his heart the flock would pick his bones dry.

Watching on from his matured state, the distorted memory that unfolded like a movie reel, Damien shuddered. In a blanket of uncertainty, the more his life's reflection replayed before him the more it dawned that everything had been an utter chaotic farce.

Sure, he remembered going to a new school. He recalled difficulty fitting in. Nothing like this. Sitting in the vast concrete, steel and wooden prison he could tell the atmosphere was swiftly swallowing his soul. How could should a crucial, monumental episode in his life be so remarkably inaccurate in his mind. To the best of his recollection it took a few days to meet some new friends, to find a confidant and someone he had something in common with. Damien had no memory of being so alienated from the get go so painfully isolated.

The recess discussion with Mrs. Breen went as predictably as could be expected. It didn't take long for his admiration to grow for his mentor. She had voiced empathy for his situation and expressed a deep understanding for difficulty in adapting to a very adult situation as a young child. In closing she made him vow to concentrate on the work, the homework assignments and the rest would slip into place in time. Placing a tender hand upon his slumped shoulders Mrs. Breen said she was there for him anytime he'd needed. Her door was always open to him. As she glanced upon the wall mounted clock, just below the ceiling on lingering somewhere in perpetual limbo above the chalkboard she beckoned him to go outside and enjoy the fresh air for the remainder of the recess period. The other children would warm up to him. Just try and see if they didn't.

Damien shook in reluctant protest. The outdoors harbored any number of undesirables. He just wanted to go home. He just wanted to put this dreadful nightmare behind him. He just wanted father.

Shuffling his sneakers along the dusty checkered tiles he retreated to the classroom's doorway. As an almost after thought he glimpsed over his shoulder. In a whisper so faint he thought she'd never had heard him, "Thank you Mrs. Breen. I'll try not to let you down."

Along the bridge of her nose her glasses had slid. Across the room she smiled while pushing them back into place.

"Anytime Damien."

His tiny heart hammered within the cage of bones. Sweaty palms left slippery streaks along the baby blue painted cinderblocks along the hallway. Within his fragile frame he grappled with catching a breath. He didn't dare approach any of his intimidating adversaries. What did they have against him anyway? Damien supposed he could make himself scarce, ideally invisible. This was a concept that was hardly foreign to his upbringing.

There couldn't possibly be a whole lot of time left in the recess period anyhow. Yet to a young, impressionable individual, the seconds passed like eons, let alone the minutes. Taking a deep sigh and beckoning a silent prayer for strength young Damien pushed the retractable steel bar in the front door and made his journey into the unknown.

CHAPTER THREE

After the Galligher Family, Aunt Julia, Danny and his bride to be Elise had deduced Damien wasn't coming, they'd taken the liberty of embarking upon the motions of the wedding rehearsal. Father O'Malley had suggested that perhaps it was in vain to continue to wait and if he'd arrived he could be brought up to speed.

The formalities of the rehearsal went off without a hitch. Occasionally there was a lapse in organization and rhythm as Danny's groomsmen scoffed and joked about missing last call at the infamous Chulka Thong bar.

Aunt Julia had rolled her eyes in disdain while Joy had silently basked in her sister's offspring in all his indignation. Once rivals, always rivals.

Even in their casual apparel, the wedding party looked striking in their places. In such an awe inducing spectacle such as St. Timothy's Church, any event could appear majestic.

Many of the rituals and mannerisms made no sense to Joy whatsoever. She did her best to convey significant restraint. After all this was not her soiree. Never would it cross her mind to rain on the parade of her nephew Danny and his beautiful blushing bride to be Elise. They made a handsome couple. She had to be some sort of saint inside to tame the perpetual party animal inside Danny. Silently, she commended her efforts and knew full well she had to have been a lady of Moxy.

Standing off to the side along the rows of pews she appraised her family before her. They were certainly a diverse tribe if anything. From sibling to sibling, each was as different as night and day. From cousin to cousin, each was as unique and remarkable than the last. Joy was proud of her loved ones. A pain of sadness constricted her pulse. How she'd wished Damien was here. A cocktail of worry, anxiety and shame. What was it about her sister's family that exuded such togetherness, such unity? Sure, they had their issues, their dysfunction and they were far from perfect. Yet there was almost always someone of her children that was forever leaving her in limbo.

Glancing at her eldest daughter Kaitlin, she smiled, and her gesture was reciprocated with beaming delight. Such an emotional prodigy, was Kaitlin. She was the rock in her instability. If it were not for her first born she never would have had the courage to pick up the pieces of the family's horrific tragedy in her last husband's brutal demise. Kaitlin adapted the role of surrogate mother to the remaining kids. She never complained and carried on with such an intestinal fortitude it quickly became the very fiber of strength the family needed to nurture and grow. It was at that moment of reflection Joy had vowed to express her gratitude and love for all her selfless actions. Watching her and reminiscing she began to permeate with pride.

Standing next to her, amongst the bridesmaids was Kassandra. Oh sweet, unbridled, uncensored Kassy. She always possessed such an unapologetic free spirit, it often made others frown in confusion. Others were simply intimidated by her ability to live in the moment, embrace life and wear her heart on her sleeve. She'd found genuine happiness and love of her own. Kassandra was one she could always depend upon to cheer her up in the most precarious of times. Her outrageous sense of humor and spontaneity kept Joy on her toes. Kassandra was not one to simply mother, she was a friend and brought out the best in everyone around her. She was ecstatic that she managed to carry on from such an onslaught of post-traumatic stress that it only made her and the others stronger.

Peggy stood with the other cousins, listening attentively and unleashing bouts of infectious laughter. If anyone had been affected or broken from a childhood life of abuse, Joy had bet it would have been Peggy. Her zest for life, passion for interacting with others and kind, giving spirit warmed Joy to the core. She regarded her youngest daughter as an inspiration. An unprecedented ability to embrace life and bask in the energy of others while offering her own unconditional radiance was beyond words.

Damien, such a tortured soul. Life was never the same for him since the terror that transpired thirteen years ago. All the world's consoling and assurance in love for his heroics would never be enough to easy his afflicted conscious. All the years of therapy, patience, sharing and interaction would never be enough to ease his karmic burden. She often questioned if he'd ever be the same, or ever measured up to be all he could be. The universe was at his disposal, the skies at the limit for his tenacity, determination and raw will. She'd recalled in any of their most recent telephone discussions that gratefully uninterrupted by Jade, he often talked about the old house, almost transcendent in thought, hypnotized with all it stood for. Perhaps he'd never rest at ease until he revisited the old home. Maybe, just maybe it was the only way to exorcise his restless demons.

A wave of nausea washed over Joy. Sweat permeated upon her brown. Stumbling in her heels she reached frantically for the edge of the pew. Leonard stood to steady her shakiness. Joy virtually collapsed into his lap.

While Father O'Malley was wrapping things up in the make shift congregation putting his seal of approval on the rehearsal, the others darted their expressions of concern to their mother and aunt. Danny made an inappropriate remark about happy hour starting early.

The girls rushed to her side to be of comfort. Ever dependable, reassuring loves they were. She wondered how such magnificent souls had started with her. They were almost paradoxes in their own reality.

"Mom! Are you alright?" Peggy almost shrieked in evident concern. Kaitlin and Kassandra shouldered one another to get to her first.

"You're shaking life a leaf. What's wrong?" Leonard had mused whisking bronze tufts of hair from her clammy brow.

"Quick! Someone get her a glass of fucking water!" Kassandra screamed, her echoes ricocheted off the cathedral's rafters.

In an absurd observation Joy realized Kassandra would offer exactly whatever was in her uncensored soul, regardless of the environment.

Joy grappled to steady herself. Her nails screamed along the veneer polished pews. The skin along her arms and shoulders quivered taking on a life of its own. The bout of dizziness gradually subsided, the double vision gracefully diminished into one.

"Oh, for heaven's sake! Everyone just take it easy. I just got a little light headed that's all. "Don't get yourselves all up in a ruckus. It's likely just an empty stomach, and all of this heat." Sitting upright, she rubbed her thighs nervously, resentful at being the center of attention. "I'm fine. I'm fine."

With a volleying sense of reluctance each of her daughters eased off glancing at one another for clarity.

Leonard gazed into her eyes searching for any semblance of recognition.

Joy found it impossible to return his look, darting away her eyes.

"Well let's just not sit here everyone. Let's go and eat before Joy has a fit of starvation," Julia interjected.

Her diversion was all the remaining inhabitants of the church needed and engaged in carefree laughter.

Standing slowly to her feet, Joy waved off Leonard and met everyone else's expression of concern.

"Well you heard the lady. Let's go and celebrate. What is it you young people say these days? Let's get our groove on."

Joy's proclamation was engaged with a round of applause. Smaller groups gravitated towards one another. Excited decimals of chattering rose shimming along the stained-glass windows. Couples made plans, cousins argued over venues, siblings ribbed one another over picking up the tab. The groomsmen slumped their shoulders in obvious defeat thinking their bachelor party soiree was out of the picture after all.

From the alter, Julia regarded her sister and wondered if her episode wasn't entirely over. She seemed to push aside the incident before completely ensuring she was alright.

Joy glanced over her shoulder and met her sister's gaze. A look of thinly veiled turmoil exchanged between them. What was it they said, you could never hide her lying eyes from your blood.

Taking the long strides towards the exit of St. Timothy's, Joy contemplated stopping this whole debacle, this whole sorted charade and announcing what she knew full well in her heart. The shame she carried was like the weight of the world upon her fragile shoulders. The indignity she felt for posing an imposition on her nephew's parade would remain undenied.

For in her heart, she knew where her only son was. Deep inside herself there was no arguing that Damien wasn't late. He hadn't simply lost track of time or been convinced by Jade not to come. He had gone to lengths to make himself right again. She knew she had to tell someone that Damien had decided to go home again.

CHAPTER FOUR

By the time Dr. Rhys had pulled up in Jade's circular driveway to her apartment in his '86 Cadillac Deville, she was already waiting outside. Looking blanched and beside herself with anxiety, Jade paced back and forth. The good doctor figured he'd arrived in not a moment too soon.

She had only a back pack with her. A hasty compromise for her anticipated weekend getaway, everything else seemed beyond trivial at this point. Reaching between her lips she hesitated for a moment, dropping the gnarled fingernail before any more damage could be done. As she grasped the door handle Jade leaned against the beige exterior, a last-minute effort to compose herself.

Just as swiftly Dr. Rhys unclasped his seatbelt and flung open the driver's door. Onto the cracked asphalt he dashed to her side. Jade shuddered at every foot fall as they grew nearer.

Offering a momentary semblance of comfort, they embraced. The good doctor glimpsed into her teary eyes. He caressed her reddened face in a nurturing and platonic sort of way. With a deep sigh Jade felt instantly at ease.

"Come now Jade. Everything's going to be just fine. I apologize if I'd over reacted on the phone. You see I care a great deal for young Damien,' oddly enough the doctor seemed to be stammering on his own words. "I'm sure all of this is going to be one crazy, spontaneous wild goose chase. It's just a precaution to ensure everything is copacetic and Damien hasn't done anything extreme."

Motioning her into the ample interior, he offered her an expression of reassurance before closing the door behind her. As he walked briskly over to the driver's side Jade wished she could buy into his gestures of comfort. Until she laid eyes on her beloved there was no easing this sensation, this all-consuming state of dread.

As the doctor situated himself once again he seemed distracted or unsure how to proceed. Jade noted he must have checked his rear-view windows a half dozen times before putting the gear into reverse and backing out the circular drive.

Cruising along the solemn street, they'd sat in silence. Dr. Rhys had just about forgotten to flip on his head lights. Upon the steering wheel he drummed his fingers, considered turning on the radio then resigned accentuating his uncertainty.

A cursory glance at her lap, Jade flushed at the realization her skirt was perhaps a little inappropriate for this endeavor. The hem hiked at least mid-thigh and she sucked her teeth wishing she'd paid more conscious attention to her last-minute apparel decisions. Lost in complete thought and worry over Damien, she was surprised she wasn't waiting with just the towel from her shower tucked around her bust.

"Dr. Rhys, I can't thank you enough for picking me up. I think I would have driven myself nuts sitting there alone wondering where Damien is." She sounded foolish, even childish in her own head. As an afterthought, "Sorry. No offense."

For the first time since he'd pulled off the highway on the closest exit to detour back to Toronto Dr. Rhys had laughed.

Offering another gesture of tenderness, he glanced at her through his peripheral.

"Think nothing of it. Although nuts is a term we try to steer clear of in my profession my dear."

"I'm guessing crackers and bananas are off the table too huh?"

Together they laughed. Not a nervous jittery laugh, but a full belly, unbridled bout of side splitting laughter.

"Yes, my personal favorite, coco for cocoa puffs is generally frowned upon too." The diversion felt good, an escape into the seemingly inevitable. Through the still air their collective facial muscles and abdominal cavities eased once again.

"Dr. Rhys is there something about Damien you're not telling me? I hate for this to sound like an inquisition and would never underestimate your kindness but, oh I don't know I guess I'm just rambling."

"Oh, I understand your concern Jade. It does seem highly un-orthodox for a former doctor, although now a close friend would drop everything and race on over to collect you to determine his whereabouts."

"It's just that you sounded so alarmed on the phone I thought maybe- "Jade interjected

Scores of transients, street lamps and newspaper boxes whipped by the glass.

"I assure you the origin of my alarm dear Jade was of friend-ship and not of the professional sense." The good doctor sighed and seemed to be grappling with some sense of ethical morals.

"Let me ask you has Damien suffered an unusual number of nightmares as of late?" He flipped on his indicator signal perhaps a little more dramatically than intended. "Any loss or increase of appetite? Any drastic change or alteration in behavior at all?"

She gazed at him a little bemused. One had to admit the doc-tor had an uncanny ability to divert questions and spawn his own inquisitive line of thought. Running a hand through her hair she twirled the ends as though just the right words would grow right out of them.

"Well sure. I mean yes. His nightmares almost seem nightly as of late. He wakes up in a cold sweat, fighting to catch his breath. From time to time he even screams himself awake. Good God Dr. Rhys, Damien's such a withdrawn man he hates like hell to show what he thinks is weakness, especially to those he loves. Many times, I've pretended to be asleep to spare him of embarrassment. I've tried to comfort him, and it just seems to get a hold of him more, you know?"

"And does he discuss these nightmares with you? Or does he remain detached from the whole horrific endeavor?"

"He doesn't really discuss them. I think he's ashamed of them. I know full well, I mean we both know they're about his father and the guilt he has over..' she peered at him with an icy stare that could stop a beating heart. "-as far as I'm concerned Damien's father got exactly what he deserved. No scratch that. He got off too easily. The hell he put Damien and his whole family through. I sure hope he got what's coming to him in hell."

If the doctor was alarmed at her candor he demonstrated no evidence as such.

"I believe that is a perfectly healthy response Jade." He smiled and clasped her hand with his own. Checking his blind spot, he signaled before merging into oncoming traffic on the parkway.

"What I am about to tell you can be considered a direct breach of patient doctor confidentiality."

The statement clung in the air thick with tension.

"I don't want you to compromise your integrity doctor, but if you feel it's relevant here please take confidence in the fact this will remain forever between you and me and never leaves this car."

"Very well. I had a feeling you would react that way." Dr. Rhys frowned as he glared through the windshield focusing on the perpetual yellow lines. "You must understand that Damien had sustained an immense trauma, a trauma that no one should ever have to experience even as such a tender age of seven."

"Well yeah, no shit Sherlock."

Dr. Rhys flinched from her lack of verbal filter. She exchanged the look with a grimace of regret.

"Clinically speaking, he suffered from post-traumatic stress disorder accompanied by dissociative personality disorder."

He allowed the impact of possible ramifications settle in for a moment.

Jade unleashed a low, astounded whistle.

"I do know a little bit about that. We studied a little of it in our abnormal psychology classes in college."

"Yes, well." Dr. Rhys fidgeted in his seat, adjusting this and rearranging that. "What you read in a textbook could not possibly do any real justice to-"

"That's sort of like multiple personalities or something like that, isn't it?"

The good doctor's eye brows arched.

"Correct. Yes, right once again,' he flinched as a red Mustang barreled on past honking its horn and muscling ahead of him. Evidently this line of reminiscing was beginning to distract his driving just a little. "You see many disorders that originate within the mind are a direct result of a coping mechanism. Which is to say, if the mind cannot function, with the stimuli presented to it, a chemical imbalance may occur in some cases to compensate for lack of better words a metamorphosis occurs to protect itself."

"Forgive me if this sounds like psycho-babble, -mumbo jumbo. What I'm trying to say is Damien could not face the emotional responses of his guilt and bereavement of his father. Quite literally he invented another version of himself. Someone who could cope and face the eyes of adversity, no matter how dire they may have appeared on the surface."

Once again, the tension in the air could be sliced from velour cushions to felt ceilings.

"So, what does this mean? I'm a little confused." Jade nervously toyed with the armrest between them. "Obviously he got better. I mean there was treatment wasn't there?"

With a distracted wave of the hand, the good doctor brushed the thought aside. If he was offended at her near accusatory stance, he never showed it.

"Well, yes of course. We engaged in a sturdy regimen of therapy. Damien and I had engaged in extensive counselling and he was prescribed medication throughout the duration. We made leaps and bounds together and had a real break-through."

"So, if he's cured. If he's better than why is it, you seem every bit as worried as I do?"

"There are two things that concern me Jade and I will never be able to live with myself if I don't express each to you."

Within her fragile frame, Jade's heart hammered and threatened to burst through her ribcage.

In a choked whisper she offered, "Go on." It was barely audible to the untrained ear.

"You see. I had developed a romantic affiliation with Mrs. Galligher, Joy."

Jade gasped, unable to conceal her unease. Suddenly she'd felt like she walked right onto the set of a Jerry Springer episode already in progress. She found it very difficult to breathe.

"It wasn't something planned I can say that much. It wasn't as though I'd methodically set out to fall in love with Damien's mother. The very notion is as preposterous, as it must sound to you at this moment." The good doctor quivered for a moment. Was he sobbing? Giggling hysterically? This whole scene was beginning to get a little too surreal for Jade.

"I resisted with everything I had but Joy was every bit as much as in love with me as I with her. We made a pact, a vow if you will, for the better of everyone, to terminate further treatment with Damien as it was a direct violation of ethics."

"So, you mean you just dropped Damien like a hot potato because you all of the sudden got the hots for his mother?" Clearly flabbergast, Jade waved her arms in the air, her voice finding its full muster once again. "How could you?"

"Please...." he muttered and pleaded to her as though she were a higher power. "You have to understand. Damien had far excelled beyond what I could do for him as a psychiatrist. Any other reputable doctor would have discharged him from further therapy as I had."

Feeling immensely violated and cheapened next to this man that her beloved had looked up to his whole life, Jade really wished she had something more comfortable to wear or better yet, be out of this whole sorted affair to begin with.

She shook her head, looking on in disbelief.

"Alright, so let's say for sake of argument, that he didn't need your help any further and could move on. So, what's this second thing you said you wanted to say."

"From time to time a patient who had endured Dissociate Personality Disorder can have a relapse or can experience something equally traumatic to trigger the coping mechanisms further."

"So, what you're saying is Damien might be out there right now as we speak and have no conscious awareness of who he is, or what he's doing?"

"I'm sure that isn't the case and.."

"Dr. Rhys! Enough of the bullshit!" Jade virtually screamed into his ear, causing the Caddy to swerve on the parkway. "I think you better step on it and you better pray to God that nothing's happened to him."

"Yes, my sentiments exactly."

CHAPTER FIVE

The burst of sunlight made young Damien squint his eyes. Somewhere, just outside the outer reaches of hell current, adult Damien took in shallow, sullen breaths. His body still functioned in the tangible, yet he relived all his distorted memories in uncanny, lucid detail.

A sensation of extreme ambivalence permeated him to the core. The other children's reception to him wasn't exactly stellar when in the classroom. If they were prone to be ruthless in a controlled setting, there was no telling how primal they could be, left to their own devices at recess.

He wasn't sure why they'd regarded him with such disdain. It wasn't as though he was all that different. Sure, he was tall and gangly. Let's not mince words, young adolescent Damien Galligher epitomized awkwardness. But weren't most youths awkward at least in some sense of the word? An overwhelming sensation of utter loneliness imprisoned his fragile heart. Why was it so important to fit in? Why did he thrive to be accepted by these judgmental gang of hyenas?

Feeling like a thousand eyes were fixed upon him, he shuffled nervously through the gravel shoulder, along the tarmac leading to the playground. Hands in pockets, he ventured on with each tentative step. The sun felt good against his skin. Perhaps Mrs. Breen was right in suggesting some fresh air after all. Emotional scavengers or not, if they let him be, he'd be just fine.

His mood even elevated, if even just for a moment as he walked along the basketball court's perimeter whistling a tune to himself. A gentle breeze ruffled his out of place feathered hairstyle. Perhaps if he relented to look at them they'd reciprocate the same small favor.

Instead of succumbing to their inevitable leers and sneers, he diverted his attention elsewhere. He longed for his inaugural day at his new school to be over. He'd race home, up the long driveway and fetch the largest bowl of black cherry ice cream ever and watch Gilligan's Island or Three's Company. The new country home his Mom had moved them into with her new boyfriend Leonard wasn't so bad. A kid could just be a kid there on his own terms.

Just as a ghost of a smile was beginning to rise upon his lips, a whirling sound bombarded his perception. A catastrophic sphere collided with the side of his head with epic proportion. Rendered completely off guard, Damien pin wheeled his arms in desperate attempt to right his failing balance. He shrieked in a pitch much too high for his ordinary maturing voice box.

A gaggle of invading laughter swarmed his senses. As his ass end collided with the dirt, the sounds reached impossible levels of intensity. Through bleary eyes the world swam in and out of focus.

"Ha ha mongoloid! Walk much?" Chants of degradation wormed their way into his delicate psyche. The day was barely half over and already his questionable self-esteem had been bruised, battered and bludgeoned beyond recognition.

A much smaller, rubber tetherball bounced in rhythm to the heart beat that clouded his hearing. It didn't appear half as menacing as it felt, yet onward it smacked against the pavement taunting his every movement. A flash of white hot rage blinded his vision. Gripping tufts of grass and dirt, his body trembled from scalp to toe. As he grappled with getting to his feet some hot shot jock he vaguely remembered from class shimmied to the edge of the court to retrieve the object of malice.

"Loser," he grumbled under his breath. The boy, Jeff, Geoff or something like that turned with nonchalant grace that any ballerina would envy.

Like tiny garter snakes, the veins upon Damien's forearms writhed and twisted threatening to burst free of his flesh. Into tiny fists his hands clenched and unclenched more rapidly by the second. Inside his mouth, his teeth grinded back and forth as his head convulsed in seething indignation.

"What did you say?" He growled in defiance, a voice foreign even unto himself.

Geoff or Jeff, or something like that flinched even if ever so slightly and looked over his shoulder. His comrades looked on with their goofy smiles waiting for their chum to volley the ball back over. He took a step towards his compatriots.

"Hey kid!" Damien's bellow froze the other youth in his tracks. "I said, what did you say?"

The fury within his boyhood host quivered on, blurring his vision and dominating his stance.

"I said, loser," the boy retorted with a snort. "Jeez get a life."

"That's what I thought you said," Upon final release of the last couple syllables, Damien launched himself at his adversary. Feet completely off the ground, he propelled his body feet first towards the object of his perpetual mockery. The crook of his arm collided with the back of his head, bull dogging his face into the pavement courtyard.

With a fistful of hair, Damien clutched hapless Geoff, Jeff or whoever, and grated his face back and forth against the hot, bumpy surface. Screaming into his ear his bounced his head off the unforgiving surface in time to each of his proclamations.

"Get a life? Get a life? You live my life then we'll see who has a life. We'll see who the loser is. Who the mongoloid is!" Blood pooled in all directions beneath the boy's head. Sounds of walnuts crunching filled the silent air.

Damien was back on his feet kicking and stomping in a flurry. The boy was helpless to the onslaught and feebly raised and arm to try and ward off the brutal attack.

"Stop it, you freak, you're going to kill him." Someone in the distance shouted. A crowd of ravenous onlookers ran to the scene and hovered above the gruesome spectacle. With each heart beat Damien thrashed, kicked and stomped harder and faster. He resorted to dropping knees to the back of his foe's head while frothy white spittle flew in clusters from his lips.

"That's enough! Enough children!" A frantic, authoritative voice beckoned while rifling through the cluster of youths.

"Damien Galligher, you get off him this instant!" It was Mrs. Breen herself, clearly harried in her actions to break up the melee.

Tiny hands splashed in blood, not his own blood, but the blood of Geoff, Jeff or whatever drizzled from his fingertips.

Mrs. Breen opened her mouth again to reinforce the severity of the situation. The gesture seemed to flash young Damien back into consciousness. Scrambling and scurrying away from the horrific spectacle, he averted his gaze and began to gag and retch. The motions initiated a series of walling sobs. It was as though he was impervious to what had happened before him.

"Shelly, run to the principal's office and have him call an ambulance." As an obvious after thought, "Hurray!"

Her star pupil did as she was told, and the crowd gradually began to dissipate.

The afternoon recess bell sounded breaking everyone free of the onslaught before them.

"Show's over children, line up as usual. Mrs. Corden will see you into class."

Mrs. Breen sighed. An all too consuming sigh, she looked as though she'd aged ten years in the last three minutes. Her stylish frock was disheveled, and glasses sat askew upon her face. To an outsider she looked helpless, uncertain as to what to do next.

Turning towards her newest student she regarded him, appraised him, unsure of what exactly to say. See avoided direct eye contact. No amount of schooling or training prepared her for this.

"Young man, I'm not going to sugar coat this for you. You're in big trouble. No, you're in a whole sea of trouble. The big trouble ship sailed long ago." Raising one trembling arm, she gestured to place it around her shoulder and appeared as though she'd reconsidered at the last moment. "Let's get you to the principal's office, call your parents and deal with this one step at a time."

Damien sniffled and simply nodded, resigned to his consequences.

As he took the long walk back to the school house, Mrs. Breen would have been grateful to have missed the prominent sneer forming upon Damien's lips.

CHAPTER SIX

The drive back to the hotel was one of relative no consequence, borderline solemn. While Seagrave, the small villa in which most of the Gallighers still resided, was a mere twenty-minute drive from the where the wedding was to be at St. Timothy's Cathedral in Port Perry, it seemed only logical for each of the attending family to get rooms. Once the reception was in full procession the alcohol would flow like a babbling brook. No one needed the heavy burden of drinking and driving.

Joy and Leonard rode in their familiar custom silence. A silence that was brandished and forged of years of marriage. Although she was a little disappointed that Leonard had refused to come to her aid during her heated discussion with her sister Julia, it hadn't surprised her. It was any wonder the old coot still had a pulse in moments such as these.

As they'd pulled into the parking lot, Joy had sighed, unfastening her seat belt and fussing about her skirt. She hadn't even realized that she'd sighed an audible emittance, one with dramatic flair until Leonard rolled his eyes. He was already out of the car, retrieving his electric key card for their corresponding room.

"Something the matter honey?" He whistled into the cool, post dusk air, almost as a distracted after thought.

"Oh, nothing you need to concern yourself with Lenny, darling."

He flinched at the Lenny remark, knowing full well she only reserved these endearments for when she was being condescending with him.

"Well if something's on your mind Hun, let's talk about it. No good to keep things bottled inside." He gestured a swirling motion with his abdomen and made a queasy face.

Joy couldn't resist giggling at his efforts. Never one to hash out feelings, the man of wealth was more prone to buying his loved ones something shiny when turmoil had arisen. Feelings and expressions thereof just weren't his thing.

"It's the boy isn't it?" He slapped his beefy yet well-manicured hand upon the roof of the '86 Cadillac. "That boy just refuses to grow up, always abandoning any sense of responsibility. I swear he'll drive us to an early grave and be the bane of our existence until then."

"Oh Lenny, darling. Go easy on him. We don't know what happened."

Leonard fought the urge to engage in heated rebuttal. Knowing full well his expression of disappointment in his wife's son would get him nowhere fast aside from the dog house.

Together they'd walked hand in hand, through the parking lot towards the quaint Inn's entrance. A gesture of tenderness that was so elusive it warmed each of their collective hearts.

"Damien has always had coping issues. Maybe I had gone wrong somewhere and been too hard on Jade. I mean she might be all wrong for him but maybe none of that matters if he's happy. I can't blame her for not wanting to come and I can't blame him for staying away. If only I'd been more kind to her, more open minded."

Joy's eyes began to glisten beneath the twinkling stars above. Leonard gasped at just how beautifully vulnerable she'd looked. He gazed into her eyes and brushed aside the streaks of tears.

"Now no point in jumping to conclusions sweetheart. It will just drive us crazy going in circles like this." He grasped her shoulders and pulled his wife into a firm embrace. Joy stiffened at first and at least resigned, feeling feeble yet protected in her husband's arms.

"I tell you what. If we haven't heard from him by the morning. I'll personally send someone over to his apartment to check on him and get to the bottom of this once and for all ok?"

Joy silently nodded, relieved that her husband, Damien's elusive step-father had intervened at last. He may be emotionally detached but his resources somehow made many matters just right. At least he was trying, in his own way, he was trying.

"Now what do you say we go have a night cap and don't give this a second thought until morning?"

Joy visibly brightened at the thought of a martini and smiled. Even though her smile seemed forced. She couldn't shake the sensation there was something much more sinister at hand.

Kaitlin, Damien's oldest sister busied herself about her hotel room by unpacking. Of course, subscribing to the stereotypical woman's embodiment of travelling, she'd brought far too much clothes, make up and acccssorics. After all they'd only be here for the wedding at the day after. Sunday, a day to recoup and then back to the grind once again. Her husband Cam was even conspicuous by his absence and wouldn't be joining her until tomorrow afternoon at the ceremony. Although Cam was not in the wedding party, it still irked Kaitlin to no end how everyone made a fuss about her only brother's absence, but no one even bothered to question where Cam once.

It didn't take long to brush the irritation aside as she too began to worry about Damien. When they were children, well she a teen and he a child, she was twelve years his senior after all, she was somewhat of a surrogate mother to the boy. Joy was often working two or three jobs to support her four children before meeting Leonard at last and their rags and impoverished lives had become one of riches in no time.

Unfolding and refolding skirts and sun dresses neurotically she lost track of what she was doing and couldn't shake the feeling of unease she had about Damien. She knew full well how he felt about Port Perry and Seagrave especially. There was nothing but a legacy of poor, traumatic memories for him there and well the others for that matter. Each sibling had their own way of coping with the nightmare Bill Galligher had put them through. It was years before Kaitlin was able to have a normal, functional relationship with any man. She resorted to reckless post teen partying and promiscuous sex with countless less than worthy gentlemen suitors. Although she never sought out professional therapy she knew in her heart of hearts she had Daddy issues and always tried to save them broken men she was with.

Kaitlin managed to repress much of the horrid violent memories of Bill yet still struggled on a deep subconscious level of the countless unspeakable acts he'd inflicted upon her. Yet she pressed on, a survivor hell-bent to prove she'd never succumb to be a victim or product of her environment. Now a successful nurse in the emergency ward of Port Perry General Hospital she transcending her caring nature in to making others better and it therefore bettered herself.

While others had dismissed Damien's absence as one of irresponsible behavior, Kaitlin knew otherwise. For the tenth time she unfolded a sun dress went to hang it up on the closet then walked it back over to the bed and folded it one again. She considered calling Cam but didn't want to anger him bothering him at work. She knew there was no point in calling Damien's number. Countless messages had already been left. If he was going to call, he was going to call, persistence would only freak him out further.

At last she resigned to the bedside in a heap next to the half-unpacked suitcase. It bounced upon the far too soft mattress. Toying with the remote she ran her finger tips along the buttons considering some mindless television viewing. It may be a welcome distraction. Yet she couldn't bring herself to it. Abandoning the remote it bounced upon the mattress and toppled unto the plush red carpet.

Pacing the room, she walked the confined perimeter to the washroom, back to the front door and around the bed again. Where would she be if she were Damien? What was on his mind?

Returning to the town he barely been to since high school graduation was far more of a deal to him than anyone recognized. Kaitlin's eyes brightened as though a light bulb had just burst into full luminosity within her cerebral cortex.

"Of course! That had to be it." Speaking aloud to the empty room, Damien's oldest sister knew exactly where he'd disappeared to.

Within the barren confines of the old Galligher family basement, Damien sat overwhelmed, drained. His conception of reality and illusion eclipsed over one another, creating a constant shade of grey. Caressing the surface of the virtual scrapbook he took a deep breath and exhaled. How could it be possible his whole existence has been a lie? Was it conceivable his entire life has been so dramatically distorted that he remembered things only the way he had been instructed to remember them? A lot of fresh questions cropped up in his weary mind. Damien began to second guess the authenticity of his good friend and therapist Dr. Rhys. Could it be possible the good doctor had ulterior motives? Was brainwashing completely out of the question? Crazier things have happened within the four walls of a therapy session; that much he was sure. Even the estrangement from his own mother, for lack of better words seemed to make sense now. If her whole genuine personality had been a clever disguise, a rouse of sorts than what exactly was he to believe?

The empty rolling deep within his abdomen did little to satisfy his appetite for understanding. Constant, nagging light headedness accompanied by an undeniable nausea plagued him. How much merit could his biological father have? This was the very man that he was forced to intervene and accidentally kill as a tender child. It seemed from that point forward nothing at all was the way it had appeared.

Gripping the bridge of his nose, he shook his head back and forth, fighting back the tears of frustration. He had returned to the scene of his all-consuming symbol of coming undone in hopes of an epiphany or at very least emotional closure to memories that repelled his very nature against any kind of healthy coping and thriving in day to day life. Now it appears everything had become more chaotic, increasingly amok.

If there was anything left within his empty stomach he would have wretched its contents all over the dirt floor. He sat there instead rocking gently back and forth, back in forth, adapting his long ago forgotten behavioral defense mechanism as a child. A casual observer would have pegged him as an autistic child, so transfixed in his own distant thoughts yet mumbling incoherently to himself and swaying forever more back and forth.

Absently his hand scanned the page once more before turning it. A repeated ritual in hopes of plucking the answers directly from the dust and fibers within the paper and making sense of each. A weathered and dog-eared pendant stared back at him in defiance. The cheap, felt material public schools issued to commemorate levels of achievement. In faint non-descript font the purple lettering read: Swim Club: Participant. Damien smirked at his observation realizing this was the school board's political way of summing up, "thanks fella for coming out. Here's this badge for being there.

Better luck next time." It was the quintessential reminder of having virtually no level of achievement at all.

The plastic, cellophane wrap, barely translucent from all the dust began to breathe above the page of pendants, photographs, keepsakes and sentimental bric-a-brac. In and out it began to undulate. Damien's eyes swam in and out of focus. His vision swirled around in spiral fashion around the violet hued font. Moans of indecipherable origin escaped in steady rhythm to the rippling page. From his scalp he felt numb then a pleasant sensation of tingling. The feeling descending down the sides of his head, unto his face and neck. It was like his whole body was getting pins and needles, but it wasn't exactly unpleasant. It was like a state of heightened suggestion. Gradually his own breathing back in synch with the page before him. It wasn't long before his hazy eyes burdened from sleep deprivation succumbed to their inevitable retreat. Into the abysmal beyond Damien escaped once again into the void.

CHAPTER SEVEN

"Everything's always got to be all about him, doesn't it?" Kassandra stewed as she slammed articles from her duffle bag up and down the length of the motel's dresser. More items than not teetered and toppled onto the floor unceremoniously from her tirade. A plume of baby powder erupted into the stagnant air, swirling particles of while granules trickling to the carpet below.

"I mean whose wedding is this anyway?" Beneath a crimson mask of frustration, she gnawed her bottom lip.

Mick, her husband sat adjacent on the modest room's queen-sized bed. Traditional, loud floral design adored the bed spread which was now bunched up in waves of varying dishevelment. For the most part he was oblivious to her escapade. The level of his desensitized demeanor was like a badge of honor having endured many years of outburst just like this.

Mick was the yang to Kassandra's ying. Always the cooler head to her heated fury, he took the Zen approach to life and always managed to level his wife in the end. He busied himself with crumpling copious amounts of dried out "Cush" on the surface of the motel's complimentary Gideon's New Testament bible, on hardcover no less. Pinching the contents between his fingers he sprinkled the fine herbal dust back onto the book and repeated the ritual all over again for posterity. He was so caught up in his own design he barely registered anything Kassandra was saying.

"Do you hear anything I'm saying, you big doofus?" Perhaps with a little more stank than intended Kassandra slugged her husband on the shoulder.

"Hey, what the hell…. dude…." Mick rubbed his arm vigorously, with theatrical flair.

She resigned to diverting her wrecking ball ways of unpacking to sitting across from him on the bed instead. Still she was agitated, unnerved. Her bobbing knee was evidence to a human walking time bomb.

"I mean why's everyone all up in arms over where the hell Damien is anyway?" She flailed her arms in the air in case extra, added emphasis was in order. "It's not like the prodigal son that never misses a family function and gives two shits one way or the other what anyone does but himself? You know?"

She waited not for Mick to answer.

"And did you see the way Mom argued with Auntie Julia about the whole thing? The little shit causes skid marks even when he isn't even around. If anyone in this family gave a half the shit about me like they did with him……" Kassandra's babbling at last got the better of her and even to herself, she must have sounded nonsensical and ridiculous.

Between a canvas of cigarette papers, Mick was steadily shifting his au gratin piece de resistance. He shifted his gaze to his distraught wife and grinned the child like exuberance of a perpetual stoner. Looking like a myriad of an Allman Brother's band reject and Lurch of The Addams Family he licked the adhesive upon his creation and grunted his sing-song emission of empathy that only a married couple could possibly comprehend.

"Yeah, I know," Kassandra continued, seemingly on queue. "I shouldn't let the little squirt get to me. I did have some things I wanted to talk about with Mom though you know? I mean we're way behind on our rent again and I figured the church would have been the perfect place to hit her up you know?"

Mick's non-verbal response came in the form of sparking the mastodon of a joint and swiftly inhaling three draws before passing it to his wife.

She reached out, spotting the cannon from her peripheral. Pinching it between index and forefinger she held it to her lips and dragged languidly. Billowing clouds rolled across the ceiling as she exhaled. In that strained exhaled voice she blathered on, "Instead it's all Damien this and Damien that."

"Babe, why don't we forget all about your little brother for the night? Why let him ruin our night right?"

Kassandra seemed to soften. It was tough to tell if it was the weed's time lapsed effects or not, but her agitation was dissipating by the second.

"I mean look around you. We've got plenty of smoke, wine's chilling as we speak. Cable T.V. and a righteous free room with no kids. All on Step Daddy Warbuck's dime."

She began to giggle at the clarity of her husband's obvious observation. Of course, Step Daddy Warbuck's was the secret moniker the couple had dubbed for Kassandra's wealthy stepfather.

"Now why don't you and I forget all about family until the wedding tomorrow and have a little honeymoon of our own, what do you say?" Mick flashed his best boyish, mischievous grin.

"You're right babe. Forget that little psycho, probably got lost on the way here if he even had the balls to walk out the front door."

"I don't know about the front door, but I'll show you the back door in no time flat." Just as the lewd entendre was out his lips, Mick mock wrestled his wife to the bed where the two bursts into bouts of carefree witless bliss until dawn.

Peggy, Damien's closest sister in age felt they were also the closest in terms of bond. It always pained her throughout their childhood years, adolescence and into young adulthood how their tragedy had affected him. Withdrawn, reclusive Damien had few friends and would often choose the sanctity of his own bedroom. Whether it was reading comic books, listening to metal records and just lying on his bed staring at the ceiling, Damien brought all new meaning to the expression introvert. As they grew further apart she always loved him dearly and couldn't possibly fathom what kind of life each of the sisters and he would have led if their father wasn't abruptly stopped that night. The memories inspired many a nightmare waking and otherwise and often sent shudders of revulsion through her core.

Now, thirteen years later awaiting the matrimonial ceremony of their oldest cousin, Peggy toyed idly with her crystal pendant upon the motel room's dresser. Her husband Dale was oblivious. Sure, she loved him with all she was capable of. Somewhere deep inside she felt an undeniable void that he was unable to fulfill. Dale came from a cookie cutter family for lack of better description. His parents ran a hardware store, God fearing, avid church goers. They resided across the rural road from where she and Dale had lived. Although Peggy had admired their sense of values and morals they just seemed a little too one dimensional for her taste. They rarely discussed their emotions, hopes, dreams or fears. Instead they simply went through the motions with Sunday night roast beef dinners and NFL blaring on the widescreen TV. She held not any conscious resentment. After all it was only their genetic makeup. Sometimes however she wished she could reach out to Dale. She needed a confidante. She needed someone to talk about her demons, her father and the unsettling spiritual unbalance she carried around with her twenty-four seven.

Although Seagrave was only a mere thirty-five-minute drive from where she and her husband resided now she really didn't want to come back to the realm of shattered dreams and raped hope. She felt safe in her cookie cutter house and home. As estranged as Damien was she knew in her heart he wanted to be there at the wedding if for no other reason than for closure. Now in his absence she felt gravely deprived of her own closure.

Twiddling and fidgeting with the crystal necklace she'd spin it, almost as a subconscious after thought. Her mind wandered. In between spins she'd sigh in resigned defeat. Hoping her husband would stir from his snore infested slumber to ask her what was wrong. She smiled a bitter sweet smile remembering how Damien had envied her ability to sleep as children when he battled the infernal monster of insomnia.

"How the tables of turned, sweet little brother," she whispered into the musty, pine scented room. Silently she said a prayer for his own well-being wherever he may be. Kissing the crystal, she lied down in the darkness next to her husband and wondered if her brother could sense her state of dread.

CHAPTER EIGHT

The over powering scent of chlorine was enough to steal young Damien's breath away. An all too familiar recollection unraveled before him. As far as the eye could see an Olympic sized pool stretched the horizon. Bobbing and swaying, separation lines of buoys taunted him, threatening to smother any sense of stability and confidence. Beneath him the tiles felt cold and hard not entirely unlike the crowd of pupils donned in their trunks and rainbow of colored one-piece suits.

The adult, conscious Damien could not fabricate as to why this memory would unnerve him so. The scene as he'd recalled was rather insignificant. Ten years old, his class along with a sister school Epsom P.S. was bused in once a week for swim lessons. As far as he knew Mrs. Galligher had scribed a note, signed by his therapist Dr. Rhys that he was to be exempt from participating because of his extreme phobia to water. Strike that as another mark to the forever growing tally that father had never gotten around to doing, teaching his boy how to swim. This little note was his holy grail, avoiding inevitable humiliation at the hands of his classmates for being a baby and not being able to even get in the water let alone a simple doggie paddle or breast stroke.

A churning and relentless iron grip fastened in his lower abdomen. Damien relived every nuance, sensation and stimuli his childhood host had felt. This whole sorted scene was playing out very, very differently from the way he'd remembered it.

The instructor, a drill sergeant in her own right paced the edge of the concrete pool brandishing some sort of torpedo like plastic apparatus. Unrecognizable letters and words spewed out of her gullet that Damien couldn't decipher if he'd tried. Upon his face he'd flushed red. His entire body grew hot, like he was on fire from the inside out, threatening to spontaneously combust at any moment. The pack of jackals around him, not a solitary ally amongst them unleashed a full onslaught of uninhibited, roaring bouts of laughter. Their faces morphed in and out in trippy fashion from feral canine to human and back again. Childhood Damien cringed and flinched. Light eons away his adult cortex grappled for the reason as to why this obscenity was unfolding. He was supposed to be in the next room working on English assignments or reading the latest Hardy Boys novel. Even his casual acquaintances had abandoned him. The one's he traded lunch with or shared the latest Star Wars anecdote with. No Judas reared their ugly heads as well as they cackled on at his indifference. Some pointed, some jeered while others heckled with words for too mature for a ten-year old's mouth. The instructor did damned little to put a halt to the injustice. No. Instead she only seemed to fuel the fire of indignity holding an accusatory finger at him and wavering in tongue that made no sense to him. He expected little to no intervention from his traitor peers. The kids from Epsom were no better as he was still getting over the sting of being ridiculed on the bus ride over from Steve and Kane over his lack of accurate professional wrestling knowledge.

"Come, come now Damien. This is indeed swimming lessons. If you want to learn something, you know you have to get in the water."

A sinking sensation rattled everything to his core. In unity the adolescent scene before him accompanied by the adult passenger in observation cringed in anticipation.

Onward the gallery of gluttonous laughter ensued.

Sitting cross legged, Indian style he gazed up at his supposed authority figure. From his scalp to toes he shivered and shook, praying this humiliation would end with a simple act of opening his eyes. Pinch me, just pinch me and make it all end.

Her towering stature blocked out the sizzling florescent lights of above. Cellulite and varicose veins glistened and bubbled upon her legs. An intimate exploitation, thatch of hair burst free of her one-piece swim suit. A sight far too unknown for any child to have to witness mocked him. Upon her hips her hands resided, clenching, white knuckles brandishing a hatred that no words could describe.

"Damien Galligher!? Do you hear me? Now! Into the water."

With one foul swoop of humiliation she grasped the youth under the arms and tossed him like yesterday's garbage into to shimmering chlorine abyss below.

Frenzied upon impact, the tiny host wailed and flapped his appendages. He grappled for purchase, anything to be spared of this indignant monstrosity. On reflexive instinct his eyes squeezed shut warding off the over whelming chemical fumes. Gasping and spurting against the rippling waves, his tiny mouth let in more water than expunged.

The external sounds around him, the hyena like jeers and militant instructor infused together. Like some sort of demonic, ritualistic chant the sounds forsaken him for being the odd duck. Always on the outside looking in young Damien's peril may very well cost him the breath inside him this time out.

Blackness silhouetted Damien's field of vision. The harder he struggled to breathe the more water came in. The stronger he thrashed the more futile his efforts became. At last he began his inevitable descent to the cement floor below.

"Jesus lady! Do something! Can't you see he can't swim?!"

"That's quite enough out of you, young man. Mr. Kane Barber if you don't want a visit to the principal's office back at school I strongly suggest you mind me!"

Even the unlikely intervention of Damien's nemesis ignited a fresh roar of cheers, whoots and howls from the rest of the children. As the swim teacher turned her back, he saw his opening and plunged into the pool after him.

Kane, no expert swimmer by any stretch of the imagination maneuvered himself in choppy circles. A modified doggy paddle, it appeared, and no one could argue in all likelihood felt like he didn't give his rescue plan a whole lot of thought before delving in. Just when his awkward spastic like strokes would too be his own demise, Kane breathed in deep, contorted his body and submerged into the depths with one powerful stroke.

Bubbles floated and spiraled towards the surface from Damien's mouth. A good sign. He wasn't exactly drowning at first glimpse. But his lungs probably took in much too much water and he blacked out. Kicking and scissoring for all he was worth, Kane plunged deeper narrowing in on his target. He grasped his ordinary adversary Damien first by a shock of rippling hair. As he drifted towards him he hooked his hands under the arms and chopped once again towards the surface.

His own ribcage was on fire, his body's way of sending rapid messages of urgency. Breathe and breathe now. Somehow, he ignored the oxygen deprivation and thrust onwards.

With a climactic eruption he burst through the surface. Gasping and panting, Kane sucked in air. Frothing at the mouth he jerked his head back and forth. The sting of the chlorine left their mark.

Onto the pool's lip the students cluttered and scrambled to get better look at the drama unfolded before them.

Conspicuous by her absence was the instructor. Kane kicked and paddled for all he was worth with his free hand towards the nearest edge. Pure adrenaline must have taken over for he too now was bobbing up and down and inhaling far too much water. Damien was virtual dead weight and far more difficult to manipulate than one may imagine.

At last his head conked audibly against the ledge. Thankfully the collision wasn't enough to prompt his own descent. Steve, another Epsom regular and Kane's best friend clambered to his aid. He clutched the seam of Damien's trunks and hoisted him up and out of the pool. With a wet slap Damien's flesh met the tiled perimeter and Steve discarded him without incident.

Now coughing and sputtering in his own right, Kane placed his hands upon the pool's edge and heaved himself up and over. His chest rose and fell in rapid succession. Teetering on the edge of blacking out Kane steadied himself.

A lightning fast crack silenced the entire class. Again, and again. An aluminum pole dented and disheveled was tossed into the pool.

"Well well, we'll just see how insolence is dealt with around here," the swim instructor returned from God knows where shrieking with a new-found exuberance.

"So, Mr. Kane Barber, you want to defy me and play hero. Why don't you show the rest of the class CPR?"

The rest of the class Epsom, and Damien's alma mater Greenbank P.S. moaned and chimed with Ew's and Aw's.

Kane gripped the bridge of his nose, a gesture ordinarily reserved for someone well beyond his years. He squinted against the sizzling florescent above.

"Lady. You just about let this kid drown. Now I don't particularly like him, but no one deserves that."

"Oh, and what exactly qualifies you to dictate who deserves and doesn't deserve what?"

Kane simply shook his head and turned away from her.

"Don't you turn your back to me young man! See this through! You want to be a hero, we don't need a dummy. The dummy's lying right there. You go on ahead and show the rest of the class how to administer Calibrated Preemptive Response. Go on now." Her eyes bulged out of her head. Each accented syllable reverberated between her teeth. "I suggest you get a move on mister. I'm not entirely sure if your dummy is breathing."

Kane darted his attention to the other boy. His condition momentarily overlooked in all the chaos. Damien was lying still. His skin had taken on a bluish, sickly hue.

"Now you don't want to be responsible for killing this young man do you? It seems as though there are plenty of witnesses here to testify exactly that. I suggest you get moving!" With a left of her left foot she shoved at Kane's back until he virtually sprawled over the incapacitated body of Damien.

"I don't know when or how,' he whispered concealed against the commotion "but I'll kill you for this." Upon his proclamation, Kane lowered himself to Damien's lifeless lips.

CHAPTER NINE

The sounds of crunching gravel were infuriating to Jade. All sense of time and perception seemed to have slowed to a murky, maddening rate. Every little pop and grind sizzled upon her last nerve. She fought with everything she had to refrain from lashing out at the good doctor once again.

"I can't help but sense your unease dear Jade," Dr. Rhys. Once again, he gave her his best reassuring smile as foreign as it felt upon his own lips. No degree of training, vast level of knowledge or experience could fabricate his own unsettling thoughts towards Damien's well-being. To accentuate his assurance, he once again patted her thigh with tenderness. His affection was of fraternal instinct and never one of a creepy nature. Thankfully Jade too regarded his efforts this way. Her mind was far too fixated on what possible fate lied for her elusive boyfriend.

"We're almost there. I promise you once we arrive we'll find our dear boy safe and sound. Worst case scenario he'd slipped into a little melancholy and nostalgia from old memories."

"Well that's where I'd have to beg to differ Doc," Jade hoped her razor-sharp sass stung as much as it was intended. "I think if you were able to identify all the queues earlier today and intervened on a professional level let alone as a friend, none of us would be here right now. Would we?"

He darted his gaze in her direction. Still he found it difficult to meet her eyes.

"I suppose I deserved that. And you're quite right. I feel horribly responsible for Damien and I never should have allowed emotions to get in the way of ethics so many years ago." Dr. Rhys cleared his throat a time or two and seemed to search for composure before carrying on.

"Damien is resilient and will preserve. That I promise you. I'm sure an hour from now we'll all have a good laugh and put this behind us."

Through deep brush and acres of barren fields they followed the narrow gravel road. Past culverts and ravines they ventured onward in the night zeroing in on the infamous Galligher family home.

Clicking off his high beams a little prematurely Dr. Rhys had to plunge onto the brakes to avoid colliding with the back bumper of a car he'd become all too familiar with.

The two shuddered in synchronicity gasping for breath. A collision had appeared inevitable right up until the very last second. Jade's finger tips went bone white from clutching the door's plush handle.

"Who would park their car out the in the middle of nowhere like that?"

A sigh of resignation escaped the good doctor's lips

"Jade. I'm afraid that is my receptionist's car, Caroline."

The two glared at one another sensing the unfathomable.

"You mean..." each reflected at once.

"When your call had been terminated earlier, or she simply could not hear you, it must have been from inside the house. Oh, I pray to God Jade that her battery simply went dead."

Gripping his wheel to the left, he maneuvered the sizable luxury sedan around his devoted assistant's park job. Onward he crept at a snail's pace. His tentative action only managed to heighten Jade's pulse. The pit of her throat had grown arid dry and she wouldn't dare speak now in fear of nothing coming out.

"Yeah you better pray that's all that went dead," Jade muttered beneath her breath. Her stomach tossed and turned rivalling the most crazed of tilt a whirls from any carnival. "Doc, all of the sudden I don't feel so good."

Dr. Rhys flinched then grimaced from the stark white complexion that overcame Jade's ordinarily olive facial hue. Her lips trembled, while her hands shook, grappling for the door's release. Not a moment too soon, Jade projectile spewed all over the wild sweet grass growing in the ditch.

Slamming the Cadillac into gear with more authority than intended, Dr. Rhys burst open from the driver's door and raced around to the other side. He knelt a little reluctantly at first then adapted his best bed side manner voice on reflex.

"Jade, dear. Everything is going to be just fine I promise you. We'll have a quick look around the old house and I'm confident there's a rational explanation for all of this." He produced a bottle of water from seemingly nowhere, handed it to her while caressing her long auburn hair. "Now take your time. Take a few deep breaths and we'll be on our way in no time."

She managed to feign a sarcastic retort and resigned to nodding instead. Sometimes the silver tongue didn't have a golden opportunity. Shuddering once or twice she inhaled deeply then let it all out while envisioning all the negative energy disposed. Her key to all around wellness spawned from a more new age school of thought as opposed to all this psychological mumbo-jumbo. She supposed when questioned about her eclectic beliefs that it had something to do with her Asian roots. It did damned good for her on the most part, well at least until now.

Jade accepted the doctor's hand and slowly began to rise. Midway through, she waved him off.

"Ok, ok Doc. I'm not some sort of damsel in distress. I'm fine." She met his gaze and frowned in indignation. "A little personal space please?"

Silently the doctor backed off and slid a little. His three hundred-dollar loafers nearly found him backward summersaulting into the ditch. Great for the office, impressive even. Brandished for searching unstable former patients in the still of the night in the remote country? Not so much.

For at least the thirteenth-time Jade regretted donning such casual apparel. Her dress left little to the imagination and held absolutely no practical merit to an environment such as this. She blushed furiously catching the doctor steal a glimpse. Reflecting she grappled with the reason why she put on this get up to begin with. Oh yes, Damien's reaction. The way his face lit up upon seeing her at first sight was more precious than anything in the world. For that very reason, coupled with the fact she wanted to give Mrs. Joy Galligher a mild cardiac arrest was the sole reason for her fashion regrets.

The two seemed to come to a nonverbal unity and walked single file along the Cadillac, and gravel shoulder. Dr. Rhys considered putting a consoling arm around the young lady than just as swiftly rejected the gesture. She seemed a little agitated with him now and was harboring resentment and any variety of other issues towards him. He didn't need to provoke any hysterical interaction, not at such a vulnerable threshold. Jade needed his trust as he needed her. He couldn't resist what a fascinating subject she would make for a preliminary session. He could only imagine what sorts of deep and dark things she was repressing behind that varnished, hardened exterior of sarcasm, razor sharp wit and innuendo. Perhaps when this was finally all laid to rest he would recommend couple's therapy.

As the two strode in indifferent silence along the roadside, a murky object came into view. Neither one of them had to voice their collective unease at the prospect. The sea green, rust exterior was familiar enough to Jade and the good doctor needed not a Ph. D. in anything to speculate what it could be.

Jade gasped while smothering her face with each of her hands. Tears began to stream between her fingers. She sobbed in succession over and over realizing the inevitable she did not want to face.

"Dr. Rhys," she wailed while hammering her fists into his chest.

This time he discarded any sense of ethics or trained ordinances and became a human being in the here and now.

"I know Jade. I know. Well that's his car. We know he's here. Now the question is just exactly where?" He held her close and waited for the initial shock to subside.

CHAPTER TEN

G olden rays of sunshine burst through the stained-glass windows of St. Timothy's Church. Fragments born of each the colors of the rainbow splashed the walls and pews within the house of holy. The ceremony would commence in mere moments as the procession filled to an alarming capacity.

The happy couple to be Danny and Elise, could not possibly pray for a better, more fitting day to be bound in eternal matrimony. Outside not a single wisp of white swirled through the sky. The deepest of blue harnessed the most luminescent of sun's inspiring each of the guests to brandish a varying selection of sunglasses to complement each individual formal attire.

Just before the massive staircase leading up to the church Joy Galligher paced back and forth smoking cigarette after cigarette. Donned in a modest but chic turquoise dress, she rocked back and forth upon her heels. On cusp of extinguishing her smoke, she just as swiftly retrieved another and lit it fresh from the sizzling embers of the prior.

Puffing billowing clouds into the sky, she grappled with the unsettling sense of unease that would not depart her thoughts for a single moment. Damien was still nowhere to be found. No one has heard from him and the anxiety and worry swirled within her abdomen, more pushing than the pot of coffee she had consumed at the motel room prior.

The ceremony would begin at any moment. Elise's family was in attendance to full capacity. While Danny's extended and immediate family along with significant others, made for a formidable crowd as well. How she longed to see her boy dressed in his finest tuxedo, walking arm in arm, with each of the guests to ensure their seating for this glorious event. She signed between trembling, dry and chapped lips resisting the need to cry. There had to be more to this whole scenario, there simply had to be. Her boy could be elusive at times, but nothing like this. Now even his questionable choices in a romantic partner such as Jade, has gone off the radar as well. Just what in the hell was going on here? Had they walked into the Bermuda Triangle of family reunions? Was this a living and breathing episode of the Twilight Zone? She made a very committed pact to herself, that once she laid eyes upon her only son she would not even scold or be angry with him, she must hug him tight and assure him everything would be just fine. Maybe he would still make the reception afterwards. After all, what was it that the youth of today had lived by? Party like there is no tomorrow, or something like that. She highly doubted the boy would pass up on an opportunity to blow off a little steam with some liquid fun. She just hoped with everything that she had, that his sisters would keep their cool and refrain from reigniting any sibling rivalries. How tacky would a fight at such a beautiful event like her nephew's wedding be? She shuddered at the thought of her children ruining such an affair. With such a wide myriad of personalities the possibility and concern were a most valid one.

Inside Peggy and Dale were already seated. The summer heat was not a deterrent in each of the couple's wardrobe selections. Dale looked most distinguished in his three-piece suit. Earlier, Peggy had straightened his tie for him at their motel room and mused that it was a shame that it took someone to either wed or expire for their family to get together like this. She made a silent promise to herself that she would make more of an effort to plan, invite and coordinate more family outings. In her sundress she beamed with pride knowing if anyone in this dysfunctional debacle was capable of such things it would be her. Absent mindedly, she twirled the crystal necklace laced around her neck, twirling it ever more between her thumb and forefinger. She had not the clearest conception of its magnitude as rays of white light danced against the walls off the alter, this way and that.

Kaitlin fussed with her skirt and blouse seated in one of the back rows of pews. The scent of polish and lacquer was strong but not entirely unpleasant. With her free hand she grasped her husband's palm, Cam. She was very proud of their love and cared not what the rest of the family regarded him as. The important thing was he was there with her now. He would talk some sense later after the ceremony regarding Damien. His cerebral logic always managed to balance her. She smiled awaiting the organ music to chime.

Kassandra and Mick sat around mid-point within the pews. Their seating was provided with little protest from a substitute usher. To herself she smacked her lips in recollection that this reception on the horizon better not be all about Damien or lack thereof. The little snot didn't deserve all the limelight and she vowed not to have his reclusive nature reign on their parade. She drummed her fingers rapidly, picking up nervous tempo upon one of the bibles. Snarking aloud, she wondered how Iron Butterfly's In la Gada Davida would sound in a place like this.

Outside, Joy on her own, with no Leonard anywhere in sight. Where was that old coot anyway? She had almost decided to retreat herself to settle her restless mind and spirit and visit the old homestead. If she didn't find her boy surely, she would get some closure herself. Although she did not dwell on the memories of her horrible relationship it was in ways a part of her, a battle scar that could never be removed.

Perhaps a divine intervention, a blue and black sedan pulled up in the final moments of Joy's revelation. The door swooshed open and Julia stood with the bride to be. The glasses upon her wrinkled profile just about slid off when she spotted her sister distraught and disheveled.

"Joy for heaven's sake what on earth are you doing out here? We're just about to begin."

In silence Joy wrapped her arms around her older sister's shoulders. Softly she wept. Julia returned the embrace and feigned the temptation to sigh in utter frustration. It seemed this side of the family did their best to ruin just about any event.

"What is it sister? Surely it cannot be that bad. Is it Damien?"

Sobbing, Joy eventually pulled back from Julia. Her bleary eyes had somehow managed to age her ten years over night. She shook her head in resignation.

"It is not exactly that, well certainly a big part of it."

"Well can't this wait? As you can see, I am about to become a mother in law here. We can work this all out right afterwards."

Joy gazed down at the ground, shoulders slumped, head hung in shame and defeat.

"It's not just that dear Julia. I can't shake this utter sense of doom and dread. Something just plain awful is about to happen. You know how I get these gut feelings."

"Oh, for heaven's sake." She snapped her fingers and motioned someone to lead the bride to be, Elise up the stairs. "Ok, let me set your mind at ease, Joy. We are in Port Perry, in perspective, nowhere really all that near Seagrave. We are about to walk into a church, a holy good to green's earth house of the lord. Everything will be fine. I swear on our mother's grave everything is going to be just fine."

"Then why is it I cannot shake the vision of these three crosses bathed in blood standing in the church before us? There is death and destruction in our wait Julia." She shivered nearly convulsing from head to toe.

Julia cackled beneath the ice blue sky. Her laughter sounded maniacal, creepy to her sister. This did precious little to ease her nerves.

"For the love of God Joy, this is a church. A Catholic Church at that. Of course, there are crosses. Oh goodness there may even be some images of Jesus and oh my maybe even some holy water and roseries."

"You're just making me sound like a dummy now."

Julia embraced her once again.

"Trust me, everything is going to be just fine." She grabbed her sister's hand and lead her up the long staircase. She grappled with her own declaration, wishing she could believe it knowing full well she did indeed have her own cross to bear.

CHAPTER ELEVEN

Dr. Rhys flinched from the mutual revelation he and Jade had mere moments ago. His chest felt bruised and battered from her onslaught of fists. All things considered he really couldn't blame her reactions. They had to get to the bottom of this and fast. Perhaps when this was all over and done with the good doctor would seek out council for himself. This just got more disturbing around every twist and turn.

"Jade maybe it is best if we give the grounds a once over before checking the house." The expression upon her face was one of utter defeat the glimmer of hope slowing swirling down a drain. "We don't want to act out of haste and put ourselves in danger in the decrepit old home if he is just outside somewhere reflecting."

She sighed, a heavy, burdensome exhale into the late summer night. The crickets in the surrounding underbrush had begun their evening sonnets. Ordinarily a tune most serene, all it managed to do was gyrate upon her nerves.

"A little more action and a whole lot less words doctor." She shook her head in disbelief. "As soon as we find Damien and get the hell out of here, the better."

Together they walked up the short driveway, void of any kind of landscape manicure or attention in over a decade. Cracks along the concrete slabs and formidable potholes from natural erosion, encompassed each of their steps. Dr. Rhys produced a flashlight seemingly out of his sleeve. Tentatively, ever so cautiously, the two walked closer to the infamous home.

A garter snake slithered and writhed between blades of timothy. Jade jumped backwards and nearly leapt off the ground into Dr. Rhys's arms. In retaliation he stumbled backwards, caught off guard. The two managed to smile an awkward exchange before submitting to a hysterical bout of laughter.

"If that is the most notorious we have to encounter for the rest of the night then I think we are in pretty fine shape."

"Yeah, well regardless Doc, I think after all this is said and done you best reserve some extended time on your couch for me."

Dr. Rhys patted her on the shoulder affectionately, a display that everything would be fine.

Each step along the driveway brought them closer and closer to the front door. Just off side in their peripheral, they spotted the old decayed tire swing. Although the still of the night delivered no breeze, Jade could not help but notice the rotted rope still swung ever so slightly. She deduced the observation as her mind playing tricks on her.

Not far beyond the tire swing, was an old rusted out car, barely visible through the long grass. It was nothing shy of a miracle there was anything left to it at all. As Dr. Rhys shined his flashlight over the hood he wondered if the wreckage had any kind of chassis at all beneath the over growth.

Silently, the two decided they had seen enough of the outdoors and crept ever so gradually towards the front door. It took just a few seconds to realize, indeed the entrance has been compromised and upon closer investigation not that long ago.

Is it possible that each Caroline and Damien had made it into this condemned structure that appeared capable of collapsing at any given moment? As though Jade and Dr. Rhys shared the same epiphany they shuddered in unison. A brief glance is all it had took to crouch down and wriggle through the disheveled boards into the great unknown.

CHAPTER TWELVE

Deep within the confines, in the bowels of the infamous Galligher home, Damien sat in an agonized heap. Rocking back and forth, he hung his head in despair. Idly, he rolled the swim participant pendant between his fingers. It all but disintegrated.

He remembered not this swim lesson unfolding anything remotely like this. To the best of his recollection, it was traumatizing but he made it through and even his mother was proud of him for persevering and learning the doggie paddle on his first day. He had previously considered it an achievement, milestone to bask in his parent's approval. Now it was all tarnished, violated. It appears his monster of a father was showing him the reality of all his upbringing in his absence. How could he be so dreadfully wrong? So brainwashed. It made perfect sense why his very spirit was in constant state of unease. Now as the truth was being unveiled, what possible kind of reality could behold?

Between quivering thighs, he clutched at the scrapbook's edges. In the dank and condemned basement of the Galligher home, creepy crawlies twisted this way and that, their constant depraved

dance of unworldly celebration. Damien was oblivious to such festivities. They seemed to blend in every bit as much as any other home's wallpaper or decorative keepsakes.

In a weathered, dusty envelope that was stapled to the page, Damien resided his touch. A pulse surged through his fingers. Something most ominous awaited. Yet what could possibly be more brooding, more visceral than the other memories? Damien was just about to drop the curtain on precisely that notion.

Inside was a crumpled-up Valentine. One fashioned with more personal attention than of commercial purchase. A red heart was crudely cut from construction paper and glued on with one of those sophomoric glue sticks upon a white doily. A cupid's arrow was drawn in a crooked line directly through. Contemporary Damien had speculated that his younger version must have had the shakiest of hands putting together such a vulnerable contraption. In floral yet wiggly script the handmade card simply read: "To Shelly, Be Mine."

A lurching sensation gripped the very core of his abdomen. How he had managed to suppress this terrible memory was beyond him. Then again with extensive therapy from the good Doctor Rhys, not to mention his mother's hokus pokus, it was no wonder his memories were so distorted.

Through bleary, saturated eyes he peered across the room. The adjacent wall suddenly rippled and swirled in spiral type fashion. Wisps of white smoke swirled from the basement up then cleared just as quickly again. As though hypnotized, he discarded the scrapbook in a heap, tumbling askew onto the floor. He stood, albeit on shaky legs, his consciousness was impervious to his battered body. As though succumbed to rigor mortis, his strides towards the wall were mechanical, lumbering. He missed not a heartbeat transfixed on the rapidly swirling target. Pausing ever so briefly, Damien crossed the threshold with crumpled up Valentine within his grasp.

CHAPTER THIRTEEN

Through the deterioration, destruction and debris Jade and the good doctor managed to crawl through. Silently a plan came together. Perpetually devoted psychiatrist would go first. It seemed more practical. Should anything go awry, chivalry would prevail. The very notion Jade was wearing a skirt left little to the imagination seemed incentive enough.

Into the visceral vestibule they rose. The energy emitted from each of their nerves became a prominent entity unto itself. Dr. Rhys bothered not to even dust off his casual, yet expensive sport jacket. Jade feigned emotional turmoil.

An undeniable odorous blend of rot, decay and death clung defiantly in the air. Over a rusted barbeque hood Dr. Rhys almost fumbled. In other circumstances Jade would have burst into care-free laughter.

The good doctor shot his new found companion an expression of progressive fortitude. Onward they must go. Do or die. It was now or never.

Jade trembled with each step. Dr. Rhys exhaled grappling with composure. Dread accompanied the stifling stench. Their combined pulses would rival any percussion sections. A cold sweat began to permeate Dr. Rhys's brow. Jade hugged her arms, shivering on verge of convulsing.

Something was amiss in the kitchen. To Damien's sweetheart it was just a hunch. To the doctor however, who on many occasions embarked upon an afternoon delight with mother Galligher the scene was imprinted within his grey matter. Even to him something was foreboding, ethereal.

The pinnacle of illusions, the kitchen was still in relative tact. For an abandoned home, little seemed out of place or out of the ordinary.

The hellacious pit that swallowed Damien mere hours ago was now non-existent. Any trace of his descent had all but vanished.

Around the infamous room, cupboards still were intact. Constant devotion to the walls were a morbid contrast to the emotional dynamic of The Galligher family. Counters and grout were evidently more reliable than the head of the household ever was.

Plumes of dust and mold spores swirled into the still of the night. Utilizing immense caution, the tandem approached the core of the room. Eerie silence had to be a ghastly prelude.

Almost on anxious cue, the temperature plummeted. Should a mercury thermometer be present it would not only crash to the base, it's very stem would freeze solid then shatter. Frost and miniature icicles formed and dangled along the doctor's bushy eyebrows and beard. Jade coughed violently. Her puffs of vapor expanded into clouds.

They held one another steadfast. Attempting to rationalize the scene before them, either refused to take a step further. Somehow the room went darker. An unseen blanket eclipsed the only source of light from the moon outside the grimy window.

A tiny sphere appeared in the distance. Whirling towards the duo, its brightness glowed. Orange and red hues burst into life. Its shine lit up the room. It hovered just inches from their faces. Then another appeared and then another. Dipping and swaying dozens of orbs all but erupted the room in red.

In the faint distance a cry beckoned. Each of the orbs hummed and vibrated in chaotic frequency. the cries intensified. Then within a heartbeat the orbs ceased. Frozen.

One by one the mystic spheres exploded. Gallons of crimson blood splashed everything within vicinity. From head to toe each Jade and Dr. Rhys were drenched. She shrieked into the mayhem.

A banshee like wail hushed her scream. The sound of a thousand talons upon unfinished steel ricocheted off the walls. Through the pale moonlight a skeletal form appeared void of virtually any sustenance save for its hair and clumps of dangling skin.

A footstep behind stood the master to the marionette. Dr. Rhys gasped recognizing the coiffed hairstyle of his receptionist anywhere. Through her punctured skull an unseen hand manipulated her jaw.

"At last. The good doctor is in. Oh, and look what we have here! He's delivered the harlot among harlots as well."

CHAPTER FOURTEEN

"You may now kiss the bride," Father O'Malley bellowed in his baritone voice. He'd likely recited the very same verbatim hundreds of times This time seemed unique

In synchronized unity, each sides of the procession, rose in a standing ovation. The crowd's clapter and cheers was near deafening. Danny's side was infectious with enthusiasm, while Elise's matched cheer for cheer.

Father O'Malley regarded the impressive turn out. Not entirely impervious to sin, a bitter taste slickened his tongue. How we wished such a crowd would attend his sermon. He knew the world would be a better place.

Wearing two hats, pulling double duty, the devoted man of God was also the appointed master of ceremony. The reception with dinner and other wedded bliss rituals was slated to take place at the Sun Dial motel and convention hall. Many of the guests had rooms already. A certain irony could not be denied as the locale had a tawdry reputation. O'Malley's very presence would surely stick out like a sore thumb.

"If everyone would care to meet out in the side courtyard, the wedding party will assemble for some photograph opportunities." O'Malley's syrupy tone chimed into the guests. "Once again, I give you Mr. and Mrs. Daniel Lawless."

Confetti was thrown. Hearty claps ensued. Eager extended family could not wait to get to the open bar.

Beatrice Redgrave, devote Catholic and organist tickled the ivories. Pounding the keys for matrimonial unity prompted the guests to clap even louder. For the first moment as man and wife, Danny and Elise clasped hand in hand, descended from the alter.

A red rivulet splashed and spread into frantic abstract upon Father O'Malley's bible in hand. Another. Then another. Oblivious at first, as he was watching the happy couple ascend the aisle, he flinched, feeling the wetness upon the back of his hand. Elise's lace and silken gown swept back and forth along the plush runway.

Stealing a glance towards the cathedral's ceiling, another splatter exploded onto the lens of O'Malley's glasses. On instinct he closed his eye. Primal reflex. The vision to behold from his remaining eye threatened to challenge his entire belief system.

The elegant and masterfully crafted ivory statue of Mary was crying tears of blood, profusely. Not just an illusionary or metaphorical, solitary tear. No. The mother of Jesus unleashed a stream of blood.

O'Malley grasped his cross within his hand. The necklace keepsake grew white hot. Branding into his flesh, he screamed into the church's rafters. He darted his gaze to Beatrice, the organist who was frantically attempting to seek salvation in his gaze as well.

Her fingers had adapted a life of their own. The tempo slowed dramatically, while she regarded her foreign hands in disbelief. Through the brass pipes, the universal funeral march of dum-da-dum rattled the stain glass windows.

Guests, family and the happy couple seized in their tracks. Clutching their hands over their ears, everyone fought against the audio onslaught. Just as swiftly and obscure as it came on, the music and madness came to a halt.

Beatrice gasped for breath, her eyes on verge of bursting through their sockets. Father O'Malley clutched his chest, his seared palm sizzled and steamed on.

The Gallighers, Joy, Kaitlin, Kassandra and Peggy along with their respective spouses clambered through the melee to find comfort in one another. Remaining guests in attendance wandered in utter confusion, disoriented. The blast of music all but pulverized everyone's equilibrium.

An eerie silence fell upon the church.

Just as swiftly as it has ceased, the carnage resumed.

Beatrice shrilled as her bony appendages pounded on the organ, on verge of snapping each in two. Defenseless and helpless, she plunged faster and faster until the church's air was filled with lunacy type carnival notes. Her eyes swelled, popped from their sockets as black grime streamed down her weathered cheeks.

An all out riot ensued, as guests stormed towards the oak doors. Razor laced chains fell from the ceiling, slashing countless faces, scalps and tore formal attire of all varieties to shreds. Screams consumed the air.

A massive oak cross fell from above, spearing diagonally across the doors. No one could enter, no one could leave.

An ominous fog seeped through the vents, descending upon the church's floor. Even St. Timothy himself had not a prayer in hell.

CHAPTER FIFTEEN

Each of Damien's strolls down memory lane seemed to have a different component to each. Sure, there was always the element of watching as a third party. Yet each seemed to have a different mystical flavor to the next.

Now as he had stepped through the rippling porthole, with crumpled up home made Valentine card in hand he pondered what this could possibly be about. The memory as vague as it was, was a pleasant one. He had given his friend Shelly the card and she loved it so much they became smitten, his very first crush morphed into his very first girlfriend what could possibly go awry in this recall?

Through the porthole Damien's adult host stood. He was on the opposite side of a massive chalkboard, sort of like a two-way mirror you would see in any of those cop television shows. The classroom before him was more of an auditorium. What was the word he was looking for? Oh, that's right. A core. Three classrooms in his grade eight class had been formed in a V-shape. One class was in the center while an additional two others had branched off. Thirty kids sat in each class for a combined ninety students. Of course, Damien's class was in the middle of it all. This class was History with Mr. Hewitt, if Damien recalled correctly. It was Valentine's Day and the instructor was going to give a lesson on Al Capone and the St. Valentine's Massacre. This seemed right up even young Damien's alley. Adult Damien looked on through the chalkboard towards the class. He spotted his fourteen-year-old version instantly. He sat next to David McIntosh, his newest friend. Shelly sat directly in front of him.

David and Damien were the unlikeliest of friends but seemed to hit it off. Of completely different cliques and groups, David was in the A- crowd. Not exactly a football player or jock but still popular among everyone. Shelly was in the same group. Although she wasn't a cheerleader or trendy like some of the other snotty prep girls Damien despised, she was well liked by most everyone.

Damien was previously in with the metal heads or headbangers if you prefer. Sort of outcasts to some, losers to others. Wearing rock t-shirts and ripped up jeans, studded jewelry and growing their hair long. Some of them even smoked! Their rebellious nature was hated by each social group in school. Damien began to drift from his comrades in exchange for acceptance and adulation. He changed his look a little bit much to David and Shelly's encouragement. He couldn't bear to cut off his shoulder length locks though.

Adolescent Damien was gazing down at the card and contemplating the courage to give it to his crush. Shelly was something else. Just one of the guys. She liked video games and bike riding even sat with Damien in the bleachers for the school's first homecoming football game. She gave him her phone number and with mother Joy's permission they talked for fifteen minutes after their homework was done. She would often say, "Damien why do you hang out with all those losers like Steve and Kane anyway? They are just going to hold you back. Don't you know that?"

Damien felt torn. His best friends were always there for him when he needed them. Why couldn't they all be accepted? He made a conscious decision to try to spend time with both and convince how awesome they were. So far it had failed miserably.

"Class, the overhead projector seems to have blown a lightbulb. I will have to run down to the AV room for another. In the meantime, any volunteers to write your homework answers from page 57 on the board?"

Some eager beavers, or nerds if you prefer, shot up their arms and groaned in agony to be picked. Most of the remaining teen demographic looked down or away, silently praying not to be picked. Damien was one of them. Oh, how he hated doing anything in front of large groups of people. The very thought of talking or doing anything in front of more than a couple people rendered him paralyzed.

"Oh good. Mr. Galligher, why don't you come up and prepare your answer while I collect the projector bulb. I won't be long."

Wait. What?

"But Mr. Hewitt-I, I, I."

"There is no I or U in team Damien, go on now. Keep the class engaged while I get back."

Mr. Hewitt was a sports nut. He coached practically all the extra circular leagues as well as taught physical education. Damien bet he broke the bulb on purpose, so he could go out and bet on the latest track and field race.

"Go on now. You don't need another trip to the principal's office now do you?"

Slumping his shoulders and nearly sliding right beneath his desk Damien muttered, "No sir."

His heart jack hammered within his chest. Upon his palms virtual geysers of sweat streamed. His hands began to stain the pink background of his gift for Shelly. His throat grew dry while his tongue stuck to the roof of his mouth. Shaking violently, he was afraid to stand.

David clapped him on the back. A gesture of a true friend would merit. Damien flinched not accustomed to such brotherhood.

"Come on man. Piece of cake. Don't let these losers get to you."

Damien nodded, the color draining from his cheeks. He supposed it was do or die time. It would make an ideal opportunity to drop his gift on Shelly's desk discretely.

Clutching each sides of the desk, veins upon his forearms bulged out like slithering snakes about to strike. His knuckles turned bone white while trembling all the while. He stood, cleared his throat. The cruel act of puberty made it sound more like a fog horn. The kids laughed. Thankfully only his immediate peers thought he was hysterical. He wasn't sure if he would die or not from the ridicule of almost one hundred students.

Shaking so badly, he just about dropped the card from between his fingers. He exhaled and cracked his neck. Instantly he felt a little better, taking his first step to the gallows of pubescence. Before he could take a second stride, Laird Barron stuck out his foot. Damien's shin collided simultaneously sending him sprawling to the floor while his arms wound around and around like a malfunctioned windmill. He just about knocked his front teeth out on the floor.

A fresh bout of cackling laughter burst into the room. This time the adjoining classrooms joined in on the fray. Adult Damien inside the chalkboard could barely continue to watch. What a travesty.

The card went swaying back and forth onto the floor. It had not a nanosecond to rest before Laird snatched it up in his hand. Damien bolted around still half lying on the floor in utter terror.

"What a second, what's this queerbait?"

"Give it back Laird. That's not yours." Damien bellowed a little louder than intended. He flinched from his own raucous outburst.

"Huh? Yeah, you're right. It ain't mine. It says, to Shelly. Hey everyone!" Laird shouted out to the remaining entire grade eight student body.

"Laird please,' an almost whisper. "Please for the love of God, don't."

"Oh God isn't here queerbait. And he wouldn't touch a piece of garbage like you if he was." He yanked up the elegant construction paper and lace and held it high on his tip toes. Laird wasn't taking any chances. Exercising his athletic abilities, he pivoted just like they do in practice in scrimmage drills. Damien had no hopes of retrieving his gift.

"Hey everyone!" He bellowed even louder to the core. "Little baby Damien Gayyy-ligher wants Shelly to Be Mine!" He started cackling like a hyena. Damien's face flushed crimson red. The rushing blood to his complexion could very well had exploded at that moment. His scalp grew hot and he thought he could cry at any given moment. From beyond the chalkboard current Damien could watch no more.

The class roared in laughter on and on. Spit balls were pro-jectile launched in Damien's direction. Someone threw an apple another a half rotten orange. He couldn't conjure the courage to even glance in Shelly's direction. He didn't have to. She stood up and walked over to him, ever so gracefully. Her long hair swayed back and forth. Her strides, the stuff that Amazons are born with. She'd give Laird a piece of her mind alright. She'd shut up this flock of sheep all at the same time. Was there any wonder why this kid was so smitten?

She stood before Damien, eye to eye with the most tender of bashful smiles creeping up on her lips.

"You,' she stammered ever so slightly. "You...don't actually think I like you. Do you?" She joined in on the laughter with everyone else. Hers was just as loud as everyone else's combined. Smacking her side repeatedly. "I mean come on, loser. Who could ever like a gross dweeb like you? Get a haircut gay boy."

David stood at this moment and rushed over to where the two stood. Laird was laughing so hard by now he was doubled right over.

Damien knew he could count on David. Bro's always stick together. Especially in scenarios like this.

"Dude, relax man,' he clapped Damien on the shoulder making him relax ever so slightly for just a moment. Maybe this was some bizarre initiation or something? The popular kids can be cruel after all.

"Maybe you just need to change your tampon or something?" He turned on one foot at the same time getting directly behind Damien. "You freakin faggot." To enunciate the point, he clutched the waistband of his briefs and reefed for all his might.

Damien spun around completely perplexed. What a God-awful betrayal! The whole class laughed on harder and harder. His ears rung as though he were at a concert right in front of the speakers.

Spinning around to confront who he thought was his new best friend, his gangly legs caught David's shoe was well. Laird pounced into action seeing perfect opportunity to pants the hapless Damien right to the ankles.

Everyone pointed, laughed, clapped and cheered. For some reason, fate's cruel design had prompted Damien to don his Batman fruit of a looms this morning. The bat symbol brandished his narrow buttocks, now divided with a vicious wedgie.

Shelly took opportunity to unleash her sentiments. "Oh, be still my beating heart caped crusader. Oh wait. Maybe you fancy Robin instead, you little creep."

This prompted the class to laugh longer, harder without relent. Damien jumped to his feet and yanked his cords back up. Hiding his head in shame, utter humiliation, he now knew why he never cut his hair. So, he could conceal his complete and absolute heart break. He tore off out of the class, tears streaming down his smoldering cheeks.

How could he ever go back there again? He slammed the swinging door to the washroom and bent over with hands on his knees, gasping for air.

Up towards the stalls he heard a familiar voice, irritated but somehow detached and calming.

"What are you doing in here man?"

Damien looked Kane straight in the eye and had no idea what to say.

———+·+———

"You've got some nerve thinking you can just crawl back to the rejects after those, those preps drop you like yesterday's garbage." Kane's complexion became red hot, even over his landscape of freckles. "What were you thinking anyway?" With bulged out eyes and animated hands he regarded Damien.

He had taken the last couple of minutes to relive the horrible degradation that unfolded mere moments ago.

"I mean just look at you. Beige corduroys, loafers. You're wearing a god damn pink polo shirt Damien! Who the hell are you?"

For the second time in less than a half hour, Damien hung his head in shame.

"I was always still your friend you know. I mean I wanted them to accept all of us. Aren't you tired of always being on the outside looking in?"

Kane shook his head in disdain. To accentuate his point, he punched the cubicle door. A small yet prominent indentation provided evidence of his hostility.

"I don't give a shit what those preppies think of us. They can all drop dead as far as I'm concerned."

Damien didn't know if he should reach out in a token of comfort or stand his ground.

"And this was all over a chick, Shelly? That bitch."

He chuckled to himself. The utterance was one of pure mockery and void of any humor. Kane began to pace the bathroom floor.

"Yeah well, I guess she showed her true colors, didn't she?" Damien grappled with feigning from a fresh bout of tears. "Kane, what are you doing in here anyway?"

Distracted in deep thought, his shoulders visibly tensed. He wasn't sure if his old friend could be trusted let alone confide in him. It seemed betrayal was the entrée of the day. Cafeteria or not, a dish served with a cold, bitter aftertaste.

"We had to put my dog down last night."

"Kane, I- "

"Save it lover boy. I don't want or need your pity."

Damien stood agape fully lost as to how to react.

"Yeah those jerks in shop class found out about it. Mark and Kyle and have been making whimpering and barking noises all morning. I was going to kill those fuckers. Mr. Preston sent me to the office. Screw that buzzard. I came in here instead."

"Look Damien, you're on your own bro. I don't need any little shit's acceptance or phoney friendship or anything." Kane now trembled in utter fury.

"Kane, man. I'm sorry. Let me make it up to you."

"Yeah, you really want to make it up to me." With eerie swift precision, lightning fast speed, Kane produced a switch blade from his jeans pocket. In a flick of the wrist the shiny blade twinkled beneath the washroom's florescent lights.

Damien retreated a step back or two. He was just about to hold up his hands to avoid anything drastic. No one needed this to escalate to this degree.

"Relax fucker." He laughed a maniacal laugh, unfiltered and harsh with vengeance.

With his free hand he held it up at shoulder height with theatrical flair. In an agonizing slow arc, he sliced across his palm. In seconds a bead of crimson formed and drizzled down his wrist. Discarding the knife into his cut hand he grasped Damien's forearm with the other.

Pulling him with alarming strength, he slashed across Damien's palm as well. Perplexed Damien looked on in bewilderment. He glared at his on and off again friend, unsure of how to react.

In a thunderous clap he clutched Damien's bleeding palm in his own reddened clutches. "You want to get these assholes?"

Damien nodded ever so vigorously, saying not a word.

"Then we'll make them sorry they ever laid eyes on the likes of us." Then just like that Kane and Damien forged a bond, a pact in the bloodiest of unholy brotherhoods.

CHAPTER SIXTEEN

"Dr. Rhys, just what in the hell is going on?" Jade croaked from her chapped, ice crusted lips. "If you have some sort of brilliant plan, now would be about the time to use it."

The doctor looked on in utter bewilderment and awe. Grasping Jade's shoulders, he all about threw her behind him, creating an impromptu barrier between her and the horror before them. On shaky ground he stood but defiantly nonetheless.

From beyond the darkened recesses of doom, despair and kitchen Father Galligher stepped. A toxic cocktail of sweat, blood, translucent strips of flesh, veins and glistening, pulsating muscle shimmered from frame. His eyes, crystal ocean blue, returned glimmering with a stare fit for damnation towards them.

"Ah, ah how endearing dear doctor. A prescription for chivalry,' he walked languidly, punishingly cerebral each stride threatened to squeeze the life out of each Jade and Dr. Rhys's racing hearts. With skeleton puppet still in hand, he drifted towards his adversaries. "But alas I am afraid this particular prescription ladies and gentlemen has no refills." To accentuate his point, he tossed Caroline's cadaver with alarming force, sending her carved out bones directly into their last stand.

A fresh bout of hysterical screams emitted from Jade. She was dangerously close to passing out. Right on her feet, as God as her witness she could not faint. She would never see the light of her life Damien, or the light of day tomorrow. Into her palm she dug her remaining long finger nail as hard as she could, trying to revitalize her presence.

Dr. Rhys grappled with the innate need to evacuate any digestion from his system. He stood above his fallen secretary, his friend, his confidante now deduced to a pile of bones and rubble. Dizziness began to now taunt him as well. His mind scrambled for any shred of rationality.

"What's the matter dear Dr. Rhys? Doesn't your secretary give you a boner anymore?"

This proclamation dropped the room's temperature an additional ten degrees. The demonic host of Bill Galligher laughed into the air. His cackles cracked the home's drywall sending clouds of dust into the air while debris spiraled to the floor.

Composing himself with a deep inhale, the demon unleashed green clouds of breath. Each step he took towards the tandem, they were further petrified in utter terror. Demise seemed to be the only fate for the two.

"Oh, and how can I forget the harlots of harlots, dear Jade. Such a silver tongue, this one." He placed a bony, blood streaked finger upon her cheek and caressed. Jade cringed, bolting back in revulsion. "My dear boy Damien chose you well. Your servitude in hell will reign for eternity." Then as an afterthought, he descended his gentle yet hideous touch to her lower abdomen. Under ordinary circumstances almost an enticing whisper, "Too bad about your unborn fetal son. But not to fear, not a life in vain. His sole destiny will serve as an entrée before our disciples of the Dark Messiah." Bill Galligher licked non-existent lips. "And a most tasty morsel at that."

Gliding away from Jade and back around to the good doctor, he took his time, reveling in their combined unease, drinking in their collective dread. Jade quivered and convulsed, she shouldered Dr. Rhys again and again begging him to act. Best he could retort was a subtle nod. His gaze said otherwise. Any shred of hope was virtually slaughtered before them, much like a prelude of destruction.

"And the good doctor, ah yes. You're such a miracle worker, you've done a real bang up job with my family in my absence haven't you Doc?"

Rhys gagged and wretched. The odor that enslaved him was more revolting than a sea of rotted corpses.

"Not so quick to the diagnosis, now are we?"

His reaction was enough to falter the demon's step even just for a fraction of a second.

"If it wasn't for you and your wretched excuse of a life, your family would have no need for me. They'll never be the same no thanks to you. You got everything you deserved and have coming to you." Rhys screamed in a final attempt to thwart the demon's confidence.

A guttural roar swirled within the inner depths of Bill Galligher. An ear shattering belch unleashed, sending not only the hair upon the doctor and Jade's head billowing backwards but their skin upon their faces rippled and danced as though sky diving, plummeting through the clouds to the earth below.

"Ah, so we agree on one thing at last dear doctor," he resigned once again to an almost hypnotic whisper. "You're quite right. The Galligers will never be the same again. Now your antics bore me, I'm afraid." The demon yawned ever so theatrically. Beneath them, the floor boards trembled, threatening to give away any moment. "The results are in doctor. It looks like the prognosis is terminal."

With dizzying precision, unseen hands split the flesh on Dr. Rhys's forehead from scalp to throat. An audible, wet suction sound ignited, as the flesh tore back and flopped to the floor. Not entirely unlike a Californian earthquake, the psychiatrist's skull cracked and split open. In rapid, frenzied breath stealing ease, the demon extracted his brain from behind, devouring half its girth in one bite. Jade screamed on verge of utter and submissive madness. The devil spawn looked her directly in the eyes and offered, "A little nutty but ever so sinfully delicious."

Mere feet away, beneath them Damien catapulted back through the oceanic porthole like wave in the wall. Swiping globs of thick gelatin from his eyes, he gasped for air. From his fallen heap he erupted into action. He knew not how, but felt deep inside somewhere, somehow, he was desperately needed.

CHAPTER SEVENTEEN

Through the bowels of depravity Damien ventured. The mystical scrapbook rendered unchartered for, so many years once again was abandoned. Its pages rippled and pulsed in the piles of dust, decay and despair. All that remained were memories, altered or otherwise. The photos within eclipsed reality and the yellow weathered pages that housed them. Knick knicks and scrim shaw fit strictly for only the most sentimental of fools, faded away into oblivion. The participant pendant and talisman of rejection in the valentine singed into ashes and blew, morphed into the gentle breeze within the basement. All evidence of the boyhood unknown had crumbled to a fine powder gone with barely a trace as though they'd never existed. Along the rugged ceiling, two by fours rotted and swelled on verge of splintering into a haphazard trestle. The duct work configured above, long ago lost its purpose, rusted out raining clouds of coppery debris onto any unforeseen traveler. The House of Anguish saw few guests and accommodated even less visitors. Cobwebs draped around each corner, their creepy drapery of death's décor clung precariously.

Undeniable globs of gelatin still clung to Damien, threatening to intervene with each of his extremities making this path to righteousness, his walk to epiphany even more bombarded with convolution. His sense of unease need not be one of a paranormal or psychic nature. Somehow, deep within his marrow he knew something was awry. Something threatened to exhume every fiber of evil that lurked beneath the foundation. Damien was drawn to very nexus of what had transpired at that very moment. He had to act. The consequences may very well be catastrophic.

From the outside looking in, an unbiased observer would be mystified just at how aligned Damien was with his demonic father one level above and his horrified girlfriend Jade, immobilized with the scene and her sanity unwound before her.

Within the kitchen, each of the walls morphed into a life of their own. As the demon continued to devour every pore of Dr. Rhys, his soul consumed, replenishing the decayed flesh of his host, Jade was slapped with the cold hard reality, an instinctual need to flee.

As she attempted to run, her feet held steadfast. Each motion compounded her confinement. It was as though the surface beneath her transformed to a pit of quicksand. Every step she sunk deeper, every reaction excelled her descent into madness. Choreographed in a lewd skin crawling fashion, each of the kitchen walls cracked and ripped open wide. Tentacles of varying sizes, girths, textures and scales slithered free from the inner recesses of damnation. The worm like entities blindly slithered this way and that, each as foreign to the next as the one before. Only one variable remained a collective common. They squirmed and wriggled towards the center of the room where Jade had struggled to leave the scene. Galligher's gluttony on Dr. Rhys intensified, Femurs and clavicles snapped and crunched beneath his onslaught of appetites.

The conquering worms seemed to sense their demonic master's obsession and slithered faster with a prominent purpose.

Beginning at Jade's feet the tentacles wrapped, intensifying in speed and strength. If she had had the faculties to unleash a scream she may very well never stop. She had not the chance, as a suction cupped base smothered her lips. Intertwined in scaly flesh and serpent like chains, Jade was hoisted high into the air. An inconceivable height that seemed to surpass even the chipped stucco surface above, she became prisoner of hellfire and brimstone, silenced to anything below.

From within the parted clouds of fog, Damien stepped into the room. Each step was cerebral, concentrated and held every movement with purpose. He regarded the profile before him. Standing in the shadows, the host now rejuvenated in a sheen of reanimated epidermis, he returned his gaze.

"Father. I heard your call," between trembling lips, "What do we do now?"

CHAPTER EIGHTEEN

"I didn't so much hear a commotion but felt something." Damien's voice croaked, a virtual whisper. His eye lids were droopy, black half-crescent moons smeared beneath his lashes. In a way his gestures and movements had become robotic like a former shadow of himself.

"Damien, my son," the demonic host regarded him. He placed a hand upon his shoulder, a gesture ordinarily best reserved for proud, dedicated fathers. "You have had opportunity to take the necessary journey in just a few select memories of your life. I am truly sorry you have been deceived, mislead and robbed of the truth." Even Damien's blinks seemed calculated. It was not inconceivable his heart beat was no longer even his own. "Your mother and that meddling excuse of a doctor truly brainwashed you." Damien looked his father in the eyes. Unseen eyes glossed over. In reflection of his pupils, a spiral turned ever so gradually, picking up speed with each revolution. "The medications you were on were enough to wring out the fluids of any mere mortal boy." Bill Galligher sighed, a very human idiosyncrasy.

"You witnessed your birth, your parents' relationship, your sisters' care, your phobia of rats, your loss of chance to learn how to
ride a bike, failure to learn how to swim, your humiliation in attempting to attract a young lady."

Damien clenched his teeth. Life was beginning to flush back
into his cheeks. At his sides he began to clench his fists. Dead or
not dead, reanimated or slain, the young man was preparing for a
fight to the death.

"Relax son. You were robbed of each of these boyhood mile-
stones because you killed me." A guttural roar begins to manifest
within Damien's abdomen. Like molten hot lava and bile, it began
to rise his throat. "But even my death was necessary to bring us to
this very moment." Damien took a step closer almost nose to nose
with the horrific entity before him.

"Can't you see what your gift is now? Surely you must see your
power. Matched with my manipulation we will be unstoppable."
Rising his hands, he placed his thumbs upon his eyes. "I have one
more vision to unveil. Then together, as one, father and son we
will take back what has been rightfully ours all along." Damien
exhaled and awaited the fate before him.

CHAPTER NINETEEN

A murky film of cloudiness embodied in utter blackness is all Damien could see. This vision of recollection, evidence of altered truth was much different than any other that father had invited him into on this fated night. Through the darkness a hint of semi-transparent colors like a rainbow or gasoline slick splashed upon his field of vision.

In the faint distance he could hear the hint of notes from a Def Leppard song. Pour Some Sugar On Me? Rocket? He wasn't sure. Before him, he saw abstract swirls upon a flesh colored landscape. His sight was distorted, pinched and squeezed. Then it dawned upon him. Of course, he was seeing the memory before him through his contact lenses of his former self. Teenaged Damien was preparing to don his prescription eyes. Current, adult Damien was seeing what unfolded before him through the lenses. The demonic Bill's touch over his eyes enabled him to see things in exactly this light.

He remembered this memory well, like it was yesterday as he squeezed toothpaste onto his toothbrush and hummed out of tune all the while. Looking up into the mirror he saw his sixteen-year-old self, clean shaven safe for the initial signs of peach fuzz on his upper lip. His current-self beckoned his reflection to smile knowing what was in store for the evening.

In recent days and weeks, he had developed a mad crush on this girl at school, named Jade. After countless times in between, classes the two stole glances, racing against the bell and smiles to inspire the most reddened of faces. Each of the two even inquired about their situation to mutual friends. She was cool after all, I mean for a chick. She listened to Metallica, Guns n' Roses and even Alice Cooper. Sporting a bad ass tasseled leather jacket, Damien just had to find out more. At last he had written a note and dropped it into her locker, immediately regretting the action fearing inevitable rejection. He was delighted to find her best friend Christina had asked him on Jade's behalf if he wanted to go to the movies sometime. The New Nightmare on Elm Street was playing, so how fitting of a first date? Damien graciously accepted and agreed to pick her up at seven on Friday evening.

Now brushing his long shoulder length hair for the fifth time, he sprayed on far too much cologne and winked at his reflection. It was a long time since he had such a crazy crush. He took a deep breath and reminded himself that the night will go without a hitch. Just be yourself, he reminded himself. What could possibly go wrong?

An overwhelming sense of dizziness overcame each current Damien and the teenaged host of before. Just minor lightheadedness at first, then the sensation morphed into one of extreme vision altering vertigo. He grappled to steady his stance upon the towel rod and nearly collided with the floor. The origin of the boy's unease was being transcended deeper and further along the memory trail. Opening his eyes, he was sitting in a dim theatre the end credits had begun to roll. He looked over to his right and saw Jade's nervous, smiling expression. Together, silently, they ascended the sticky steps out of the concession area. Damien asked her if she had a good time as they prepared to walk out of the mall and into the bitter, frigid February night. Jade replied that of course she had and thanked him for bringing her along. They started to re-enact the film's dialogue with those classic zingers only Freddy Krueger could unleash.

Laughing hand in hand they walked the brisk, swift strides to where Damien was parked. He had gotten goosebumps wondering how his date would react if he tried to kiss her. Her teeth chattered with over dramatic clattering and the two began to laugh.

Into the frosted door he inserted his key unlocking the passenger side to let her in first. She sat down rubbing her hands furiously, while billowing out plumes of smoke into the car's interior. Damien marveled at how she leaned across the driver's seat to unlock his door. Cool, cute and thoughtful. Not at all a bad combination. Damien retrieved his keys with shaking hands, partially composed from the bitter, cold air, the remainder from sheer nerves. Having not the courage to look her in the eye he had proclaimed that he had a great time and hoped they could do it again sometime. Jade replied with an enthusiastic yes and wondered if he would mind calling her when he'd gotten home.

Damien smiled at the request and felt his face flush a little. Slipping the key into the ignition, he frowned when the motor barely even sputtered upon turning it over. He cursed inside his head only, fearing he would offend his date. With a tap, tap on the gas pedal he flipped the key away again. This time only a moderate clicking sound emitted from under the hood. Damien sighed, streams of vapor swirled up to the ceiling from his utterance of near defeat. Jade offered her hand upon his shoulder, a gesture of reassurance made him shiver, but all the while grew more irritated with himself to consider they may very well be stuck.

"Damien, can't we go back inside? I'm freezing out here." Jade clutched her upper arms practically convulsing from the cold. He felt like a perfect letch for ruining an otherwise great night. He reflected on how he'd attempted to put his arm around her at just the scariest part, she jumped, making him jump and elbow her in the side of the head by accident. Their popcorn, barely touched went tumbling to the floor. It was their only opportunity for tenderness up until now.

"Huh? Oh yes of course Jade,' he offered distracted in his own thoughts. "I'm so sorry about this. Let's go inside and call a tow truck."

Damien cringed from her expression of utter disappointment. Rage began to swirl around in his lower gut. Self-loathing rushed through his veins at the realization any other guy could just pop the hood of the car and get this baby going in no time. Other guys at school could fire it up with a matchstick and piece of chewing gum and have plenty of time left to drink a beer and smoke a joint. But not Damien, once again Daddy dearest has rendered him a loser.

He raced across the parking lot to catch up with Jade now almost back inside the mall. Hoping he could find a pay phone with a phone book he had no idea the only tow-trucking company around was Barron's Towing, the one and same operated by the high school dropout Laird Barron and his pregnant teen aged girlfriend Shelly. He deposited the coin once at the payphone and had no clue his night of hell was just about to begin.

"Damien, sweetheart? It's so cold out here," Jade shivered trying with everything she had not to complain too much. "Did they give any idea how long the tow truck would be?"

Startled from his nervous pacing, he looked up and smiled. He'd never been called sweetheart before. He guessed maybe this breakdown had a brighter side after all. Approaching with the snow and ice crunching beneath his step, he offered his most reassuring expression.

"I'm sure it won't be much longer," as an afterthought to offer any semblance of consolation, "I tell you what, why don't you take some cash and go into the mall and get us some hot chocolate, you know the ones with the little marshmallows? Then just wait by the doors." He could see her reaction was one of worry. "It's alright, I'll be fine. I'll come and get you as soon as they get here."

Reluctantly she obliged, but refused to take his ten dollars. He watched her leave, smitten and hoped over and over, he didn't ruin this night and any hopes of the two of them continuing to date. His lack of knowledge in cars, his failure at being a man would be the death of him yet.

Blowing into his hands he rubbed them back and forth with a fury. The friction did damn little to improve his conundrum. It'd be just his luck to get out of this Jim Dandy and get a cold, the flu or worse.

Just when he was considering chasing after Jade, he heard a horn blast behind him and a rackety old diesel engine clunking away. Turning to the abomination, Damien was blinded by the high beams blazing into his eyes. This had to have been them.

"Well shit on a stick and Jesus H. Christ," the tow truck's door slammed shut. A phlegmy hoarking sound erupted and the driver spat onto the icy ground. "If it ain't little queerbait Damien Galligher." Laird Baron strutted on up to where he was standing. "What's the matter fag boy get your wiener stuck in the tailpipe?" His old junior high school nemesis spit bile colored chewing tobacco on the ground.

Damien sighed, hanging his head in defeat. Great, just great. Of all the lousy places to see this guy again, it had to be in a vulnerable moment where he needed him.

"Look Laird, I don't want any trouble. If you can't give me a tow or lift back into town, I'll find some other way." Damien was almost proud of himself for taking a stand against his former bully.

"Ah come on now, no need to get your panties in a bunch." He clapped his hand a little too enthusiastically on Damien's shoulder. He cringed at the odor of pepperoni, whisky and pot on his breath. "Fuckin' Gay-lligher never could take no God damn joke anyway."

Damien leaned against the hood, retreating a step back or two, not of fear but just to get away from the stench.

"So let's see here," Laird produced a tire iron from seemingly nowhere. "Little rust bucket like this, front wheel drive, about 200 horse, suspension likely hold, I'd say five hundred bucks for a tow ought to do it."

"Jesus Laird, you know I don't have that kind of cash. I'm a student for Christ's sake."

He held up a beefy hand in front of Damien's face. Halting him from continuing any longer. "So what ya sayin, think you're better than me for stayin in school, that it?"

Laird poked a taunting finger into Damien's chest.

"Don't play dumb with me faggot. I know your step Daddy's got all the gold in Scotland Yard. This ain't a drop in a piss bucket to him."

"Laird let's just forget it. I can find another way."

"Oh, little late for that, queer. Hey Shell," Laird belched over his shoulder. "See who we got here. We gots us a real live one." From back in the cab, Shelly, Laird's girlfriend screeched.

"A live one, for sure Hon, squeeze that gay boy for all he's got. Surprised he ain't drivin' the bat mobile."

From across the lot, a cry shot into the still of the icy air.

"Damien, sweetheart, you alright?"

Laird frowned, his reddened, blistered nose just inches from Damien's face.

"Sweetheart huh? Who's this, fag? That your bitch or something. I mean not bad for a chink but-"

Damien didn't even let him finish the thought. He hauled off and delivered a haymaker of a right cross straight to Laird's nose.

He went sprawling to the tarmac, sliding on the ice and snow. He clutched his nose, now running red and snot like a faucet.

Shambling and shuffling, Laird got back to his feet.

"You're so dead fag, you don't even know it yet."

With his icy threat, two of the cabs' rear doors burst open. To the ground both Mark Szechuan and Kyle Irbine jumped. Damien didn't like the looks of this.

"Fuckin' fairy broke my nose," Laird spit blood into the snow. Mark wrapped a chain around his fist while Kyle grabbed Laird's fallen tire iron.

"Damien no!" Jade shrieked from the mall's doors. She dumped the hot chocolate cups into the snow. The steamy trail of sugary goodness ran down the ice and grime. In a flash she ran over to the melee.

"Get him up." Laird barked orders to his flunkies. Kyle and Mark went for Damien's upper body. Huge mistake. With a crescent side kick his heel connected with Kyle's knee cap in mid stride. A sickening crunch was heard as Kyle screamed. His leg bent the wrong direction contorted and twisted. Marc went to swing his chain, Damien ducked easily and placed an excellently executed head butt to the sternum. The wind rushed out of him, but the chain still came smashing down onto the back of Damien's head. He saw stars instantly but shook them away knowing his life could depend on it.

Before he had a chance to shake off the cobwebs and stand, a sized twelve steel toe boot collided with his forehead. Into a heap Damien fell. Like a pack of hyenas Mark, Kyle and Laird kicked, smashed and punched.

Jade raced over to the tow truck, running by the passenger side window. Shelly clutched and yanked on a handful of auburn locks. Screaming into her ear.

"Where you think you're going you little gook bitch?" To add insult to injury, she spat in her face.

Just when Damien was rapidly losing consciousness, a whirling sound whipped by, then another and another. The windshield of his decrepit car caved in.

From across the mall's parking lot, a shadowy figure stood high on a snow bank, sling shot in hand.

"You fuckers want to dance, you better start lovin' metal real fast." Kane laughed his maniacal laugh into the cold February night.

⊷⊶ ⊷⊶

A sizzling sound emitted from the demon's finger tips. Smoke billowed, precariously close to where Jade was cocooned high in the rafters above the kitchen. Damien's eyelids scorched, singed beyond recognition. His body quivered, convulsed uncontrollably. Rapid snippets of his entire life from birth to one humiliation, one defeat, one degradation one heartache after another and another. The intensity picked up racing over and over in his mind. Froth began to form at his lips and bubbled over running down his chin and onto his chest. Transforming into an utter invalid, Father Galligher was his sole caregiver now, in complete control of his welfare.

He released his grasp from his eye lids. Black ooze puddled at his lashes and ran free form in clumps, streams of excremental evil. Almost as a tender afterthought, he caressed his son's cheek. He leaned in close, almost intimately to whisper into his ear.

"You see my dear boy. Nothing was as you thought it was. Even your chosen companion was a farce. If not for her, you would have been beaten to a bloody pulp that day. Sure, you gave it your all. But without me in your life, to guide you, to show you the way, then ultimately you always fell short." Tufts of green swirled up from his lips, almost caressing Damien's earlobe. He stood steadfast, not entirely unlike catatonic.

"Your mother and the good doctor did their best to shield the truth from you. But the bond that runs deeper than water, our blood cannot be denied." Placing his thumbs back onto his eye lids he twisted his wrists with lightning precision. "You will need these, no further." Into his sockets he wrenched free his eyes. With a sloshing, audible pop they rolled this way and that onto his massive palm.

"I am the only eyes you will need from this moment forward." Damien collapsed into a heap on the floor scrambling for inexistent vision. His long, matted hair, streaked in plasma and blood hung over his face. Snapping out of his paralysis, he screamed for vengeance. Clambering into the abyss, the unknown he fought to grasp anything within reach. "Surely you must understand you are the dark messiah. The chosen one. The boy that cannot die. Together, you and I will rule the earth, take back what was raped and stolen from us and send all those accused before us straight to hell where they belonged to begin with." He caressed the top of his son's shaking head. "We will have our own Garden of Eden and eternal paradise will be ours."

Damien clawed and scratched searching in vain.

"But never fear. I would never dream to ask you to do this alone. I believe you are indebted my dear boy. I mean, you do remember your best friend Kane?"

From the ceiling, his forgotten comrade descended. In place of his unruly frock of ginger hair was a perpetual flame, three shades of extreme heat. Their flames flickered and glowed seemingly along with his moods.

"Geez dude, you never told me your old man sure knows how to party. The old boy gets this joint smokin' every time."

Back and forth between his hands Kane tossed a sphere of apocalyptic energy. It blazed brighter with each toss.

"Now let's say you and me, have a wedding to crash?"

Reaching out for his friend, he helped Damien to his feet. The floor below them collapsed once again sending them into a tunnel of eternal damnation.

CHAPTER TWENTY

An eerie silence clouded the air within St. Timothy's Cathedral. Deal calm. Those lacerated and slashed by the onslaught of evil intrusion scattered to higher ground, both spiritually and physically. No obvious fatalities were noted. Yet anything was possible on this hellacious evening. Everyone was so caught up and fixated on their own disdain they hadn't noticed Beatrice Redgrave; the organist had combusted beyond recognition. Even Father O'Malley was transfixed in his own world of prayer. Coddling his scorched palm, the cross indentation would surely remain until his last dying breath.

Joy had managed to somehow assemble most of her loved ones. Daughters Kaitlin, Kassandra and Peggy huddled up beneath a heap of fallen pews. The makeshift structure provided little semblance to their unholiest of dilemmas. Idly, Peggy twirled the crystal necklace between her fingers. A bona fide habit, she became so dependent upon it, she knew not consciously she was even doing it. Kaitlin seemed the only one being proactive searching the confines of the church from a far, forever assessing damage and looking for each of their respective spouses. Little did she know Cam, Dale and Mitch had formed a pack to ensure the well-being of the remaining guests at the ceremony.

Leonard was conspicuous by his absence. For all that Joy had cared at that very moment, the old coot could keel over and step into the great beyond. She had other fish to fry as it were. A nagging, almost stabbing sensation bombarded her chest and back of her skull. Somehow, she knew this was far from the worst they'd see this day. Desperately, she looked around for sister Julia. While they only embraced their Wiccan beliefs, there were no magical spells to undo the evil before them. At least their sibling bond would provide a unity of love and struggle until the very end.

At the very moment when most of the church's populous had acquired a sense of relief and comfort, the alter at the head of the church began to rattle. Rosery beads began to pop from their chain, projectile shooting in chaotic frenzy. With such velocity if anyone where to walk in its path an eye would no question be ejected.

Statues of Mary and the three wise men crumbled with others, exploded, forcing clouds of shrapnel in porcelain and clay into a dizzying fray. An urn of holy water, open in its majestic stone basin, began to bubble gently at first, then a full all and out boil ensued. Steam clouded and drifted into the high balcony and rafters above.

For a monetary second all paranormal, supernatural activity ceased. Just when everyone was questioning their sanity and scattered for higher ground, the alter erupted and burst into a thousand pieces into the cathedral's ceiling. The sculpted craftsmanship was obliterated beyond recognition. Any evidence of faith and hope was ruined with no trace of otherwise.

A cavernous pit opened beneath the alter, approximately half its size in circumference. Around the jagged edges a trembling, gloved hand slapped, clawed for purchase then began to raise the appendage's possessor inside. Bemused and terrified, spectators gasped in sheer terror as a frock of flames peered into view. Flickering multiple hues of fiery hot, an image of welder's goggles then came into perspective. Barely recognizable, Kane climbed into St. Timothy's, his free hand clutched the locks of his best friend, his unholiest of brother's Damien. Together they rose on sacred ground, ready to unleash their wraith and claim what was so rightfully theirs.

Out of pure instinct, or his rigorous training as a security guard, Dale deployed a taser from his suit jacket. Sending a trident of needles directly into Damien's chest, the strings of high voltage made his body convulse like a fish out of water. Whirling backwards he collided with two rows of oak pews sending them each into a mayhem of a heap. Dale's chest rose and fell in a frenzy. Regarding the freak of nature known as Kane he contemplated how to react.

Just as Kane was about to spring into action the fallen pews flew high up into the air. Damien sat upright. With unseen black sockets for eyes, he glared directly through the soul of Dale, in choppy, lumbering gestures he shook off the shards of wood threatening to penetrate his arms and stood.

Kane conjured a sphere of white hot fury within his palm. Its center grew hotter and hotter, ready to ignite like a solar flare. He took an authoritative step forward, prepared to scorch Dale to a crisp. From behind, Damien clutched his wrist overhead. Kane bolted backwards, in shock and taken off guard.

"What the hell are you doing?" He screamed into Damien's former shell of a face. In rebuttal he merely shook his head in painstakingly defiance. His neck snapped up and down his vertebrae with each movement.

Cam and Mitch seized the opportunity, grabbing their brother in law and raced towards the church's balcony. The remainder of the guests screamed in horror running over one another. Their riot did precocious little to alleviate the nightmare around them. As many tried in vain to break the stained-glass windows for escape, still others just fainted from pure disbelief at the scene unfolding around them.

Basking in the world gone mad around them, the cavernous pit opened further, pivoting and twirling in an almost certain eloquence the demon formerly known as Bill Galligher levitated. In his clutches was Jade, unconscious from the pure fear and evil that shrouded her and from within.

"What a perfect, perfect day for a sermon." He hovered just inches above the fiery abyss from below. "Welcome one and all sinners. The day of reckoning has arrived at last." He spewed forth a stream of green bile. He laughed while ejected a possessed gale into the rafters and all in between St. Timothy's. "I do love when we all have a time to confess." With a flip of the wrist Jade was shot high into an ivory pillar. Her lopped head indication she had sunken into a coma of primal fear. Her arms and legs spread upon impact. Nine-inch spikes spun and thrust into each of her palms and ankles pinning her in place.

To the adjacent pillar Aunt Julia already lied. Strings of barbed wire, not entirely unlike razor thorns bound her in place. Each Aunt and girlfriend to Damien, tried for their deadly sins of abomination. One of theft the other of lies. The two awaited their court of demise.

Kane and Damien had somehow shrugged off their opposition to one another. The demon in father opened his hand. Glistening eye balls with glimmering blue irises twirled this way and that, the unholiest of remote controls any mortal could fathom. Damien involuntarily obliged, lumbering and shuffling towards the direction his father pointed his eyes. Kane marched in tow, the indestructible tandem, hellbent on vengeance and bloodshed.

Along the front of the church, Damien kicked over pedestals containing bouquets of flowers, while Kane licked the stems and pedals with his heat, sizzling each to ashes. Two long, folding tables were set up, draped in elegant, white lace and decoration. Scores of expensive audio equipment along with turntables and speakers resided. Cowering behind the table was none other than Laird Baron and common law skank Shelly. It seemed the two were hired to bring along song and melody to this joyous event. Kane spotted them instantly and sneered. He punched the shoulder of his blind comrade.

"I won't offend you with asking if you see what I see, but surely you can smell the stink of shit anywhere." Damien stood, frozen. Transfixed.

"Look what the cat dragged in. Might have known a couple of gay freaks would be the center of all this." Despite the fact Laird was quivering in unbridled fear, his silver tongue always got the best of him.

With lightning fast reflexes, Kane bounded across the table and grasped Shelly by the bangs of her hair. The two and a half bottles of hairspray she unloaded into her grimy do, burst into flames instantly. Kane pulled her forward and kissed her smack on the lips. The kiss of death if there ever was one. On reflex, Shelly tore free taking most of several layers of flesh from her face. Kane leaned back preparing to finish her. Damien burst into action stepping in front of his unholy brother.

"Oh, for Christ Sake, Damien. What's gotten into you?" He shoved his hellacious ally backwards, moving the table almost a foot or so. In the meanwhile, Shelly raced for relief, dunking her head in holy water. But the damage was done. In all the confusion, Laird pounced into action and buried the cake cutter deep into the back of Damien's neck. Blindly, he scrambled to retrieve the hilt for precious release, as he fell into a heap on the floor.

Kane and Laird glared at one another. Their stare could cut all the evil energy and tension within the church. Damien rose next to his brother, the hilt snapped in half and the blood all about dried up. He squeezed Kane's shoulder. He shook it off, refusing interruption. With a thunderous clap he slapped on a choke hold across the table onto Laird's throat. Twisting his head sideways he regarded Damien in defiance. He returned his stare then bolted his perspective back to Laird. He met his brothers grasp, smothering the grip on Laird's throat with his own. Their adolescent bully croaked for mercy, his eyes swelled within his skull. Without another single word, each Damien and Kane hoisted Laird high above the table. Their grip refused to falter. Kicking his feet in rapid succession proved futile, as he was crashed straight through the table, busting it in two. To the side a turntable still spun, its warped revolutions refused to repent.

In the throes of unearthly Armageddon, Elise crawled before the alter under overturned tables and pews. She knew full well her special day would be ruined leading up to this. But what person could possibly foresee this? She crawled into the clearing, attempting to flee for sweet release. The demon spotted her within seconds and ignited a formidable boomerang talon. Into the air it diced off her forefinger. The golden ring funneled over and over, before handing next to Damien's eye balls within his palm.

"Ah yes, you won't be needing this any longer. After all, Till Death Do Us Part." His laughter shook the very foundation of St. Timothy's "Children!" He thundered to Kane and Damien. "Gather around. The ritual is a hair away from complete. Come claim the garden of Eden that was always yours. Come exile these sinners straight to hell." Effortlessly an unseen force yanked Joy Galligher from the tent of wooden pews across the floor to the brink of the cavernous pit below. She fought off succumbing to utter arrest in terror. It was now or never.

Together Damien and Kane stood before her, the evil alter and the maestro of macabre hovering above. The irises drained blood red from within the demon's palm.

"Damien my son, you know what to do. Free us at last. Banish those who had forsaken you, but it is only you that can sentence your mother for eternity."

The sockets darkened within Damien's skull. With unseen eyes he looked down at his mother. His chest rose and fell in heavy succession. In his mind the scenes of deception and betrayal whirled repeatedly.

"Damien please!" She pleaded for her life. "I know you are in there. I know you know, none of this is real. You defended my honor thirteen years ago and saved each of us. This devil spawn has brainwashed you." Her speech grew on verge of hysterics and then pole-vaulted over the top. "I know we were far from good parents to you. But don't you understand? None of those memories were real. You became the man you are today not because of us, but despite us. I am so very proud of you. Please! This is not the way!"

He appeared to soften. Tenderness returning to his face. All over his body he slackened, void of defense and tension. Stepping forward to the edge of infinite damnation, he reached for his mother for a heartfelt embrace.

At the last second his fist raveled around her dress he hoisted her high into the air above his head. The most primal of laughter erupted from each the demon and Kane.

"At last conquer all that opposes us son!" Kane responded with an applause that ignited his palm and shot off flickering flames.

Across the church, Peggy crawled out, unable to take the onslaught any further. She knew not what to do, but a beam shined off her necklace, reflected off Elaine's wedding ring and lit up Damien's face.

"Please understand Damien," Joy chirped off as methodically as she could muster. "There is an angel that awaits you. The angel of mercy. Known by most simply as Aida. She will appear to you one day upon the horizon. She is your salvation, the answer to everything. Open your heart to her, let her love in. She will sing from the heavens and listen closely for it. "Should you take a step towards me, you will take my breath away." Please Damien, humanity depends upon it." Tears streaked down Joy's face. She prayed it was not too late. Damien regarded her with a blank expression. He cocked his head sideways staring up at her blindly. We walked to the abyss's edge. Kane and father clapped and cheered, deafening everyone inside. With a simple flip of the wrist he tossed his mother clean over the cavernous pit onto the safety of the organ behind them. Taking a step back in retreat, he glared at the opposition of his father. The unholy had not the chance to utter his eternal disappointment. Damien launched himself at his father, spearing the demon off his feet, father and son spiraled head over heels deep into the dark abyss below, sealing off the porthole to hell.

Virtually everyone inside St. Timothy's collapsed. Across the church, a disheveled turntable burst into life. It's needle piercing the air with its harmonious song, a classic rock tune, this version covered more contemporary. Chirping into the air, the refrain of Simple Man spun lazily in revolution after revolution.

EPILOGUE

Hydraulic doors popped open against the hospital walls with an earth shattering crash. The gurney whipped by with dizzying speed. To the sweat ladled Jade, the overhead lights became a blur. She fought consciousness with realizing the pinnacle of pain. Her contractions were mere minutes apart. To her side, Joy Galligher held her hand, keeping pace with the EMT's. In the last several months she had taken her under her wing, accepting her as her own.

It had been just over eight long months since the tragic day, the union of Danny and Elise's wedding. Few spoke about it anymore, many succumbing to post traumatic stress disorder while others preferred to just put it behind them. The memory of Dr. Rhys lived on. He would have made a killing in these trialing times.

Jade and Joy had put aside their differences, their common love for Damien and keeping his spirit alive was enough to strengthen their bond forever more. For a first child, Jade's labor proved to be relatively at ease. Four hours later, she gave birth to a healthy ten-pound two-ounce boy. Joy caressed Jade's forehead. Never had she envisioned the two would become so close. She was very proud of the daughter before her, even more so to the precious gift in grandson she held so tightly. Jade looked up through teary eyes.

"Mom, would you like to hold him?" She smiled sweetly, strengthening their bond even further.

"Thank you dear." She cooed and swooned as any proud grandmother would at that moment. Rocking gently, she regarded Jade once again. "He has his father's eyes." The two exhaled in unison remembering their fallen love. "Have you thought of any names?"

Jade smiled. "Yes Mom. I shall name him David."

"That's perfect dear, just perfect."

⟞⟨+ ⟩⟞

On a remote tundra highway, a transport truck came barreling through the ice and snow. Many miles left behind. Many more left to charter. The driver could barely recognize the insanity before him through the blizzard. At once he depressed the air brakes bring the mastodon to an eventual stop.

A mysterious figure loomed, walking along the ditch's edge. The transport pulled up as close as possible. What kind of fool would wander in such conditions? Wearing just a flimsy jean jacket, it was baffling how such clouds of steam rose off his shoulders. A pair of aviator glasses donned his face, protecting from snow, but how could this stranger see anything? At any rate, the wanderer grasped the cab's door handle above his head, depressed and opened the steel entry with flawless execution.

"To je vani mećava. Će se smrznuti!"

The tongue should have been one unable to decipher to the stranger, yet somehow, he knew it fluently. He began to shiver in the seat. The driver stared at him in disbelief. A gesture the stranger was unaccustomed to, the driver appraised him once more.

"Imaš groznicu. Moram te odvesti u bolnicu."

"Thank you, friend," the stranger responded in English. Leaning against the glass window he added, "You could say I have had one hell of a night." The stranger in strange land knew his journey had just begun.

AUTHOR'S NOTE:

What can really be said about writing this novel that can truly do it justice? This is a special project to me that I have been working on many years, lived with many more and endured my entire life. I had abandoned the writing process for House of Anguish many times, failing to believe in myself. A remarkable tale with elements that have enough power to merit a novel within its own transpired one day.

Something had returned to me that I had thought I had lost once and for all. More specifically someone had returned that I thought was gone for better part of a decade. The love of my life, my angel Aida came back into my life. Without her constant support, encouragement, enthusiasm, advice and nourishment I know full well, none of this would be possible. All the gratitude goes to her. I can never thank you enough my angel. Vas vole Aida med. I love you Aida Honey. More than you will ever know.

David W. Gammon August 13, 2017

As of publication date is has become apparent indeed Angels and Demons are best left apart. I'll always hold the highest gratitude for getting a glimpse of heaven, Aida. May happiness find you eternally.

February 2, 2018

ABOUT THE AUTHOR:

David W. Gammon has been a contributing columnist, film and novel critic for horrornews.net for the past six years. In 2016, deciding, to take the bold leap into more creative endeavors, he submitted and published his first short story, The Evil That Men Goo, that was included within the anthology Splat by J. Ellington Press. Other creative endeavors include Keep The Change and Through the Dark, found in Morbid Metamorphosis and Grey Matter Monsters by Lycan Valley Press. In late 2017 he launched his own self-publishing endeavor CanAida Publishing as a tribute to the phenomenon of a relationship he had with a beautiful soul from Sarajevo named Aida. His inaugural release titled CanAida: A Tale of Love Lost, Rekindled, Redemption and International Romance tells their tale in poetic prose. House of Anguish is CanAida's second release, the premier in horror. The mission statement remains the same: Whenever you feel like you cannot, guess again. You can always CanAida.

Connect with a demon:
https://www.facebook.com/dave.gammon.54
http://horrornews.net/author/dave-gammon/
https://twitter.com/slamsta